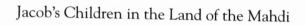

Jacob's Children in the Land of the Mahdi

Jacob's Children in the Land of the Mahdi

✧

Jews of the Sudan

Eli S. Malka

Produced and Distributed by
Syracuse University Press

Dedicated to the memory of my beloved parents,
Solomon Malka,
Chief Rabbi of the Sudan,
and
Hanna David Assouline Malka

Eli S. Malka was born, raised, and worked in the Sudan. From his youth, as a son of the Chief Rabbi of the Sudan, he has been an active participant both in Jewish affairs and causes and in commercial activities. In the Sudan, he not only had strong ties with other members of the Jewish Community but also conducted business with and counted among his friends many Sudanese, British, and others in the international community. As an active member and supporter of the Sudan Jewish Community, he served as president of the Community, vice-president of the B'nai B'rith Khartoum Lodge, and member of the Grand District B'nai B'rith Lodge No. 16 of Egypt and the Sudan. In business, he became senior director and CEO of Gellatly Hankey Trading Co., Ltd., a member of the leading British shipping, engineering, and trading companies in the Sudan and the Red Sea region, the Gellatly Hankey International Group.

He is one of the last living eyewitnesses and authorities on Jewish history in the Sudan and neighboring countries during the period from the end of the nineteenth to the end of the twentieth century.

After leaving the Sudan in 1964, Malka immigrated first to Switzerland and then to the United States; and in each country, he continued his business and Jewish Community activities.

Throughout his life, Mr. Malka has read extensively on all subjects in which he was interested. He earned a diploma in accounting and auditing from the Finance Department, Khartoum; a Bsc. in commerce, from Comboni College, Khartoum; and a degree in mercantile law from Wolsey Hall, Oxford University.

He has traveled widely on business and pleasure throughout the Middle East and Europe and in neighboring countries to the Sudan, especially Egypt, Eritrea, Ethiopia, Kenya, Uganda, and the Belgian Congo (now Zaire). He made his first trip to Eretz Israel in 1928, when he was nineteen, and has visited many times since, both before and after independence.

Contents

PART TWO
Eighty-seven Years from Omdurman to New York

Illustrations

Preface

Now go, write it before them on a tablet,
And inscribe it in a book,
That it may be for the time to come,
For ever and ever.

—Isaiah 30:8

The recent history of the Jews in the Sudan dates back to 1898. In 1885, half a dozen Jews who were then living in the Sudan were caught in the turmoil of the Mahdi's rule and were forcibly converted to Islam. In 1898, General Sir Horatio Herbert Kitchener, later Lord Kitchener, of former Sudan fame, defeated the Mahdi and reconquered the Sudan. The resulting Anglo-Egyptian government established in 1898 provided the opportunity for these forcibly converted Jews to return to Judaism. Joined by other Jews from Egypt, this small nucleus of Jewry grew into an organized, vibrant Jewish Community with its own achievements and institutions. Much later in time, as the Arab-Israeli wars made life difficult for Jews throughout the Arab countries, they similarly impacted on this small but vigorous community, so that almost the whole community gradually left the Sudan.

I was born in the Sudan. My father, Rabbi Solomon Malka, was the chief rabbi of the Sudan from 1906 to 1949. I was deeply involved in the Jewish Community of the Sudan and served as honorary secretary, vice-president, president, and member of the Executive Committee of the Sudan Jewish Community for thirty consecutive years, extending from 1934 to the day of my final departure in 1964. I lived among the Sudan Jews; shared all their activities, struggles, joys, and sorrows; and maintained their friendships after we all left for the Diaspora and Israel.

Reaching by the Grace of God the age of eighty-seven and seeing no written record of the Sudan Jewish Community, I find it incumbent on me to write the history of this relatively small but unique community from its start in 1898 to the continuing activity of its members and leaders as they spread to the United States, United Kingdom, Switzerland, and Israel.

This book also presents my eyewitness account of the governments in the Sudan under which these Jews lived, the institutions they established, their individuals and leaders, and some information about the neighboring Jewish communities in Egypt, Ethiopia, and Eritrea. It includes my personal memoirs of the Sudan and its people and the happenings during that period.

It is meant to preserve a place in history for this mainly Sephardic Community as one of the Sephardic communities that dispersed and disappeared from the Middle East Arab countries. It is also designed for the American or English reader interested in the history of the Jewish people and to give the descendants of the Sudan Jews information on their families and ancestors.

The early part of this history was given to me by my father from his own Sudan records written in Hebrew. These were lost, but a sample is preserved in an article I sent in 1936 from Khartoum to the B'nai B'rith International Headquarters in Cincinnati, Ohio. I was at that time serving as vice-president of the B'nai B'rith Ben-Sion Coshti Lodge No. 1207 in Khartoum (of which more later). When in 1986 I visited the B'nai B'rith International Archives in Washington, D.C., I found it published in the October 1936 issue of *B'nai B'rith Magazine* (now *Jewish Monthly*) and indexed under my name.

The rest of this work is from my personal knowledge and records and from information supplied to me by Sudan friends and published works, some of which are mentioned in the Bibliography.

I would like to thank the Paris-based association Mémoires Juives—Patrimoine photographique, which is dedicated to the preservation, enhancement, and promotion of photographs and other documents belonging to Jewish families for use as historical, sociological, and ethnological testimony, for their permission to reproduce some of the photographs in *Juifs d'Egypte—Images et Textes*, published by Les éditions du Scribe, Paris, France.

I would also like to acknowledge my debt to Henry N. Feingold, professor emeritus of history at Baruch College and Graduate School of the

City University of New York, author and editor of American Jewish history and the history of the Holocaust, for recommending my manuscript to Syracuse University Press "as the indispensable source of everything a historian would like to know regarding the impact of certain events in the recent past"; to Jane S. Gerber, professor of Jewish history of the Graduate School of the City University of New York and director of the Institute of Sephardic Studies, who led me to Professor Feingold and to Syracuse University Press; to Robert A. Mandel, director of Syracuse University Press, for finding it worth his attention and for producing it in the high standard of the Press; and last but not least, I wish to express my special gratitude to Joyce Atwood, managing editor of Syracuse University Press, for her inexhaustible patience and superb advice and guidance in editing my manuscript.

I am also grateful to my wife, Bertha, for her patience and encouragement, without which this work could not have been undertaken; to my deceased wife, Dora, who shared my life in the Sudan and Switzerland; and for the encouragement of my daughter, Evelyne; her husband, David Klein; and my many American friends.

In particular, I wish to acknowledge the tremendous contribution of my son, Dr. Jeffrey Solomon Malka, to this book. He was fascinated by my manuscript and spent many hours editing it and imputting it on his computer to ready it for publication. Along the way, he made suggestions and contributed many additions and changes that improved the book enormously and served as my editor in preparing the final manuscript. His wife, Susan, also expressed helpful ideas, not the least of which was the title of the book.

In conclusion, I bless the Lord who has privileged me to see the rebirth of the State of Israel and the promise of the gleaming of peace on Holy Jerusalem. I thank Him for His abundant mercies and for the health and vigor He has given me to conclude this book. May it be a heritage for posterity and a new addition to the annals of the history of the Jewish people.

Eli S. Malka

White Plains, New York
November 1996

PART ONE

The Sudan Jewish Community

Separate not thyself from the Congregation
Judge not thy fellow-man until
thou art come to his place.
—Hillel, *Perke Aboth*
(Sayings of the fathers), 2:5

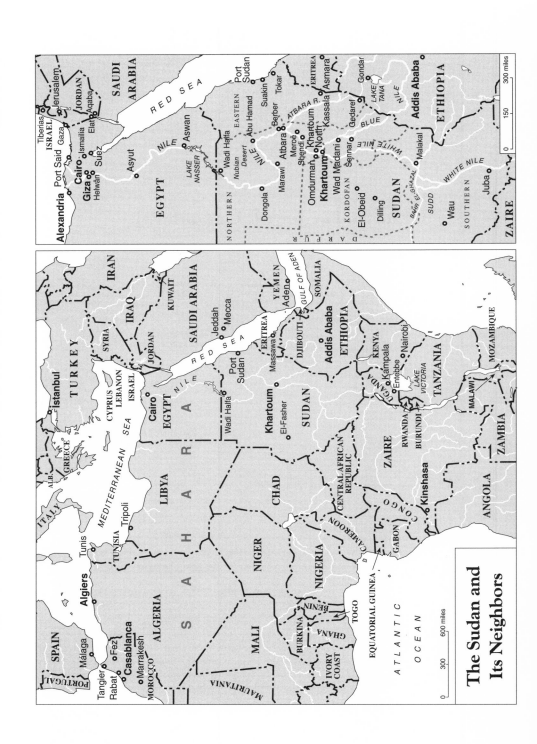

The Sudan and Its Neighbors

1

❦

The Sudan

The Sudan,[1] the largest country in Africa, is bounded by Egypt on the north; Ethiopia and the Red Sea on the east, Uganda and Zaire on the south; and Libya, Chad, and the Central African Republic on the west. It covers nearly 1 million square miles in area, approximately one-quarter the size of Europe, or, the size of Texas, Alaska, and Massachusetts combined. Because of its large size, its climate runs the gamut from desert in the north to the swamps of the *Sudd*[2] in the South. The northern population is Muslim, largely urban, and the dominant governing group. In the south, the population is black African, land of the tall Shilluk, Dinka[3] and Nuer tribes, more backward, essentially nonurban, nomadic, and of various animalistic or missionary-taught Christian religions. The differences between these two populations remains a source of conflict to this day.[4]

---

1. *Sudan* comes from *Bilad al-Sudan*. *Bilad* means country, and *al-Sud* means the blacks; hence, country of the blacks.

2. *Sudd* is an anglicized word for *sadd*, (Ar. barrier), a testimony to the formidable nature of this swampland.

3. The Shilluk and Dinka tribesmen are tall and lanky, frequently ranging from six to seven feet in height. A member of the Dinka tribe, Manute Bol, was recruited in the Sudan and made a career as a professional basketball player with the NBA in the United States. He frequently told interviewers that his father and brother were taller than he was, and they probably were!

4. It is of interest that under British rule, these differences were consciously accentuated by the government, which encouraged the English language and Christian missionaries in Southern Sudan and discouraged Arabic and Islam. In fact, the region was closed to Northern, Arabic-speaking Muslim Sudanese. The Nuba Mountains District in the west and the Southern provinces of Equatoria and Bahr el-Ghazal (Ar. Gazelle river) were classified as "closed districts," to which entry from the North was only allowed by hard-to-get permit.

Two Niles enter the Sudan from the south and join to form the main Nile. The Blue Nile originates in Lake Tana, 6,000 feet above sea level in Ethiopia and enters the Sudan in its southeastern border. The White Nile originates in Lake Victoria in Uganda at a much lower height of 3,000 feet above sea level. Both the White Nile and the Blue Nile course through the Sudan from its southern border combining halfway through the country to form the main Nile, which then flows on to the northern border into Egypt and finally into the Mediterranean Sea. The outline on a map of the Blue Nile and White Nile as they meet to form the main Nile creates the silhouette of an elephant head with the main Nile playing the role of the elephant's trunk extending north into Egypt. The Sudanese capital is located at that junction point, hence its name, Khartoum (Ar. elephant trunk).

The Blue and White Niles get their names from the color of their waters. The White Nile has a turbid, muddy, white color, whereas the Blue Nile is bluish in color. At their junction point in Khartoum, the two Niles combine to form the Nile. For a short while, they flow together with the waters seeming to remain separate, so that they present a fascinating visual image of a river with a clear dividing line in its midst that separates the two streams; for a few miles, with the left half of the river remaining distinctly whitish and the right half blue.

The Nile is the source of life and prosperity both in the Sudan and in Egypt, with most of the settlements being found on the banks of the White, Blue, or main Nile. Annually, the Nile overflows its boundaries to flood the surrounding areas. Rather than a curse, this is the agricultural life source that brings fertile silt and water from its origins in the highlands of Ethiopia and Uganda down to the desert regions of the Sudan and Egypt. In the 1860s, as a consequence of the Civil War in the United States, there developed a scarcity of cotton in the world markets that greatly increased the value of cotton grown along the Nile. The British responded to this situation by encouraging the planting of cotton along the Nile. The delta area of the Nile in Egypt and the area between the White Nile and Blue Nile, just south of their junction in the Sudan, were ideally situated for cotton plantations. Irrigation in this inter-river area in the Sudan, known as the Gezira (Ar. island) was developed and expanded with the building of the Sennar Dam on the Blue Nile in 1925, and cotton became a primary source of wealth for the Sudan economy.

Historical Background

As early as 2000 B.C.E., ancient Egyptian records speak of the kingdom of Cush in Nubia in what is now Northern Sudan. Cush, or Kush, was then a prosperous kingdom; and its ivory, ebony, gum, hides, and ostrich plumes were carried along the Nile to Egypt and across the Red Sea to Arabia and Mesopotamia. These remained the same exports from the Sudan along the same caravan routes until the nineteenth century and Mahdiya times.

Cush was conquered by Egyptian pharaohs in the sixteenth century B.C.E.[5] For a long time, it was an Egyptian dependency; and ancient Egypt's influence, religion, language, and culture extended into Cush as far south as the junction of the Blue and White Niles, near present Khartoum. Cushite elite adopted Egyptian gods and built temples to Egyptian deities, and ancient Egyptian language became widely used.

In the eighth century B.C.E., Cush rulers threw off their Egyptian overlords and once again became an independent kingdom. In the seventh century B.C.E., however, they withdrew their dynasty to their ancient capital Napata[6] in Cush; and by 540 B.C.E., they transferred their capital from Napata to Meroë, 180 miles north of present-day Khartoum and just north of the ancient market town of Shendi. From the royal city of Meroë, they developed their own distinctively African civilization but retained Egyptian culture and traditions, building monuments and stelae and erecting pyramids to be buried in. Today in Meroë, there are the ruins of about two hundred temples, pyramids, palaces, and baths. I have not had the occasion to visit these ruins of Meroë; but on a visit to the

---

5. The Egyptian pharaoh Ahmose I (1570–1500 B.C.E.) conquered Cush and ruled it as an Egyptian province governed by a viceroy. Loyalty of the local chiefs was ensured by having their children serve as pages at pharaoh's court and tributes of gold and slaves were exacted from them.

6. In 750 B.C.E., the Cushite king Kashta conquered Upper Egypt, and his successor, Painkhy, conquered the delta. Cushite monarchs then ruled Egypt for the next century. Following conflicts with the Assyrians, the Cushite pharaoh Taharqua (688–663 B.C.E.) withdrew the dynasty back to Napata in Cush and concentrated on extending its dominion to the south and east. Because of Egyptian military pressure, they moved their capital to Meroë but retained Napata as their religious center. For the next few centuries, Cush and Egypt had separate histories. Greek and Hindu influences came to the kingdom of Cush from traders on the Red Sea, and there is some evidence that metallurgical technology may have been transmitted westward to West Africa from Meroë's smelteries.

other Marawi,[7] further to the north on the curve of the Nile to Dongola, I enjoyed visiting three or four pyramids of the ancient Egyptian type. In 350 C.E., a conquering army from the kingdom of Axum, in what is now Ethiopia, conquered and destroyed Meroë city, bringing an end to the Meroë kingdom.

The Christian period in Nubia started in the sixth century C.E., when three kingdoms that had emerged in Nubia (centered around Dongola and Meroë) were converted to Coptic Christianity, tradition says, by a missionary sent by Empress Theodora. Archeological remains have shown that colloquial Greek was spoken into the twelfth century, but Arabic was gaining prominence after the seventh century. Muslim Arab invaders conquered Egypt in 640 C.E. but were unable to conquer the Christian Nubian kingdoms, which reached their greatest military power in the ninth and tenth centuries. Muslim domination of Egypt caused the Nubian kingdoms to become isolated from the Egyptian Coptic Church.

Having failed to conquer Nubia, there was a relative peace between Arab Egypt and the Nubian kingdoms that continued through a series of treaties well into the thirteenth century, despite some occasional incursions by Nubian kings to free imprisoned Coptic patriarchs or beleaguered Christians in Egypt. In the thirteenth century, through gradual intermarriages, Muslim members of the royal family gained control of the combined northern two kingdoms in Dongola; and it became a satellite of Egypt.

In 1504, the black sultanate (*Al-Sultana al-Zarka*) replaced the third, southern Nubian kingdom of Alwa. This was the beginning of the Funj Empire, based in Sennar, which at its height extended thousands of miles up and down the Nile, all the way to the Shilluk tribes in Southern Sudan and most of Kordofan. It was ruled by a *mek* (Ar. king), and the land was divided into vassal areas called *dur* (ruled by a nazir), with which the local populations identified into quasi-tribal groups, some of which persist today.

About the same time, the Fur kingdom developed in Darfur with its capital in El-Fasher. It was made up of horsemen tribes related to the Kanuri of Bornu in Nigeria and was ruled by sultans who competed with the Funj for control of Kordofan.

---

7. Marawi is not to be confused with Meroë. Marawi, much further to the north of Meroë, was the site of the original Napata capital of Cush before Napata was moved to Meroë in the South, near Shendi.

Because of the Nile and caravan routes, the Sudan shares a long history with Egypt, going back to pharaonic times. Expeditions were sent south from Egypt to the Sudan from ancient times to as recently as 1820, with the purpose of bringing back slaves, ivory, ostrich feathers, and gold. But despite its long history, the Sudan was largely unknown and unexplored by Europeans, except for some intrepid adventurers from the 1800s onward. Maps drawn as late as the 1920s still showed parts of the southern Nile, particularly in the gorge of the Blue Nile near its origin, as a dotted line with uncertain location. The Sudan gained its strategic importance to Europeans shortly after Bonaparte's expedition and his attempted conquest of Egypt in 1798. Bonaparte's engineers proposed to build a canal across the Suez; and though they never got to build it themselves, the implications of such a canal relative to the route to India were not lost. The British government realized the need to protect this new route to India and thereafter took a great interest in the countries bordering the Red Sea.

Khartoum

The present capital of the Sudan is Khartoum, located approximately in the center of the country. Khartoum was still a small, insignificant fishing village on the Blue Nile when in 1820 Muhamed Ali Pasha sent his son Ismail on an expedition from Egypt with specific instructions to conquer the Sudan and to bring back slaves for his armies and ivory and gold for his coffers.[8] The Egyptians, realizing the strategic importance of Khartoum between the two rivers, decided to move to Khartoum and make it the capital in 1826. While I lived there, Khartoum was a large, modern city on the banks of the Blue Nile with broad, shady avenues. Nile Avenue, heavily shaded with banyan trees because of the heat, runs along the banks of the Blue Nile and was a favorite of mine for cool evening drives. At its midpoint lies the Palace of the Governor General of the Sudan, on whose ceremonial steps General Sir Charles Gordon Pasha

---

8. Ismail, was extremely brutal and unnecessarily savage in his tactics and conquest. He made a fatal mistake that cost him his life when he snubbed a local king (Ar. *mak* or *mek*) called Mak Nimr, (Ar. tiger or leopard), who was coming to offer his submission. Mak Nimr, the king of Shendi and descended from a lineage dating to the sixteenth century, got his revenge in a night raid, in which Nimr warriors set fire to Ismail's dwelling and murdered his bodyguard. Ismail burned to death in the blaze.

1. Governor's Palace in Khartoum.

was felled by the spear of a Mahdi dervish warrior. On either side of the palace, the shady avenue stretches pleasantly along the river.[9]

Running south of the palace and a couple of miles farther, past numerous elegant structures, the riverside drive passes by several distinctive buildings, including the Sudan Club, situated in spacious grounds. The Sudan Club used to be the private preserve of the senior British officials, on whose grass tennis courts were played the annual tennis tournaments. Next to the Sudan Club is the large Catholic Cathedral, with its attached "Sisters school" for girls and "primary school for boys" run by the local convent. Another 5 or 6 miles farther, it reaches the grounds and buildings of Gordon College, which subsequently became Khartoum University, with several soccer fields, and so forth. The avenue then continues its leisurely way past the bridge crossing the Nile to Khartoum North and Halfaya, to pass by the grounds of the British garrison, the

9. Although the Nile still has abundant crocodiles, hippos, and the like, the Jebel Awlia Dam that was built on the White Nile, about 30 or 40 miles upstream from Khartoum, prevents their passage into the Nile through Khartoum and on to Egypt. Occasionally when the water level was unusually high, a crocodile or two would slip into the protected waters but would soon be detected, captured, and returned upstream. The name Jebel Awlia comes from *jebel* (Ar. mountain) and *awlia* (Ar. pl. of *wali* (Ar. *faki*, or religious person).

Navy, Army, Air Force Institute (NAAFI), and the movie theater. After the Sudan gained its independence from the British in 1956, the British garrison grounds became a Sudanese Army Barracks and the movie theater was transformed into a commercial open-air movie theater called "The Blue Nile Cinema."

On the north side of the palace, the avenue again runs past numerous colonial buildings, to the Grand Hotel and its Annex on an adjacent anchored steamer in the Blue Nile. The Grand Hotel is a classic colonial hotel structure, reminiscent of such structures as the Raffles Hotel in Singapore. It is a spacious, sprawling, two-story edifice, with a large parade ground lawn where outdoor society and government parties took place, attended by turbaned waiters in white *gallabias*,[10] or caftans, and red or green cummerbunds. At times, government military bands played in the background. Men in smoking suits (tuxedos), attended formal lawn parties wearing black or white sharkskin jackets during the mild winter season or shirt-sleeves and black tie during the hot summer. Women outdid each other in the finery they would wear for such occasions.

Beyond the Grand Hotel, the avenue continues past the Khartoum Zoological Gardens. Although very spacious, the Zoo actually developed from a holding station for captured African animals on their way elsewhere. It contained a wide collection of permanent animals, mostly of African species. A few miles farther down the avenue one comes to the Moghren,[11] a large treed and green park at the point where a 1926 colonial-era bridge crosses the White Nile on its way to Omdurman. The Moghren was a popular place for leisurely open-air weekend breakfasts, served by the Moghren's kitchen, or picnics on the banks of the beautiful Blue Nile.

Arising perpendicularly from the Blue Nile at the level of the palace, runs Victoria Avenue, renamed Kasr (palace) Avenue after Independence. This too is a tree-lined avenue extending from the Blue Nile to the Khartoum Passengers Main Railway Station. On this main avenue the Khartoum Synagogue was built.

10. A *gallabia* is the traditional dress for men in Northern Sudan. It consists of an ankle-length, white buttonless tunic worn free-flowing, except for waiters and butlers, who add a cummerbund. In waiters, the color of the cummerbund indicates the rank of the waiter (captain, red; waiter, green, assistant waiter or bus boy, no cummerbund).

11. *Moghren* is the Arabic word for junction and is so named because at this point the meeting of the Blue and White Niles can be seen running along side each other with unmingled waters.

2. Downtown Khartoum, which was rebuilt as a modern city after General Kitchener recaptured it from the Mahdi in 1898.

3. View of Khartoum, showing the Blue Nile and the Blue Nile Bridge.

The Khartoum *souk* is a large colorful, covered market located in the center of town next to the main Khartoum Mosque. In its open-air stalls, one could purchase fresh produce as well as colorful spices, live chickens, and other livestock. In contrast, the older *souk* in Omdurman sold more exotic goods, such as leopardskin or cheetah leather goods, Sudanese *khanjars* (daggers), spears and shields, carved silver utensils, and hand embroidery, Dongola stallions and asses; and in the background were the rolling dunes of the open desert and sometimes a camping or passing caravan, complete with unruly grumbling camels. In its crowded streets, cars vied with passing camels, donkeys, or horse-drawn carts.

Except for the heat, life in Khartoum was inexpensive and comfortable. Most households had at least one servant; and many had several in the positions of butler, assistant butler, cook, maid, and gardener. Homes were spacious and surrounded by cool yards and gardens. Evenings were spent socializing at home parties or in the clubs. Some of these garden parties were very formal, but most were informal, friendly affairs. Members of the foreign communities intermingled freely, though the British tended to stay somewhat aloof. Going to the movies was very popular, as was a leisurely drive along the river in the cool hours after sunset. Because of the midday heat, schools and businesses closed down at noon and did not re-open until four o'clock, when the temperature was cooler, and then stayed open to six or seven at night. The weather was dry nine to ten months of the year, with nightly a brilliantly studded sky filled with a myriad of bright stars unobscured by any pollution.

In February 1995, the total population of the Sudan was 30,120,420,[12] up from 15–16 million in 1964. The population of the three-town metropolitan area of Khartoum, Omdurman, Khartoum North–Halfaya is up from about 1 million in 1964 to an estimated 7 million in 1995. Of this number, Khartoum accounts for about 2 million; Omdurman, with its suburbs Wad Sayedna and Omdurman Thowra, for 4 million; and Khartoum North–Halfaya for about 1 million.

---

12. According to the CIA *World Fact Book 1996/97*, 398.

2

꙰

The First Jews and the Mahdiya

The history of the Jews in the Sudan starts with eight Jewish families living in Omdurman. Living under Egyptian-Turkish rule, they were in 1885 free to practice their religion.

In 1881, Muhamed Ahmed Ibn Abdulla El-Mahdi appeared in Aba Island, located in the White Nile south of Khartoum, and proclaimed himself the expected Mahdi. *El-Mahdi* (The Mahdi) derives from *hada*, which means the leader and guide to the right path. The Mahdi preached that the prophet Muhamed had promised that one of his descendants would one day appear and reanimate the faith and declared, with unshakable conviction, that he was that man. He led a violent jihad (holy war) against all infidels and a revolt to oust the Egyptian-Turkish rule started by Muhamed Ali Pasha in 1820 and subsequently continued by his successors the Khedive Ismail and, in 1881, the Khedive Muhamed Tewfic.

A small force sent to Aba Island, to bring the Mahdi to Khartoum for punishment was defeated and massacred by his followers. The Mahdi then retreated with his followers to the desert Kordofan Province in Western Sudan. He called his followers the Ansar (Ar. supporters). *Ansar* was the same name used by the supporters of the prophet Muhamed when they accompanied him on his Hijra from Mecca to Medina. In Kordofan, the Mahdi was joined by other tribes. Among these were the Baggara nomads, who were cowmen and whose name derives from the Arabic word *bagara* (cow). The leader of the Baggara was Abdulla El-Taishi, who was already the Mahdi's devoted disciple, principal emir (Ar. chieftain, nobleman, prince), and later his khalifa (successor).

In the following four years, the Mahdi and his forces carried out their jihad and revolt against the Egyptian administration of the Sudan. In due course, El-Obeid, the capital of Kordofan, with its 100,000 population, its

4. Muhamed Ahmed Ibn Abdulla El-Madhi. Courtesy of the Mansell Collection, London.

Egyptian garrison, and its £100,000 treasury, fell to him. Later, Rudolph Slatin Pasha, the Austrian-born Egyptian governor of Darfur Province, and Frank Lupton, the British-born Egyptian governor of Bahr El-Ghazal Province, were defeated and captured; and the Mahdi pushed on to Omdurman.

In response to this series of events, military expeditions were sent to Kordofan under the command of both Egyptian and British officers but were defeated and annihilated. Of note among them was the Hicks expedition, under the command of the Indian army officer William Hicks, which however fared no better.

Sir Charles Gordon Pasha (Chinese Gordon) was sent back to Khartoum as governor general of the Sudan. Gordon was a religious mystic with violent swings of mood and severe bouts of depression and possibly drinking and a particular hatred for the abomination of slave trading. He had previously served in the Sudan and put a significant dent in the widespread slave trade, particularly relative to El-Zubayr Rahma Pasha, then the greatest slave trader of them all, who was enticed to go to Egypt whence he was not allowed to return. When Zubayr's son took over the trade, Gordon had him executed. On his return to the Sudan as governor general, Gordon tried unsuccessfully to reach accommodation with the Mahdi. Failing to do so, he appealed repeatedly for military troops to allow him to evacuate the garrisons and civilians; but his calls went unheeded and rebuffed. He was in fact ordered to leave the Sudan but refused to do so, on the basis that his honor would not permit him to leave the garrison and civilians behind. He decided to stay in the besieged capital city of Khartoum and defend it with the inadequate available Egyptian garrison and loyalists and continue to await military reinforcements from London and Cairo. Reinforcements were finally sent as a little flotilla sailing down the Nile under the command of Sir Charles Wilson. Ironically, it arrived on Gordon's birthday and two days too late to rescue him and his garrison. The flotilla turned back and returned north when it learned that General Gordon had been defeated and killed and that Khartoum had fallen to the Mahdi.

Omdurman and Khartoum are sister cities, located a stone's throw across the river Nile from each other. In 1885, Muhamed Ahmed El-Mahdi, having by then most of the Sudan under his control, established his Islamic rule in the older city of Omdurman. His dervish forces had captured the capital city of Khartoum and, after Khartoum's fall on 26 January 1885, had speared to death Sir Charles Gordon Pasha on the

5. Statue of Sir Charles Gordon Pasha, which, until Sudanese independence, stood before the Governor's Palace in Khartoum.

very stairs of his Governor General's Palace in Khartoum. Elsewhere in Khartoum, there was widespread slaughter of infidels. Nicholas Leonticles, the Greek consul, had his hands cut off and was then beheaded. The Austrian consul, Martin Hansal, was killed and burned in front of his home. Another Austrian, a tailor, had his throat cut in front of his wife and children when in terror he crossed himself; and his eighteen-year-old son was speared and thrown at the feet of his mother, while his daughter was dragged off to be a concubine.[1]

The Mahdi ruled a few months more and then died in June 1885, a mere five months after Gordon's death. He was succeeded by his loyal lieutenant, El-Khalifa Abdulla El-Taishi. Under the Mahdi's rule and that of the Khalifa, a period of ten to thirteen years known as the Mahdiya, all infidels, who included the eight Jewish families; Christian Copts and Greeks; Protestants; and Roman Catholics, including priests,

1. Byron Farwell, *Prisoners of the Mahdi* (New York: Harper and Row, 1967), 97.

nuns, and missionaries, were forced to convert to Islam or face death and mutilation. Slatin Pasha and Frank Lupton, had preceded them in professing the Muslim faith to escape execution.

The eight Jewish families in the Sudan at that time were all Sephardim.[2] There was a possible exception of one whose name had been Arabized to *Mandeel*. It is presumed his original name was *Mandel* or *Mendel*, which would suggest an Ashkenazi origin. All eight were forcibly converted to Islam. I think of them as having become the Anusim of Sudan, or forcibly converted ones, analogous to the Anusim of Spain, who were forcibly converted to Christianity in the fifteenth century.

The leader of the eight was Ben-Sion Coshti. On conversion to Islam during the Mahdiya, his name was Arabized to Bassiouni, which he kept after returning to Judaism and which has remained the name of his family and that of his children and grandchildren to this day.

Ben-Sion Coshti was a practicing Jew of Turkish origin. A tall, imposing figure with a striking red beard, he represented the Jews at the courts of the Mahdi and his Khalifa. He was the son of Rabbi Mayer Bechor Coshti of Hebron. Even after professing Islam, he remained secretly observant of his Jewish faith. It was told that he used to put on his tefillin (phylactery) every week day and say his shahrit prayers secretly at his home before going to the mosque. He and other forced converts were obliged to go to the Grand Mosque in Omdurman, especially for Friday prayers; and Khalifa Abdulla and his agents watched them carefully to ensure that they did so.

Besides Bassiouni, the other original Jewish families were those of Shalom Samuel Hakim; his brother Aslan Hakim; Nessim Shalom; Khidr Daoud; Suleiman Mandeel or Mendel, and about whom more later.

Seething from the defeat of British will and the massacre of garrisons and civilians in the Sudan, and shamed by the abandonment of their envoy Gordon, public demand in Britain forced the British government, who wished nothing more than to avoid further entanglement in the Sudan, to organize yet another expedition to conquer the Sudan. In the interim, the Austrian officer Slatin Pasha,[3] prisoner and confidant of

---

2. Sephardim is the name given to Jews who originally lived in Spain during its golden age and who were forced to leave in 1492 after the Spanish Inquisition. Today, it frequently also broadly encompasses all Jews from Middle Eastern countries, as distinguished from the Ashkenazim, or Jews of German and Eastern European origins.

3. Slatin had been governor of Darfur when he was captured by the Mahdi.

the Mahdi's court and emirs, escaped from the Sudan to Egypt, disguised as an Arab in bedraggled clothes. He was assigned to the intelligence service of the British rebuilt and run Army of Egypt with the rank of pasha and provided extremely valuable information about the Sudan before the Kitchener expedition. General Sir Horatio Herbert Kitchener, a then little-known British officer in Egypt, who, to the surprise of many, had been recently named sirdar (commander in chief) of the army of Egypt, was authorized in 1886 to prepare an expedition to reconquer the Sudan. By 1 September 1898, General Kitchener had arrived before Omdurman with a force of more than 20,000 Egyptian troops and fierce Sudanese battalions commanded by both British and Egyptian officers. They included gunboats of the Royal Navy, one hundred heavy guns, and a large number of camels and horses. Among the troops were Slatin Pasha; an intelligence officer named Wingate, who later became Sir Reginald Wingate, governor general of the Sudan; and young Winston Churchill.

This impressive military force engaged the Khalifa dervish forces in what is known as the battle of Omdurman. The battle took place on the Karari hills, a few miles outside the town of Omdurman, which was the Mahdiya capital. Conventional wisdom was that the Khalifa did not have much of a chance. Many of his 50,000 warriors were armed with nothing more than spears, his guns were obsolete, and his steamers were hardly a match for the British gunboats. The dervish forces, however, imbued with religious fervor, attacked en masse, rushing head on into British artillery, which mowed them down in blast after blast. Kitchener's rifles completed the job. On the left side of the battlefield, in a throwback to a previous age, the Twenty-first Lancers made a gallant but disastrous and pointless cavalry charge. Young Winston Churchill was part of that charge; and rushing intently at the enemy with pointed spear, he was almost killed by a dervish sword.[4]

4. In *My Early Life: A Roving Commission* (New York: Scribner's, 1987), 191, Churchill says, Once again I was in the hard, crisp desert, my horse at a trot. I had the impression of scattered dervishes running to an fro in all directions. Straight before me a man threw himself on the ground. My first idea was that the man was terrified. But simultaneously I saw the gleam of his curved sword as he drew it back for a ham-stringing cut. I had room and time enough to turn my pony out of his reach, and leaning over on the off side I fired two shots into him at about three yards. As I righted myself in the saddle, I saw before me another figure with uplifted sword. I raised my pistol and fired. Man and sword disappeared behind me.

On 2 September 1898, General Kitchener had defeated the Khalifa and his dervish hordes. Kitchener set up his headquarters in the very mosque the Khalifa used in Omdurman. The Khalifa had however escaped capture with 30,000 fugitives, including Osman Digna, and retreated toward their old stronghold of El-Obeid. He was defeated there one year later.

The eight Jewish families had lived under the Mahdiya rule as forced Muslims from 1885 to 1898. As soon as the Anglo-Egyptian government was established, these Jews returned to Judaism. Those of them who had in the interim married Muslim women converted their wives to Judaism and circumcised their sons as soon as it was possible for them to do so.

Suddenly in the midst of the troop up sprang a Dervish. How he got there I do not know. He must have leaped out of some scrub or hole. All the troupers turned upon him thrusting with their lances but he darted to and fro causing for the moment a frantic commotion. Wounded several times he staggered towards me raising his spear. I shot him at less than a yard. How easy to kill a man. But I did not worry about it." Winston Churchill was then twenty-one years old.

3

Ben-Sion Coshti and Other Jews

Before and during the Mahdiya, the Sudan Jews, like many others, were engaged in commerce, exporting Sudan products such as gum arabic, sheepskins, ivory, and ostrich feathers (then highly valued in Europe for fashionable ladies' hats) and importing Sudan needs such as textiles, soap, and the like. Export and import took place either overland through Egypt or by sea through the ancient Red Sea port of Suakin. The overland route taken was an ancient well-traveled caravan trade route known as *Darb Al-Arba²in*. *Darb* (Ar. road) and *arba²in* (Ar. forty), thus the forty days road, so named because it took a caravan forty days to reach Cairo. The route ran from El-Fasher in Darfur, through El-Obeid in Kordofan, through Halfaya, in the vicinity of Khartoum North, and then to the ancient market town of Shendi in the Northern Province. From Shendi,[1] the route divided into two routes. One proceeded from Shendi to the Red Sea port of Suakin. The other went to Sennar (site of the ancient Kingdom of Sennar), through Berber, to Abu Hamad, and then through the desert to Ibrim near Wadi Halfa. From there, the route continued to Aswan and Asyut in Upper Egypt, ending in Giza, of pyramid fame, outside Cairo.

Following the defeat of the Mahdiya and the reconquest of the Sudan

---

1. In ancient times, Shendi was a busy market town, where products as varied as slaves (5,000 per year according to some reports), ostrich feathers, Dongola horses, ivory, and other local produce were available. Early travelers told that one could, a couple of hundred years ago, purchase goods such as swords and razor blades from Germany and soap and other products from Egypt and Ethiopia. Because of its location on the caravan routes, traders from afar came to it as well as pilgrims on their way to Suakin and then on to Mecca. In my day, however, Shendi was an ordinary market town that had little to differentiate it from other native markets.

19

by General Kitchener, things settled somewhat in Omdurman. The Jewish families, having returned to Judaism, found in Ben-Sion Coshti, now known as Bassiouni, a father figure and protector. They looked to him for leadership, and he led them in the discharge of their religious duties. All Shabbat (Sabbath) services and festival prayers were conducted by him in his own home in Omdurman.

There then arrived several other Jews from Egypt to add to the embryonic Jewish community in the Sudan. These were followed shortly thereafter by Rabbi Solomon Malka, my father, who came from Tiberias. These early Sudan Jews joined to form and found the Sudan Jewish Community. Bassiouni was elected its president for life, a position he held from 1908 to his death in 1917.

When we later established the B'nai B'rith Lodge in Khartoum, it was named the Ben-Sion Coshti Lodge in memory of this man and what he endured and did for his faith.

Bassiouni's first wife was Bechora, a daughter of a well-established and -known Sephardic family in Cairo. Unfortunately, their union was barren. During his forced period of Islamic conversion, he married a Sudanese Muslim named Manna,[2] who bore him four children: Naomi (Arabized to Ni'ema,[3] a blessing), Esther, David, and Suleiman (Solomon). All four grew up to have distinguished careers in the Sudan. Except for David, who died in Khartoum, they all immigrated to Israel via Eritrea with their children and lived in and around Holon. In Israel, Suleiman Bassiouni, a physician, changed his family name back to the original Ben-Sion. Manna, who had converted to Judaism, was, both before and after her husband's death, a devout Jewess. She kept a Jewish home and reared her children in the Jewish faith and traditions. Manna's eldest son, David, was a friend of mine, and I recall visiting their home for lunch while in my early teens and being impressed that she was the

2. During the Mahdiya, all converts were required to take a Muslim wife. Almost all the Jews in the Sudan married a Sudanese Muslim, as did many Copts and Christians. It was even said that the Catholic priests married the Catholic nuns after both were forced to accept Islam. "There was the question of those nuns with the Austrian mission to Darfur; there was a rumor that they had been married to the Greek traders who had also been captured by the Mahdi. What a row the Pope will make about the nuns marrying the Greeks. It is the union of the Greek and Latin Churches." Alan Morehead, The White Nile (New York: Dell, 1969), 261.

3. Ni'ema, born in the year Kitchener, "the English," entered Omdurman, was nicknamed "Angleterra" by her Sudanese nanny.

one who led us in reciting the *hamotse* (Jewish grace) in Hebrew before allowing us to partake of any food.

Shalom Samuel Hakim was also married to a Sephardic lady from Cairo. Her name was Esther, and she bore him three daughters (Rose, Gracia, and Sarina) and two sons (Victor and Samuel). The daughters married fine young Jewish men, newcomers from Egypt. Rose married Ibrahim Seroussi, a future president of the Sudan Jewish Community; Gracia married Leon Ortasse, a future vice-president; and Sarina married Yacoub Ades. Victor was in business with his uncle Raphael. They were exporters of senna pods and other Sudan produce. As a ten-year-old boy growing up in Omdurman, I used to spend my summer school vacations as an office boy in Victor and Raphael Hakim's offices. I began my stamp collection by gathering all the foreign and local stamps from their business mail. Samuel, Victor's brother, was an accountant for the Sudan Gezira Board, which was the large agricultural governing body in the Sudan.

During the forced Islamic Mahdiya period, Shalom Hakim married a second wife, who was Sudanese. Her name was Rosa, daughter of Suleiman Hindi. After her husband died, she immigrated to Palestine, where she became known as Rosa El-Sudaniya (the Sudanese Rose). Her children settled in the United States; and one of them, Gershon Hakim, became a furrier in Manhattan. Shalom's brother, Aslan Hakim, also married a Sudanese wife. They had a daughter, whose name was Fortuna.

Another Mahdiya Jew, Nessim Shalom, died early on in Omdurman. His family went back to Egypt. One of his sons, who became an agricultural engineer for the Kom Ombo Cotton Plantations in Upper Egypt and later an agricultural authority on the staff of the United Nations, came to me in Khartoum in the 1940s looking for the grave of his father. I found it for him in the Omdurman Jewish Cemetery, a vast burial ground with only a few graves. Among them, we came across the grave of Ben-Sion Coshti.

Another Mahdiya Jew, Khidr Daoud, left one daughter, Rachel, who married Menashe Yousef Levy. Rachel Levy became a well-known midwife in Khartoum, delivering both Jews and non-Jews. One of her children, Joseph Levy, briefly worked for my company. Ultimately, he left to return to Egypt, where he married and died. Rachel Levy's daughters, Josephine and Victoria, left the Sudan for Asmara (Eritrea) and from there to Italy, where they were married and took up residence. On the last day of 1994, I met the son of Josephine, grandson of Rachel Levy.

A pleasant, twenty-one-year-old Italian with the name of Joseph Marnignone, he was at my brother David's home in New Jersey among the many Sudan Jews who came from Europe and other places in the United States to offer condolences to my brother David on the passing of his beloved wife, Jean Malka Bat Dannon.

A Jew who did not return to Judaism was named Suleiman Mandeel, son of a Mahdiya-converted Jew whose name was probably *Mendel* and Arabized to *Mandeel*. Despite repeated efforts by my father, Rabbi Solomon Malka, to convince him to return to the faith of his fathers, he consistently demurred. One reason he cited was that his sisters, of black complexion because of their Sudanese mother, would be unable to find husbands among the young white Jews coming from Cairo. He remained an ardent Muslim and became a prominent Arab journalist.

There was also a well-known race horse owner who lived in Omdurman whose name was Barakat Israel. His name would seem to indicate that he was a son of the eighth Mahdiya Jew, who never returned to Judaism.

4

⋘⋙

Early Settlers
and Founding Families

There was no Sudanese railway connection with Egypt until 1898. It was then that Kitchener, with his advancing army, completed the construction of the first railway line extending from Wadi Halfa, across the Nubian Desert to Abu Hamad, and then from Abu Hamad to Khartoum North. Wadi Halfa was the Nile port in Northern Sudan closest to the Egyptian border and was already connected with Aswan in Egypt by river steamers. Aswan in turn was connected to Cairo by the Egyptian State Railways.

As soon as the railway connection with Cairo was completed, a number of Jews from Egypt flocked to the Sudan seeking commercial opportunities. A few even arrived with Kitchener's army in 1898 on the first trains to Khartoum North, the final stop before the Blue Nile Bridge connected it with Khartoum in 1916.

The Khartoum North Jews

The El-Eini family were among the first arrivals to Khartoum North.[1] Mourad Israel El-Eini arrived in 1898 on one of the first army trains as army purveyor throughout the journey from Egypt. As a result, the commanding officer rewarded him with the first permit to open a shop in

---

1. At times, parts of this chapter will read like the old testament: "And the generations that went forth unto Egypt were . . . ." Please indulge me because I feel the need to enumerate the names of these early Jews as part of the reason for this book describing a Jewish Community that has disappeared.

Khartoum North given to a newcomer. El-Eini subsequently returned to Cairo to bring his parents and his bride, Farida, back to the Sudan. After his early death at age forty-six, his widow guided his sons Saleh, Suleiman, Ibrahim, and Zaki as they developed their family business into one of the larger commercial enterprises in the area. Shortly thereafter, Mourad's brothers, Daoud Israel El-Eini and Mousa Israel El-Eini,[2] who was only four years old, followed him to the Sudan.

Around about 1910, they were joined by Ibrahim Cohen from Cairo and Sassoon Ezra from Baghdad. The latter came with his older sons, and his wife stayed with the rest of his family in India until the men got established. This was not an uncommon plan for Jews from Iraq, who frequently had relatives or friends in India; it was also followed by Shaoul Eliaho, who arrived from Basra, through Cairo, leaving his wife and children in India until he too was established.

All these newcomers opened shops in the main market of Khartoum North and built homes for themselves and their families nearby. Even though moving to Khartoum North was adventure enough, some went farther afield. Shaoul Eliaho set up business in the ancient town of Marawi, in Dongola Province, where, he remained the only Jew in that isolated place. During one of my business tours, I made a special detour to Marawi to visit him and his wife, which they seemed to appreciate. Even though the Eliahos kept a home in Khartoum North, their sons pursued their education and careers in Khartoum.

The Khartoum Jews

Another group of shopkeepers coming from Egypt crossed to Khartoum and established their shops there. These were mostly retailers of cotton and silk piece goods, textiles, and haberdashery. Among these

---

2. Some Jews living in Arab countries Arabized their Jewish names in the same manner that American Jews Anglicized their names to Solomon, Debbie, or Saul, instead of Shlomo, Deborah, or Shaoul; or in France to Jean or Jeannette instead of Jonathan or Hannah.

Common Arabized names were Daoud (David), Gabra (Gabriel), Mousa (Moses or Moshé), Ibrahim (Abraham), Ishag (Ishak, Yitzhak), Suleiman (Solomon), Yacoub (Jacob, Ya'acov), Zaki (Isaac).

Other names that sound unfamiliar to a Western ear do so because they retain in fact their original Hebrew pronunciations. Among these are Eliaho (Eli), Ezra, Shalom, Shaoul (Saul), and Nessim.

were the Shoua family, led by Farag Shoua; Ishag Daoud; Elie Mashiah; Yacoub Aeleon; and Baroukh Israel, followed by Saleh and Hizkeil Baroukh; Herman Bellenstein; Charles Weinberg; Moussa Cohen; Aslan Yettah; Suleiman Kudsi; Moussa Harari; and Mathiu Sidis.

The heads of other families, Aslan Cohen and Ibrahim Ades, came about the same time; and later they and Elias Benou Jr. and Saleh Baroukh established themselves in Wad Medani, the capital of the Blue Nile Province and center of the cotton plantations, 175 miles South of Khartoum.

The Omdurman Jews

The greater number of Jews coming from Egypt however settled in Omdurman, then as now the largest Sudanese metropolis and a major marketplace and trade center. The early settlers in Omdurman in the first five years of the twentieth century included Edward Castro, Menahim Saleh, Mayer Ephraim, Yousef Arbab, Ezra Marcos, Samuel Hizgeil Wais, and Yousef Mizrahi. Among the newcomers in the 1900–1915 period were Leon Mafinfeker, Boris Kantzer, Emile Feinstein, and the Benous. The Benous, who included Elias Benou, Suleiman Benou, and their brothers who specialized in gum arabic, then the main produce of the Sudan, became dealers and exporters of Sudan produce for two generations. The Seroussis, led by Ibrahim Seroussi, specialized in goatskins, sheepskins, and other animal hides. They remain in that field now in their third and fourth generations, with establishments in Gloversville, New York, in Nigeria, and in other skin markets. Aslan Seroussi followed his older brother Ibrahim, to Omdurman and there established his own trade and family. Abraham Dwek, a pious Jew from Aleppo, Syria, led an exemplary Jewish life, and he and his family became textile merchants until their second generation in the Sudan. He, too, was followed to Omdurman by his brothers Aaron and Shabtai Dwek. Other early settlers in Omdurman were Suleiman Ani (another goatskin and sheepskin merchant) and, shortly thereafter, Elie Tammam, Gabra Cohen, Gabra Pinto, Abdalla Saltoun, Yousef Abboudi, and Obadia Safadi, all of whom were independent merchants in various lines.

During the same period, in the early 1900s, the leading Jewish firms in Cairo also rushed to open branches in Omdurman. Prominent among those were B. Nathan & Co., a major Manchester cotton piece goods wholesale importing firm, and Giulio Padova & Co., another major wholesale importer of sundry goods. Their Jewish managers got involved in and played an important part in the progress of the Jewish Community. Three early managers of B. Nathan were Raphael Ades, Joseph Forti, and Albert Forti, all of whom became president of the Sudan Jewish Community. The last B. Nathan manager, who subsequently took over the Omdurman branch for his own account, was named Czar Levy. Levy married Esther, a daughter of the first Mahdiya Jew, Ben-Sion Coshti. Esther went on to become the first female inspector of education in the Sudan.

The Jewish managers of Giulio Padova included Aaron and Shabtai Dwek, who were quite active in Community affairs in the 1950s and 1960s. One of their managers, Joseph Tammam, became president of the Community a little time after his father, Elie Tammam, had held the post.

These early Jewish families, with their Jewish brethren from the hectic Mahdiya era, formed the nucleus of the first Jewish Community in the Sudan. They were to be led by their religious and spiritual leader, Rabbi Solomon Malka, who arrived in Omdurman in 1906.

5

⚜

Rabbi Solomon Malka and the First Community Council

In August 1906, Rabbi Solomon Malka (1878–1949) arrived in Omdurman from Tiberias, Palestine, traveling through Egypt. He was then twenty-eight, *Rab Talmudi Musamakh* (ordained rabbi learned in Torah and Talmud), a member of Beth Din (religious court) of Tiberias, and had his smikhot (rabbi's ordination) from Tiberias and a Board of Rabbis in Safad. He used to tell me that all three of the rabbis who examined him in Safad were Ashkenazim; and that at the end of the exam, one of them turned to the others and said "he is a good frenk," meaning "he is a good Sepharad."

Rabbi Solomon Malka went to the Sudan at the behest of Rabbi Eliahu Hazan, who was then the grand rabbi of Alexandria and Egypt. In 1906, Alexandria was the seat of the Hakhambashi[1] (grand rabbi) of Egypt and its chief rabbinate. By the 1920s, when the population of Jews in Cairo had grown to exceed that of Alexandria, the seat was transferred to Cairo. Rabbi Eliahu Hazan, seeing a growing number of Jews in the Sudan without religious leadership, called upon Rabbi Solomon Malka to leave Tiberias for Omdurman to provide religious leadership and services to the Sudan Jews and to organize their congregation.

My father was born in Morocco of a rabbinic family and studied in its Yeshivot, or religious academies. His elder brother Yehiael, who was eigh-

---

1. *Hakhambashi* is an interesting title because it combines Hebraic and Turkish roots. *Hakham* (H. wise or sage), the common title for a rabbi in Sephardic communities, and *bashi*, or *basha*, (Eg. deformation of the Tr. title *pasha*). Hence, *Hakhambashi* became the official title of the grand rabbi in Turkey and Egypt and was recognized as such.

27

6. Rabbi Solomon Malka (1878–1949), Hakham of the Sudan, its chief rabbi.

7. Hanna David Assouline Malka, Rabbi Malka's wife.

teen years his senior and a remarkable Talmudic rabbi and Rosh (head of) Yeshiva, served as chief rabbi of the Tafilalt district, a southern province of Morocco. In about 1898, at age twenty, Rabbi Solomon Malka made *aliya* (immmigrated) to Eretz Israel (Palestine) to continue his rabbinic studies in the Yeshivot of Tiberias and Safad and because of a desire to live in the Holy Land. This was a common aspiration of many religious Sephardic Jews in North Africa, Egypt, and other parts of the Middle East. They wished to return to Zion, live, populate, and die in the Holy Land and consummate a two-thousand-year-old Messianic dream. This movement assured a continued Jewish presence in Jerusalem and the holy cities of Tiberias and Safad until the modern Zionist movement, which resulted in the Jewish State of Israel.

My father once told me that, on leaving Morocco for Palestine, his father, who was fairly well off by the Jewish Moroccan standards of those days, gave him some money, probably as part of his inheritance. On his arrival in Tiberias, my father, following an old tradition, entrusted the money to a distant cousin, whose family name was Dahan and who had traveled with him from Morocco. The idea was for this distant relative to work the money in partnership for him while my father devoted his time to studying the Torah. Unfortunately, before long, my father's cousin, whose sons, Mayer and David Dahan, I came to know in future years, lost my father's capital in unsuccessful trades. Knowing that his family owned orchards and vineyards in Morocco, my father decided to return to Morocco to fetch another part of his inheritance. The story he told me was that, on his arrival home, he was met with great festivities, including in the tradition of those days, a parade of horsemen who rode out to meet and greet him, some firing guns in the air. Faced with such an overwhelming welcome home, he became too embarrassed to ask for any more money and returned to Palestine empty handed. The need to earn a living and support his family may have been the reason for his agreeing to leave Eretz Israel to accept the position of rabbi in the far-away Sudan when it was offered to him. My father left for the Sudan in 1906, leaving behind in Tiberias my mother and my two elder sisters, Esther and Fortunée. In 1908, he returned to Tiberias and took my mother and sisters to Omdurman, where I was born in November 1909.[2]

On his arrival in the Sudan, Rabbi Malka rented a house in Omdurman in the Haret El-Masalma quarter (*haret* means lane, *El-Masalma* means those who accepted Islam). All Jews and Christians from the Mahdiya times and those who joined them in Omdurman in the early years lived in El-Masalma quarter. It was also the preferred residential quarter of many prestigious native Sudanese families.

Rabbi Malka transformed this house in Omdurman into a "syna-

---

2. This series of events is a recurring theme in religious rabbinical families as far back as Maimonides (Moses Ibn Maimon), who on his arrival in Egypt busied himself in his studies, writings, and Jewish Community affairs and let his younger brother, David, engage in trade to support the family. David became a successful merchant, engaging in risky but lucrative trade with India. On one journey to India, he was shipwrecked and lost at sea with most of the family's fortune. Because of the need to earn an income to support his family, Maimonides began to practice medicine again, a profession for which he had already previously earned high repute (Simon Novecks ed., *Great Jewish Personalities in Ancient and Medieval Times*, 208).

gogue," equipped it with Sepharim (Torah scrolls) brought from Egypt and the Holy Land, and conducted there all Shabbat, festivals, and daily services. Seeing the lack of kasher (kosher) meat, he also performed shehita (ritual slaughtering) at the Omdurman slaughterhouse; and from then on, kasher meat became available to Sudan Jews.

In one of his first acts, Rabbi Malka converted to Judaism the Sudanese Muslim wives and their children from the Mahdiya period, in full accordance with the Halakha (legal part of the Talmud) rules and principles. The first giyoret, or converted Jewess, was Manna Bassiouni. She was given the name of Hanna Bat Abraham and coverted to Judaism with her children Naomi (Niʾema), Esther, and David. This conversion occurred on 31 January 1908, during the visit and with the participation of Eliahu Hazan, the grand rabbi of Alexandria and Egypt. She was soon followed by Rosa, the wife of Shalom Hakim, another Mahdiya Jew. Soon after the early death of her husband, Rosa left the Sudan to go live in Eretz Israel.

Because there was no other, Rabbi Malka was also the mohel[3] for the Community. The first Brit Milah he ever performed was on his own son Eliaho at eight days of age. Because I apparently survived the procedure with no apparent ill effects, the parents of other Jewish children needing circumcision called on my dad when circumcisions were due.

And because of the absence of a mohel, there was a small backlog. David Bassiouni, eldest son of Ben-Sion Coshti, was three years old and Edward Benou, son of Elias Benou, was one year old when my father circumcised them. Suleiman Bassiouni, the second son of Ben-Sion Coshti, was born two months after me; and he and all other Jewish males born in Ordurman after him were circumcised when they were eight days old, according to the Covenant.

Rabbi Malka found that the salary that the Community was able to

---

3. The person who performs ritual Jewish circumcisions. *Brit* (Covenant) *Milah* (circumcision) refers to the Covenant made by God with Abraham, by which Abraham and his descendants circumcise every male on the eighth day after his birth and by which Abraham and his descendants inherit the land of Canaan and God will be their only God. "I will establish my covenant (H. Beriti, from Berit, meaning covenant) between me and thee and thy seed after thee throughout their generations, to be a God unto thee and thy seed after thee, and I will give unto thee the land of Canaan for an everlasting possession, and I will be their God" (Gen. 17:7–8). "This is my covenant that you shall keep between Me and you and thy seed after thee; every male among you shall be circumcised and he that is eight days shall be circumcised among you, even every male throughout your generations" (Gen. 17:10–13).

pay him was far too meager to live on and rear his children. He thought, however, that he could not leave the people with no rabbi, shohet (ritual slaughterer), religious instruction, or leadership. He therefore embarked on obtaining a separate source of income; and in later years he owned in Khartoum a sesame-oil mill, a factory manufacturing floor tiles, and a macaroni factory. One of the products of the macaroni factory was vermicelli, which was called sha'ria (from Ar. *sha'ar*, which means hair). The sha'ria was produced in a figure-eight shape and became popular with the Sudanese, who mostly prepared it as a dessert coated with sugar. With the income from his businesses, the rabbi was able to discharge both his religious and parental duties simultaneously.

My father owned the vast one-story building that housed the macaroni factory. It was located at the edge of the Khartoum native market area, and he rented its frontage as a row of shops. The factory, with its native workers, was located at the back of the premises. Immediately behind the factory's front gate was a pleasant, spacious room that my father used as an office, study, and meeting place.

It was in this office that my father would regularly receive Father Boulos (Paul), a priest of the Omdurman Protestant Church, who would come at least once weekly to study the Old Testament and the prophets in Arabic with my father. We liked Father Boulos. He was a friendly, robust fellow, converted to Christianity from Islam by the Church Missionary Society (CMS). His name was no accident because this society tended always to give the name of St. Paul to their Muslim converts.

Many other Christian priests, Jewish disciples, and students came to my father for study, learning, and consultation, either in his office and study in the macaroni factory or at appointed times in his study in his Khartoum house.

A visit I particularly remember was that of the Reverend Mr. Revington, one of my own teachers at the Church Missionary Boys School of Cairo. The Reverend Mr. Revington came to my father from Cairo with a small English version of the Qur'an that had footnotes on each page pointing out the Jewish sources of the Qur'anic verses, whose text was similar, or in some cases identical, to those in the Talmud or other Jewish sources. Father would soon enough find and supply the Reverend Mr. Revington with the Jewish source and the exact text that was similar to that in the Qur'anic Sura. Even though my father's English was limited, they communicated well because the Reverend Mr. Revington was fluent in classical Arabic.

Beginning in the early 1940s, I replaced my father in controlling the macaroni factory during his almost yearly six-to-eight-week lecture and preaching tour to Cairo or Alexandria, during which he would visit his daughter Fortunée (H. Mazzal), her husband, Bernard Goldring, and their children in their home in Cairo. During his absence on these trips, I would visit the macaroni factory early in the morning before my office hours at Gellatly and from a locked storehouse on the premises give the foreman the required number of flour bags by weight that were necessary for that day's production. At the end of my office hours at Gellatly Hankey, the leading British company in the Sudan, I would return to check and control by number and weight the product manufactured that day. On his return from his trip, my father, pleased with my control and results, would bless me, which was the best reward I could wish for.

I was only a child when my father first started business in Omdurman; but I know that around 1918 or the early 1920s, he encouraged a young distant relative, Makhlouf Malka, to leave Morocco and join him in the Sudan. He took this relative into partnership and opened for him a textiles and haberdashery store in Khartoum. They later moved the store to the town of Hassa Heissa, the second largest city after Wad Medani in the Gezira cotton belt, where it did very well. Makhlouf later married my eldest sister, Esther, and had his own textile and haberdashery business and store in Khartoum.

About my father's sesame-oil mill, I recall that it was one of the first engine-driven hydraulic presses in the area, at a time when the majority were camel-driven, native-made wooden presses. There were still quite a few of those camel-driven oil mills in use when I was in the Sudan, and I suspect there may still be some in use in the interior. After a few years, my father sold his share in the mill to his Sudanese partner and moved on to other things.

The tiles factory he established lasted much longer. It produced black, white, and red square tiles, which, at the time, were the most popular tile flooring used in new houses. The presses in this factory were also hydraulic and imported. They were housed in premises not far from my father's house in Khartoum and run by skilled native labor. Needless to say, my two-story house in Khartoum was floored entirely in tiles from my father's tile factory.

The macaroni factory was also one of the first of its kind when it was established by my father. Six months or so before his death, my father liquidated all his business assets and activities and wrote his will, which conformed closely to Jewish Halakha law, as if on a premonition that his end was approaching and a desire to leave his heirs a clean estate, which he did. It was at this time that he sold the macaroni factory to a competitor who had established a similar factory. The new owner bought the plant, took over the trained workers, and paid my father and his heirs rent for the premises.

Election of the First Community Council Leaders

During the visit of Rabbi Eliahu Hazan, in his official capacity as Hakhambashi of Egypt and grand rabbi of Alexandria, and under his guidance, the first Sudan Jewish Community Council was elected. The meeting took place on 27 Shebat 5688 (30 January 1908) in the Omdurman Synagogue and, as mentioned previously, Ben-Sion Coshti, the first Mahdiya Jew, was elected president. Rabbi Hazan issued two documents with a title page, the one recording his visit; the second, the election of the first Jewish Community Council under his chairmanship. Both documents are written in his own hand in the old Sephardic script, with his signature and official seal.[4]

An abbreviated translation goes as follows:

Record Book of the Jewish Community of Omdurman,
Sudan Shebat 5668 (January 1908)

Document 1: In continuation of my visit to the Jews of Upper Egypt, I traveled to the Sudan and found in the City of Omdurman a community of Jews, small in number, lenient in Halakha, but God fearing and anxious for the word of the Lord. They came with their families from Omdurman and nearby cities of Khartoum and Halfaya. In the beginning of my actions, I summoned them to a general meeting in the synagogue of Omdurman at 4 pm on 27 Shebat 5668 (30 January 1908), to raise their spirits, organize their Community, and ensure their religious acts are in conformity with the rules of the rabbinate in Egypt. There were 20 men, besides children, with their spiritual leader Rabbi Shlomo Malka, *hashem yish-*

4. As the old Sephardic script is not legible to most modern Hebrew readers, my friend and Hebrew scholar Roberta Barkan, professor of Jewish studies at Purchase College, State University of New York (SUNY), transcribed them for me into easily legible modern Hebrew script. These documents are reproduced in their original and transcribed forms in Appendix A.

mereho (may God bless him). I pointed out to them the irregularity of performing Jewish marriages without the prior permission of the *beit din* (rabbinate court) in Egypt.

Document 2: At the above Community general assembly, I counseled them to elect amongst themselves five able men to place at the head of the people. By secret ballot, they elected the following; and by general agreement they chose them to occupy the undermentioned offices of the first Council of the Community:

Ben-Sion Coshti by 19 votes out of 20, *Nasi* (President)
Nessim Shalom by 19 votes out of 20, *Sokhan* (Vice-President/Treasurer)
Edward Castro by 19 votes out of 20, *Mazkir* (Secretary)
Menahim Saleh and Mayer Ephraim by 16 votes out of 20, *Yoasim* (Counselors)

Because it was customary for a candidate not to cast a vote for himself, nineteen votes were a unanimous vote. It was also decided that in the month of Shebat in each year, the council would call a new general meeting of the Community to report and render account to the Community and elect a new council. The result of each election was to be reported by official letter to the government of the land.

Rabbi Hazan was one of the leading Sephardic rabbis of his time. Marc D. Angel, chief rabbi of the historic Spanish Portuguese Synagogue[5] of New York City and the first Sephardic president of the Rabbinical Council of America, writes extensively about Rabbi Eliahu Hazan. He states that Rabbi Hazan's philosophy of education was reflected in how he dealt with the Jewish School of Tripoli. He was then serving as an emissary to North Africa on behalf of the Jewish Community of Jerusalem. He thought that the level of religious education among the Jews of the city of Tripoli was quite low. Though he would have preferred to remain in Jerusalem, Rabbi Hazan felt the responsibility to provide religious leadership to that large Jewish Community and therefore accepted to serve as

5. The Spanish Portuguese Synagogue of New York City is the oldest Jewish community in New York. It moved to its present address at Seventieth Street and Central Park in 1897 from its original location, dating from 1730, on Mills Street in downtown Manhattan. Its Hebrew name was and still is Shearith Israel, which translates as "remnants of Israel" congregation. The name is meaningful because the congregation was founded by the twenty-three Spanish and Portuguese Jews who landed in New York in 1640–1650. They were fleeing the Inquisitiion that caught up with them when the Portuguese conquerors took over their town of Recife, Brazil, which had previously been in Dutch hands. Their Jewish cemetery can still be seen near Chinatown in Manhattan.

the rabbi of Tripoli in 1874. Fourteen years later, in 1888, he was elected grand rabbi of Alexandria and Egypt. It was in that post that he similarly felt a responsibility for the Jewish Community in the Sudan, which he visited in 1908, the year he died.[6]

After the death of my father in 1949, the Community had difficulty in replacing him. Efforts were made to get a qualified Sephardic rabbi from Israel. We first engaged Rabbi Masliah, but he did not stay long, returning to Israel before two years had gone by. We then got Rabbi Haim Simoni, who stayed an even shorter time.

Finally, we got Rabbi Massoud El-Baz, a young rabbi from Cairo, who served the Community well until his own departure from the Sudan in the early 1970s. By that time, Sudan-born Nessim Gaon had built Heikhal Haness, a beautiful synagogue in Geneva, Switzerland, and engaged Rabbi Massoud El-Baz as the hazzan, where he served until his retirement in Israel, where he died.

6. *Voices in Exile: A Study in Sephardic Intellectual History* (Hoboken, N.J., and New York: Ktav and Sephardic House, 1991), 184.

6

⚜

The Move to Khartoum and the Building of the Khartoum Synagogue

In the meantime, Khartoum, the new capital of the Sudan, had been developing rapidly into a nice, modern town, center of trade, and seat of government. Many Jews moved to it from Omdurman and Khartoum North, and with them was Rabbi Solomon Malka. He found that, in 1918, Farag Shoua had already established a small synagogue in rented premises for the then small Community of Khartoum. From that rented synagogue, Rabbi Malka conducted the services for the Jewish Community and led the effort to establish a permanent and spacious synagogue in Khartoum.

Not much progress was made until Joseph Forti, then manager of the Manchester textiles firm of B. Nathan & Co. in Omdurman, was elected president of the Community. During his four-year term, and as a result of his efforts, a large plot of land was purchased in the middle of Victoria Avenue. Victoria Avenue, now Kasr (palace) Avenue, was then the nicest avenue in Khartoum. It was a broad, tree-lined avenue extending from the Governor's Palace[1] on the Blue Nile embankment to the Khartoum Passengers Main Railway Station.[2]

A beautiful and spacious synagogue was built on that plot in the Sephardic style, with a capacity of about five hundred worshippers. In addition, the azara, or separate women's gallery, was built on the mezzanine

1. Renamed al-Qasr al-Jamhouria (Republican palace) following Sudan Independence and replacement of the British governor general by a president of the Sudan Republic. More recently, it has been renamed Qasr al-Shaʾab (People's palace).

2. In addition to the station for passenger trains, there was the Trucking Railway Station.

8. Interior of the Khartoum Synagogue, showing the teba (reader's desk).

floor, facing the Heikhal (Holy Ark). According to Sephardic tradition, the teba (middle bima [platform], where the rabbi, hazan, and reader stood and prayed, was an elevated platform with a large, eight-foot-wide reader's desk and was located in the middle of the synagogue, facing in the same direction as the congregation, toward the Holy Ark.[3] The main floor led up broad steps to the Heikhal, containing the Sepharim, (Torah scrolls), which was also on a wide, elevated stage. The door of the Heikhal was covered with a brocade curtain, called the *parokhet*, donated by congregation members and made of rich red and blue velvet embroidered with the names of the dear departed. The Sepharim were housed in traditional Sephardic cylindrical wooden containers covered with velvet cloth. These Torahs were topped with silver rimonim (pomegranate bells) with pointers to form an awesome sight when the Heikhal door was opened. The synagogue was not air-conditioned, air-conditioning having

3. This arrangement differs from the Ashkenazi tradition, where the rabbi and bima face the congregation.

9. Interior of Khartoum Synagogue, showing the Heikhal (Holy Ark).

not yet been invented; but it had ten ceiling fans and numerous windows along the walls opening onto a surrounding courtyard and garden to let the cool breeze in during hot days.

From the Heikhal and from the teba, the Torah readings and prayers were led by Rabbi Malka, flanked by Farag Shoua and the hazzan (ca) Albert Gabbai, who had a notably beautiful voice. They were assisted by the shohet rabbi student David Ohanna and the very pious Makhlouf Malka. The chanting in beautiful Sephardic melodies that originated in ancient Moroccan and Egyptian minhagim (Jewish religious customs) was very moving to the congregation, who joined in the chanting with the hazzanim in the customary Sephardic way.

Sermons were delivered on religious subjects from the teba by Rabbi Malka in Arabic, which was the language spoken and understood by most of the congregation. They were also published weekly in *El-Shams* (The sun) of Alexandria, the only Arabic Jewish newspaper in the area. Later, some of these sermons were collected and published in a book entitled *Al-Mukhtar Fi Tafsir Al-Tawrat* (Digest of Torah interpretations). These

10. *El-Shams* (The sun), Wafdist Zionist Arabic newspaper in which my father's lectures were printed. Courtesy of Mémoires Juives—Patrimoine photographique, Paris.

and other writings of Rabbi Solomon Malka, who had then become the chief rabbi of the Sudan, were translated from the original Arabic into English by his son Edmond S. Malka[4] and published in a three-volume work entitled *Frontiers of the Jewish Faith,* which included *Morals of the Pentateuch, Song of Songs Annotated,* and *A Digest of Faith.*

4. Edmond S. Malka was at the time deputy attorney general of New Jersey.

The synagogue was completed in 1926 at a cost of about E£ 3,000, an enormous sum at the time. Most of it was contributed by Sudan Jews, every man and woman "whose heart stirred him up brought an offering for the building of a House for the Lord," (Exod. 35:21–22).

Some contributions were also received from Jews in Egypt, among them the Jewish philanthropist Abraham Btesh, who contributed E£ 250 and a similar amount to another synagogue being built at the same time in Tel Aviv. Other contributions were also received from Jews in the United Kingdom through the *Jewish Chronicle of London*.

In the 1940s and 1950s, the Community was at its full strength, and the Khartoum Synagogue was filled to capacity on the festivals, particularly on the High Holidays when worshippers came to it from Khartoum, Khartoum North, Omdurman, and as far as Wad Medani, 175 miles away.

Wad Medani is the capital of the Blue Nile Province and the center of the 500,000 feddans[5] grown in long-staple cotton. This was started by the Sudan British administration mainly to provide long-staple cotton for the mills in Manchester and other markets. The plantation headquarters was in Barakat, a few miles outside the town of Wad Medani. The plantation areas were cultivated on a three-year rotation. The rotation consisted of one feddan of cotton, one feddan of durra (sorghum) and other food for the tenant farmer, and one feddan fallow to allow the land to rest. In a way, this system resembled the law of shemittah in the Torah, by which the land had to be cultivated for six years and put to rest the seventh.

Not surprisingly, Yom Kippur in Khartoum was often very hot and humid; for it usually came in September, the most unpleasant month of the year, replete with stifling heat, dampness, and the buzz of nimetti that follow the brief rainy season. In the respite between the Yom Kippur morning and afternoon prayers, the fasting congregants would flock to the cooler garden and courtyard of the synagogue, where they found seats, chaises longues, and even a few beds provided for their comfort. The elders chatted and relaxed; and the young men and women met and got better acquainted, with as in ancient times, possible future betrothals in mind—or so their elders hoped. Many years later in the United States, I remember reading in the Yom Kippur prayer book used in Conservative synagogues that, according to Rabbi Simeon Ben Gamaliel, Yom Kippur

---

5. A feddan is 4,200 square meters, or about one acre.

11. "Siddur Farhi," Hebrew prayer book with Arabic translation by Hillel Farhi. Courtesy of Mémoires Juives—Patrimoine photographique, Paris.

was a festive occasion and a most joyous day. On the Day of Atonement, maidens danced in the vineyards and sprightfully challenged the young men to make their choices based on beauty, family, or merit. That very day, betrothals were announced.

In one of the corners of the synagogue was kept *Kissei Eliaho Hannabi* (the chair of the prophet Elijah). It was a nine-foot-high and five-foot-wide wooden structure with a wooden seat across its width. When a Jewish male child was born, *Kissei Eliaho Hannabi* would be taken to his home; and on the eighth day the child would be circumcised on it. Eliaho Hannabi, the prophet Elijah of ancient times, is traditionally supposed to be present at every Brit Mila to preside as the child is entered into the Covenant of Abraham.[6]

6. In *The Legends of the Jews* (Philadelphia: The Jewish Publication Society of America, 1968), 338, Louis Ginzberg writes, "During the persecution of the pious by the wicked Jezebel, Elijah displayed great zeal for the observance of the Abrahamic Covenant. As his reward God promised him that he would be present at every ceremony of circumcision. Accordingly the 'Chair of Elijah' must not be forgotten at the ceremony of circumcision, as he is always present at these occasions, though not visible to the eyes of the ordinary man."

תְּפִלָּה לְדָוִד

PREGHIERE

TRADUZIONE E NOTE DI
DAVID PRATO
Gran Rabbino di Alessandria d'Egitto

12. Hebrew prayer book with Italian translation. Courtesy of Mémoires Juives—Patrimoine photographique, Paris.

Seekers of miracles from the presence of Eliaho Hannabi would congregate around his circumcision chair. A childless woman might sit under it hoping for pregnancy. An unmarried young lady would carry the child to the chair, dressed in a bride's white dress and veil, in hopes of finding a husband soon. The child himself would be dressed in a long, rich, white silk dress covering his underwear.

As the child was brought to the chair in a procession, my father, the mohel, would chant for him a welcome in Hebrew, "*Baroukh Habba Be Shem Adonai*" (May he be blessed who comes in the name of the Lord). Even the seniyet (tray of) Eliaho Hannabi, carrying my father's circumcision instruments, the kiddush cup, and wine, would be taken to him by someone seeking a special wish. My father would then recite the blessings for the Mila, perform the operation, and chant the kiddush with all around responding. He would make the child partake of the kiddush by putting a drop of the wine in the child's mouth, which would frequently put him to sleep and he would forget the pain. There then followed congratulations, the serving of ice cream, bonbons, and petit fours, and general merriment.[7]

As in most synagogue services, a prayer is recited on festivals asking for blessings on the rulers of the land. When the Sudan was under the Condominium rule of Britain and Egypt, my father would include King George V and King Fuʿad I and add them to the name of the British governor general of the Sudan at that time. When Sir Herbert Samuel, a Jew, became the high commissioner of Palestine, my father added his name with great joy to the other kings and rulers he called blessings on. After the birth of the State of Israel, my father was even more overjoyed to add the names of Chaim Weizmann and David Ben-Gurion, Israel's first president and prime minister respectively.

I still remember with emotion the night of 29 November 1947, when I joined my father in his house for us to listen together late into the night to the voting going on at the United Nations in New York on the resolution for the partition of Palestine into a Jewish state and an Arab state. With every vote counted, our tears ran with emotion; and when the required two-thirds majority was exceeded, we jumped with joy and happiness. The vote was thirty-three to thirteen, with ten abstentions.

Like most Sephardim, my father and I were born Zionists, consumed by love of Eretz Israel and by the old dream of returning to the land of our fathers. In the synagogue and on every other suitable occasion, my father led us in singing *Hatikvah* (the hope). In its old form before Israeli Independence, we sang, "The old hope, to return to the land of our fathers, the land of Zion and Jerusalem." In the new version after Independence, we sang, "Our hope has still not been lost, the hope of 2,000 years, to live free in our land, the land of Zion and Yerushalaim."

In the early 1950s, the Khartoum Synagogue was renamed Ohel Shelomo in memory of my father, Rabbi Solomon Malka, Zichro Leolam (may his memory be forever), and his forty-five years' service to the Sudan Jews. A large, marble memorial plaque was placed in the sanctuary wall on the right of the Heikhal, with the following inscription:

7. "A child was once brought in for circumcision and all present greeted him with the customary formula of Barukh Haba, Blessed be he that cometh, which at the same time is a welcome to Elijah, the guest expected to come" (Ibid., 338).

OHEL SHELOMO

Beit Haknaesset Hazzeh Hokam Lezichro shel
Hamanoah
Harab Hakhram Shlomo Malka—Zecker Saddik
Librakha
Asher Sharat 45 Shana Betor Rab Rashi
Lemidinat Sudan
Ve shel Ishto Hanna

THE TENT OF SOLOMON

This Synagogue was established in memory of a
righteous man the Rab and Hakham Shlomo
Malka who served 45 years as Chief Rabbi of the
State of Sudan and his wife Hanna.

Another Ohel Shelomo memorial plaque was also erected for him in
the Yeshiva Hall on the second floor of the Central Sephardic Synagogue, Yissa B'Racha, the usual home of the chief Sephardic rabbi of Israel.[8] This second memorial in Jerusalem was contributed by Sudan Jews,
led by Albert Gaon, the chief contributor, on the initiative of my brother
Edmond Malka.

Rabbi Solomon Malka died and was buried in the Khartoum Jewish
Cemetery in April 1949. It is an attestation to the impact he had that his
funeral was attended by representatives of the Sudan government and
such dignitaries as Sir Sayed Abdel Rahman Pasha, leader of the Ansar
sect and the Umma political Party; Sir Sayed Ali El-Merghani Pasha,
leader of the Khatmiya sect; the Roman Catholic bishop; and the leader
of the Protestant clergy of Omdurman. They were accompanied by all the
members of the Sudan Jewish Community and many of the poor of all
faiths, whom he silently helped and comforted. All of the above also attended the seven days of mourning (*Shibaa Yeme Ha Abel*), also known as
shiva among the Ashkenazi communities, from the word *shibaa*).

8. Located at 31 Jabotinsky Street, Talbieh, Jerusalem, this Hall is now occupied by
the Yeshiva Etz Haim from Montreux, Switzerland, who in 1980 renamed it Yeshibat
Heikhal Eliaho, in memory of their founder. In a photograph taken at the 1980 inaugura-
tion, President Chaim Herzog of Israel is seen addressing the audience with the Chief
Ashkenazi Rabbi Kahana Shapiro on one side, Chief Sephardic Rabbi Mordechai Eliaho
on the other, and the plaque in memory of Rabbi Shlomo Malka appearing behind them.

אהל שלמה

בית הכנסת הזה
הוקם לזכרו של המנוח

הרה״ג שלמה מלכא זצ״ל

נולד תרל״ה נפטר תש״ט

אשר שרת 44 שנה

בתור רב ראשי למדינת סודאן

ולזכר אשתו המנוחה חנה ו״ל

תרמ״ד-תש״י

תנצב״ה

נדבת משפחתם וידידיהם בסודאן

13. Khartoum Synagogue plaque to Rabbi Solomon Malka.

Desecration of the Khartoum Cemetery

Sadly, long after we had left the Sudan, reports came of cases of vandalism and desecration in the Khartoum Jewish Cemetery. Moved by this unfortunate news, my brothers Edmond, Sam, David, and I felt the need to do something. Joined by Nessim Gaon and Leon Cohen from Geneva; the Tammam family in London and Geneva; and the Ishag family in London, Khartoum, and Israel, arrangements were made for the 1975 air

14. Desecration of the Khartoum Jewish Cemetery.

transfer, via Geneva, of remains to Givaat Shaoul Cemetery in Jerusalem. Among the bodies transferred were the remains of my father, Rabbi Solomon Malka; my mother, Hanna; and my daughter Jenny Hanna, who died in Khartoum at age six. Other remains transferred included former Presidents Elie Tammam and Daoud Ishag, two Kohanim (members of the Cohen family of priests, Isaac and Reuven Cohen), Mrs. Rena Tammam, and other members of the Sudan Community. All the bodies were buried in a special compound of Givaat Shaoul Cemetery in Jerusalem, marked "The Sudan Jewish Community Cemetery," as arranged by the good and righteous Shlomo Ben-David, himself from the Sudan. Meaningfully, the funeral service at the cemetery was led by a nephew of my father, Rabbi Moshé Malka, the chief Sephardic rabbi of Petah Tikvah in Israel, and was attended by many of the Sudan Jewish Community living in Israel, including three of his daughters (Allegra Sasson, Sara Gabriel, and Rachel Polon) and their husbands and children.[9]

9. The transfer of the bodies was no easy matter and required numerous struggles to secure the proper permits for the excavations, permits for the transfer to Geneva, and

Honor Guard in the Khartoum Cemetery

Around 1940–1941, at the height of World War II and the British-Italian war over Eritrea and Ethiopia, the Italians would occasionally bomb Khartoum and Port Sudan from the air, fortunately usually missing their targets. Incidentally, it was during one of these air raids that my wife gave birth to my son, Jeffrey, and we therefore would subsequently joke with him that it must have been a royal birth to have fireworks and a cannonade in his honor.

One day I received a call from R. Beer, the Khartoum British district commissioner, who knew me as secretary of the Jewish Community and a member of the Khartoum Supply Board. He told me that he had heard from the commanding officer of the Royal Air Force in Khartoum that two Jewish British airmen had died when their plane crashed near Khartoum and asked if I could arrange to have them buried in the Khartoum Jewish Cemetery. Because gas (or benzine, as it was then called) was rationed, he issued me additional benzine coupons for my car to allow me to get around and make the necessary arrangements.

My father was away from Khartoum on one of his speaking tours in Cairo. I therefore asked the manager of the Khartoum Grand Hotel, who was a very religious young Jew and hazzan to conduct the burial ceremony. At the appointed hour, troops from the British Royal Air Force arrived at the Jewish Cemetery with an honor guard and the two coffins. After the coffins were lowered into the prepared graves, the commanding officer walked past and saluted each grave in turn with me at his side, following which we both lined up to receive condolences, he on behalf of the military and I on behalf of our Jewish Community.

About one year later, Mrs. Magid, the mother of the two lost airmen, came to Khartoum from South Africa and looked me up. I took her to the Jewish Cemetery of Khartoum, where she visited their graves and mourned them. On returning to Cape Town, she sent to the Khartoum Synagogue several copies of the British Empire prayer book in memory of her two sons, who were killed on 17 July 1945.

---

then on to Israel. The transfer to Geneva was necessitated by the political situation, which made it impossible to travel directly from the Sudan to Israel. A rabbi, accompanied by Zaki Daoud Ishag, went to Khartoum from London to ensure the proper religious arrangements, and they were further assisted by the few remaining Jews in Khartoum at the time.

Presented by

Mrs. Magid

in memory of her two sons

Lt. W.J. Magid

and

W/O. M.L. Magid

killed at Khartoum, 17th, July, 1945

15. Hebrew-English prayer books cover presented to the Khartoum Synagogue by Mrs. Magid of Cape Town in memory of her two sons killed in Khartoum.

Rescue of the Torah Scrolls of Khartoum Synagogue

Those who visited Khartoum for the Jewish Cemetery transfers took the opportunity to rescue the Torah scrolls from the Khartoum Synagogue, which was needed because there no longer was a minian (quorum of ten men) or services at the synagogue. About ten Sephardic Sifrei

Torah[10] were retrieved, taken to London, and then restored and distributed to the synagogues of some of the Sudan Jewish Community in London, Geneva, Israel, and the United States.

The Sepher for the United States was given to my nephew Mayer
Malka, a pious and religious man who housed it in his synagogue, Temple
Beth Abraham, in North Bergen, New Jersey, in a magnificent Siyum
Torah (Torah dedication) on 7 December 1975. It was attended by many
Jews from the Sudan who went to greet their Sephardic Sepher Torah
from Khartoum. Unfortunately, I was living in Paris at the time and was
not able to attend. Mayer Malka used this Torah in many special
Sephardic services he conducted, and it is now used by his sons, Jack and
Michael Malka, in their Sephardic synagogue, Temple Ahabat Torah, in
Englewood, New Jersey.

Sale of the Khartoum Synagogue Building

Tragically, in late 1986, the remaining half a dozen Jews still left in
Khartoum, under the leadership of Henri El-Eini, accepted a commercial
bank's offer of about $200,000 to buy the synagogue with the intention to
tear it down and replace it with an office building. Those of us living outside the Sudan were greatly distressed on hearing of the proposed disappearance of the Khartoum Synagogue. I personally made every effort to
prevent the destruction of the synagogue but soon learned that the building had already been demolished and that it was therefore futile to inter-
vene after the fact and embarrass the few Jews still living in the Sudan.
The few remaining records were apparently saved, and that unfortunately
ends the story of the Khartoum Synagogue.

The Jewish Community also owned two houses, whose rentals were
meant to maintain the synagogue and the premises of the Jewish Recreation Club of Khartoum after we left. There is little doubt that these
have met a similar fate.

10. Torah scrolls.

7

✤

Growth of the
Sudan Jewish Community

During the worldwide economic depression of the 1920s and 1930s, some of the influential members of the Community relocated to Cairo, always a coveted place to live in; but in a few years, all returned to their homes and businesses in the Sudan. In the meantime and throughout the 1920s, 1930s, and 1940s, a stream of young Jews came from Egypt to take up government, banking, and commercial company jobs for which expatriates were needed. Others came as shopkeepers, and several new businesses with either Jewish managers or owners were established.

Port Sudan is a busy port on the Red Sea. David Gaon went to Port Sudan, where he became the town clerk, or city administrator, serving under the British governor of the Red Sea Province. He was the father of Albert, Leon, and Nessim Gaon, the latter becoming the business magnate and philanthropist of whom we will read more later.

To Khartoum came David Hornstein, manager of the Khedival Mail Line; Joseph Dannon, manager of the Remington Typewriter Company; and Emile Feinstein and Bernard Goldring, at the headquarters of the Sudan Government Post Office. Others who came to Khartoum were I. Weiss; David Hemou; Cesar Belilos; Isaac Cohen; Edgar Ben-Rubi; and working for a short period at the Khartoum branch of the National Bank of Egypt, Joseph Nahum, son of Rabbi Haim Nahum Effendi, grand rabbi of Egypt. The Gellatly Hankey Group of Companies, the leading British shipping, trading, and engineering firm, attracted Henry Romy, Maurice Marcovitch, and Joseph Soriano to their Khartoum head office; Felix Harouche and Max Bergmann to their Port Sudan offices; and Boris Gwertzman to their Eritrean offices. Jack Carmona came to the

Khartoum agency of the Prudential Insurance Company; and Mathias Nahmias, who owned a roller-skating rink. Also arriving were Max Gabriel to the Red Sea Hotel in Port Sudan; Alexander Haim, manager of Debbas & Co., cotton merchants and owners of the Port Sudan Cotton Ginning Factory in Port Sudan; Israel Kaminsky, Khartoum manager and representative of Ali Pasha Cotton Company of Alexandria; R. Fishman, Victor Heiman, and Raphael Hakim, representatives of other firms in Cairo.

From Cairo also came Maurice Goldenberg, who became the first optician in the Sudan; Robert Braunstein, as manager of Pinto and Co.; Henri Farhi, manager of Imperial Chemical Company; Marc Merzan, manager of Coats Cotton Thread Company; and Edward Sheridan, manager of Sheridan & Co. N. Miara came as chief engineer of the Sudan Light and Power Co. and was responsible for the construction of all their installations in Khartoum and Wad Medani. Czar Levy came as manager of B. Nathan & Co. in Omdurman; as did Albert Gabbai, who subsequently became the treasurer and gabbai (beadle) of the Jewish Community and who, because of his exceptionally lovely voice, also became its volunteer hazzan; and David Ohanna, who became shohet of the Community. Gabbai and Reuven Cohen also maintained shops in Khartoum, as did Abramino Konein in Gordon's Tree.

Most of these young Jewish men coming from Egypt married Jewish girls born in the Sudan, founded families, and became permanent Sudan residents, swelling the ranks of the Sudan Jewish Community.

I. Segal came from Palestine and became for a short time a senior official of the Sudan Government Passport Office, a rather delicate position for a Jew and Zionist from Palestine in an Arab Muslim country, but that was before Israel's 1948 War of Independence. Also from Palestine came Abraham Benin, who established the Keystone Company and founded one of the first button manufacturing companies, making button blanks from Sudan domnuts, a Sudanese wild palm tree fruit.

J. Wolf came as inspector of finance for the Sudan government and was the only Jew to come from Britain. He also came through Egypt, where he met and married a young and beautiful Ashkenazi lady. He was a neighbor of mine in Khartoum and joined us for a while as a member of our B'nai B'rith Ben-Sion Coshti Lodge in Khartoum. On his retirement from Sudan government service toward the end of 1940, the Jewish Community gave him and his wife a very warm send-off. A picture taken at the time is a rare one showing the old generation of Community lead-

16. Farewell party for J. Wolf with Community leaders. *Sitting, left to right,* Ibrahim Ades, Farag Shoua, Joseph Tammam, J. Wolf, Rabbi Solomon Malka, Mrs. Wolf, Eli Tammam, Saleh Sasson, Ishag Gabra. *Standing, left to right,* Yousef Gabra, Albert Gabbai, Shalom Seroussi, Habib Cohen, Maurice Levy, Daoud Ishag, Maurice Goldenberg, Daoud Shoua, Victor Seroussi, Maurice Tammam, David Ani, Eliaho Malka, Suleiman Shaoul, Saleh El-Eini, Edgar Ben-Rubi, Aslan Seroussi.

ers with my father, Wolf, and Mrs. Wolf in the middle, and a large portion of the future leaders behind them.[1]

We also had our share of German Jewish refugees fleeing Nazi Germany, and for a time they were required to report their presence to the Khartoum Police on a daily basis. There were first Richard Weiss; his wife, Lisa; and their young son, Herbert. They had come through Egypt, where they had been refused residence, and proceeded to Khartoum looking for a possible refuge. They arrived deprived of all possessions except their intellect and education. We first housed them in small rooms on the Khartoum Synagogue grounds. Soon and in good time, Richard worked out of their impoverished state to the good milieu of Khartoum commercial centers and society. He went from selling potato chips in Khartoum cinemas to becoming a partner in Neophytos and Company, an important Greek import-export firm, and from the synagogue rooms to a home

---

1. Sudan government British officials were retired with full pensions at age forty-eight to permit them to embark on a new career in England or elsewhere, which they would be assisted in getting; Egyptians, Lebanese, and the like were retired on full pensions at age fifty-five; and the Sudanese at age sixty-five. As a British official, Wolf was retired on pension at age forty-eight and got the job of bursar at the English Public School in Meadi, a section of Cairo, the home of his wife.

in the best residential quarter of Khartoum, where he and his family min-
gled with the cream of Khartoum society. In the 1960s, Richard Weiss
and his family immigrated to the United States, where Richard continued his Sudan connections. When in 1966 I immigrated to the United
States with my son and daughter, Richard Weiss was one of the first to
welcome us to their Manhattan home to enjoy their hospitality and
friendship. They were secular but good Jews, appreciating and adhering
to their Judaism. When their son, Herbert, became twelve years old in
Khartoum, they sent him to my father to be prepared for his bar mitzvah,
which was of course done in the Sephardic tradition. Richard's wife, Lisa,
was a professional photographer; and on the occasion of her son's bar
mitzvah, she presented the rabbi a beautiful portrait of himself, the one
reproduced in this book.

Other German refugees who came to Khartoum fleeing the Nazis were
two artists, Jimmy Kane and his wife, Trudy. They later established the
Gordon Music Hall in Khartoum, which they owned in partnership with
another German artist. The Gordon Music Hall was the only cabaret and
night club in Khartoum and was frequented by many Sudanese and European patrons. Later, Jimmy and Trudy Kane converted to Christianity
and joined the British Church of England Cathedral in Khartoum.

I found in Richard Weiss and Jimmy Kane two contrasting types of
German Jews. The one, secular but respecting and adhering to his Judaism; the other, taking the first opportunity to assimilate and flee it.

Notwithstanding Jimmy and Trudy Kane's behavior as Jews, I did no-
tice that Trudy's father, a man in his mid-sixties and himself a runaway
from Nazi terror, used to come, year after year, to the Khartoum Synagogue on Yom Kippur, listening silently to the prayers and Sepher Torah
readings for a couple of hours or so and then returning to his quarters.
When he died in Khartoum, Jimmy telephoned me; and I arranged for a
Jewish burial in the Khartoum Jewish Cemetery, with appropriate minian
and Kaddish. He obviously wanted to die a Jew; and in his life, he had remained a Jew at heart.

8

⚜

Community Representation and Administration

The Jewish Community was represented before the Sudan government and other official bodies by its religious and spiritual leader, Solomon Malka, the rabbi of the Sudan, and by its president. With all other notables, they were invited to all leeves, ceremonies, and palace garden parties held by the governor general in his Khartoum palace. The governor general was also called the sirdar, the Egyptian title for the British commander in chief of the Egyptian Army in the Sudan, until 1924, at which time the two positions were separated.

The governor general gave garden parties at the palace to which presidents and representatives of foreign communities were invited with their spouses. This created a social outing that the presidents' wives looked forward to; and I particularly recall Jeannette Cohen; my wife, Dora Malka; and Auro Ishag going to the palace attired in the latest of high fashion and being a credit to our Community with their intelligence and elegance.

I recall once going to one of these palace garden parties in the company of my father, he as the spiritual leader of the Sudan Jewish Community and I either as its president or as director and representative of the leading British company in the Sudan. My father stood among a group of religious heads and native Sudanese notables, and I stood next to him awaiting our host. The British governor general, attired in full uniform and regalia, came down the long palace stairway, the very steps on which his predecessor, General Sir Charles Gordon Pasha, had been slain by dervish spears of the Mahdi's followers. As he reached our group, he greeted and exchanged a few words with my father and me and the other guests in fluent Arabic. I responded in English; but he ignored my English and responded in Arabic, so as not to slight the Arabic-speaking notables standing by, thus demonstrating that he was no mere soldier but was an astute politician as well.

All guests to the palace entered through the south gate, which faced a square in the center of which a statue of General Gordon Pasha, mounted on a camel, stood on a high pedestal. Not far from there, in another square, a statue of Lord Kitchener on horseback was erected as the liberator of Khartoum and the Sudan from the Mahdi's rule. Both statues, viewed as symbols of colonial and Egyptian rule, were taken down after Sudan's Independence and shipped back to Britain, where they have been remounted. Gordon's statue was remounted at the Gordon's Boys School in Surrey.

Presidents of the Sudan Jewish Community

Listed below are the names of the presidents of the Sudan Jewish Community from its inception until its demise after the departure from the Sudan of almost all its members and the disappearance of its institutions:

The first-generation presidents were:

Ben-Sion Coshti, also known as Bassiouni, the first Jew of the Mahdiya and elected for life. He served from 1908 to his death in 1917. He was a tall, red-bearded Turkish Jew with an imposing and courageous nature that he used in the Mahdi's and the Khalifa's courts to defend the Jews both during and after their forced conversion to Islam and then led them back to Judaism.

Raphael Ades, partner and senior manager of the notable Jewish firm of B. Nathan & Co. in Omdurman, the leading supplier of Manchester cotton piece goods and other material for men's and women's clothing to wholesale and retail merchants throughout the Sudan. He served from 1917 to about 1920.

Joseph Forti, also manager of B. Nathan & Co. in Omdurman. It was during his term of office and thanks to his devotion and hard work that the construction of the beautiful Khartoum Synagogue on a central site on Victoria Avenue was completed and opened for service in 1926. With his personal prestige and connections and his vigorous efforts at fund raising, he fully funded the project with contributions from Cairo, London, and the Sudan. He served from 1921 to 1926.

Albert Forti, also manager of B. Nathan & Co. and a brother of Joseph Forti, served from 1927 to 1930 and continued the work of his brother for the synagogue and the Community.

Ibrahim Seroussi, the leading sheepskin and goatskin exporter, served from 1931 to 1936. During his term of office, the Community prospered, the synagogue attained full attendance, and the B'nai B'rith lodge was founded in the Sudan.

Abraham Dwek was one of the early bastions of the Jewish Community and a noted textiles merchant in Omdurman and Khartoum. He served as president from about 1936 to 1939 and was an example of traditional Jewish life devoted to Talmud Torah. He kept an open and hospitable house to all newcomers to the Community.

Elie Tammam, patriarch of the Tammam family and a noted merchant in Omdurman, served from about 1939 to 1941 and was very active in preserving the Community's institutions.

Mousa Israel El-Eini served as president of the Jewish Community in the early 1940s. He was a leading merchant and financier in Khartoum North and started the first mini supermarket in his town. Of Iraqi origin, he arrived in the Sudan with his parents from Cairo at age four and was one of the first Jewish graduates of Gordon College of Khartoum.

It was my good fortune and happiness to have served as honorary secretary of the Jewish Community and to organize its work with all of the above from Ibrahim Seroussi onwards, having been influenced by my father to give of my time and energy to the affairs of the Jewish Community and Jewish problems at large. By the 1940s, the Sudan-born Jews and children of the early settlers came of age. Having reached their maturity and strength, they shouldered the responsibility for their Community and Jewish affairs. From here on, the Community elected the president from among the leaders of that generation.

The second-generation presidents were:

Joseph Tammam, son of Elie Tammam, served his term of office from about 1945 to 1947. He was at the time manager of the Omdurman branch of the Cairo Jewish firm Giulio Padova & Co.

Nessim Gaon, son of early settler to Port Sudan David Gaon and now the well-known international businessman and philanthropist based in Geneva and president of the World Sephardic Federation, served as vice-president and treasurer from 1947 to 1957. He was then a partner of the leading exporting firm of Albert and Nessim Gaon in Khartoum.

17. Presidents of the Sudan Jewish Community

Ibrahim Seroussi

Abraham Dwek

Elie Tammam

Mousa Israel El-Eini

Joseph Tammam

Eliaho Malka

Habib Cohen

Daoud Ishag

Nessim Gaon

Ishag Mousa Israel El-Eini

Eliaho Malka, served from about 1948 to 1950 and again from 1954 to 1955. At the time, I was executive director of Gellatly Trading Co. Ltd., part of the Gellatly Hankey Group of Companies, which was the leading international firm in the Sudan. I was twice pressured to accept the presidency after long years of service as honorary secretary and vice-president, positions I liked because they gave me the opportunity to organize the Community and its affairs along modern lines.

Habib Cohen, nephew of early settler Ibrahim Cohen of Khartoum North, served as president in the mid-1950s and again in the early 1960s until about 1964. He was then a wholesaler and partner in the Import Division of the influential Sudanese firm of Osman Saleh & Sons.

Daoud Ishag, the Sudan-born son of the early settler Ishag Daoud of Khartoum, served as president from about 1956 to 1959. By that time, he had built a trading and manufacturing empire that included being the importer and exporter of various goods and the owner of perfume and other factories.

During the period of this second generation of presidents, the Community reached its peak in performance and prestige. The Jewish Recreation Club was constructed and established and became a center for Jewish life; and as mentioned above, the B'nai B'rith lodge was founded and the generosity of its members richly contributed to our Jewish institutions and synagogue.

The last president, Ishag Mousa Israel El-Eini, the Sudan-born son of Mousa Israel El-Eini, was elected president in 1965, after most of the Community had left the Sudan, and served until his own departure to England in 1970. He held the fort after we all left and faced the harassments that followed the Six Day War between Israel and its neighbors. Then a leading businessman in Khartoum and other parts of the Sudan, he was a graduate of Comboni College in Khartoum and had studied at the American University of Cairo. He was also an Arabic poet and sportsman.

Among the many men who served on the Jewish Community Board and Committees were David Bassiouni, son of Ben-Sion Coshti, as honorary secretary; Albert Gabbai, as treasurer and gabbai and voluntary hazzan of the synagogue; Isaac Cohen, treasurer; Edward Dwek, honorary secretary; Henri Farhi, vice-president; Edgar Ben-Rubi, honorary secretary; Maurice Goldenberg, vice-president; Ibrahim El-Eini, chair, cemetery committee; and Sion Shoua, treasurer.

After my term as president, which was a continuation of my service to the Community since 1934 as secretary and then vice-president, I was elected a permanent member of the Community's Executive Board. I remained active on that board and participated in all its decisions until the day of my final departure from the Sudan in April 1964, a departure necessitated by the need for medical treatment in London and Geneva for my wife, Dora (née Goldenberg), who was suffering from terminal cancer. My dear wife died in Geneva in January 1966.

Thus I had the joy and great satisfaction of having served my Community and my people in the Sudan continuously for thirty years and to have shared their joys and sorrows, their successes, their struggles, and their deliverance. Following my father's teachings and Hillel's saying "Separate not thyself from the Congregation," I continue to join the Jewish Community and its institutions wherever I am and to serve my country, my Jewish people, and their struggle for Eretz Israel in whatever way I can.

During the 1940s and 1950s, many of the Sudan Jews made remarkable progress in their trades and professions and acquired along the way good friends among the Sudanese and members of other foreign communities in the Sudan. We served the Sudan in our different capacities and participated in its social, economic, and political advancement and welfare. In preparing this chapter, I could not fail to be impressed by the level of success achieved, in some cases from very humble beginnings, of so many members of our Jewish Community, not only in the Sudan but elsewhere.

Dr. Suleiman Bassiouni, son of Ben-Sion Coshti, became the chief surgeon of the Sudan Government Khartoum Hospital and professor at the Khartoum University School of Medicine.

Suleiman Shaoul became a senior engineer of the Sudan Government Survey Department in Khartoum and Wad Medani and had several major development projects to his credit in both areas.

I was on the Board of Directors of the leading British international company in the Red Sea area, the Gellatly Hankey Group of Companies, and was the first Jew and non-Britisher to hold such a position. I became the executive director and chief executive officer of their trading company, Gellatly Trading Co. Ltd., which I built from the ground up and which became the leading import and export company in the Sudan;

marketing director for the Gellatly Manufacturing Companies, the Sudan Soap Factory, and the Portland Cement Company; and commercial advisor to the Gellatly Companies of Egypt, Eritrea, and Ethiopia. I also served as their representative on the Board of the Sudan Chamber of Commerce and chaired many of its committees. During World War II, I served in the Sudan War Supply Board and the Sudan Auxiliary Force.

My brother Edmond S. Malka, an international lawyer, became one of the most prominent lawyers in the Sudan courts. He wrote in Arabic the book *Sharh El-Kanoun Al-Ingilisi* (English common law), which became a legal reference book in Sudan law circles. He subsequently practiced law in Israel, Ireland, and the United States, where he was for a time the deputy attorney general of the State of New Jersey. He authored many books in English, among them *Sephardi Jews—A Pageant of Spanish-Portuguese and Oriental Judaism Between the Cross and the Crescent* and the English translation of our father's book entitled *Frontiers of the Jewish Faith*.

My other two brothers, Samuel Solomon Malka and David Solomon Malka, specialized in business and trading. Sam became the manager of the Import Department of Bittar & Co. and David the manager of The Building Materials Company of Khartoum. When he moved to the United States, David became the vice-president in charge of the Building Materials Department of Borneo Sumatra Trading Corporation, a Dutch international firm. He subsequently became president of Borneo Sumatra USA Co. for ten years, at the end of which, at retirement age, he bought the company, changed its name to The Building Supply Trading Company, went into partnership with his former metals suppliers, the Polish State Universal Company, and became chairman of the new company. Always looking out to help his fellow man, David found employment in his various companies for Sudan Jews newly arrived in the United States, among whom were members of the Dannon, Ades, and Malka families, as well as non-Jews from the Sudan, such as Sarkis Kalpakian, Eugene Mazuki, Joseph Menasse, and George Kawa. In New Jersey, he was active in the B'nai B'rith and the Clifton Conservative Temple.

Mayer Malka, my sister Esther's son, also went into business in Khartoum and became director of the Import Division of Rye Evans & Co., Khartoum, an internationally known cotton company. Its chairman was a man named Alexander Ben-Lassin, a Jewish leader from Alexandria who had connections in the Sudan for many years, during which he founded several manufacturing companies there. Of note was the Blue Nile Packing Company in Khartoum North, which had another Jew, Ben-Ezra, as its manager. I had very long and friendly relations with Alexander Ben-Lassin and know that he was responsible for recruiting many of the Jewish young men who came to the Sudan in the employment of other Sudan companies.

On leaving the Sudan for the United States, Mayer Malka started a textile firm that was highly successful and is now continued by his son Jack. In every community in which he lived, he was a pious leader of his Jewish Community synagogue and an example of Jewish life. In that regard, he followed the footsteps of his father, Makhlouf Malka, who was extremely pious and at one time took on the role of shohet in the Sudan.

Muradsons was the trading name of Saleh, Suleiman, Ibrahim, Zaki, and Jack El-Eini, the sons of Mourad Israel El-Eini, one of the early Jews who came to the Sudan in 1898. Muradsons became one of the important agency and importing houses in the Sudan dealing in things from cars and tea packets to cotton thread and yarn and manufacturing various items from perfumery and cosmetics to nails and aluminum pots and pans. Another Jewish company, Daoud Ishag and Sons, also grew into a very important importing and wholesale company of a long line of commodities and owners of perfume factories. Habib Cohen, another prominent importer and wholesaler, was a partner to the leading Sudanese importing firm of Osman Saleh & Sons.

The two brothers Albert and Nessim Gaon started an export company of oilseeds, grains, oilcakes, and other produce in Khartoum. They developed it to become one of the leading Sudan exporters. From there, they branched out to Geneva, where they founded the Oleagine International Produce Company and then Nessim Gaon's internationally known NOGA group of companies dealing in international trade, construction, finance, real Estate, and hotels.

Leon Tamman[1] and his brothers Albert and Gabriel, started and developed the largest crocodile and snakeskin, hunting, tanning, and exporting companies in the Sudan. Later, Leon Tamman built the first large pharmaceutical factory in the Sudan; and then from headquarters in London, he founded International Generics, Ltd., and a group of international trade companies in the United Kingdom, Israel, and Hong Kong. His brothers Albert and Gabriel Tamman founded their own separate trading and real estate companies in Geneva.

1. The younger generation of Tammams spelled their name Tamman.

The Seroussi brothers, Victor, Shalom, and Maurice, became the most important exporters and tanners of sheepskin and goatskin in the Sudan. Later, they continued this old family business into the third and fourth generations in Nigeria, the United States, and other skin markets.

Their cousins Edouard, Eli, Joseph, and Albert, sons of Aslan Seroussi, had successful business careers in the Sudan and then later in the Diaspora. In particular, Edouard Seroussi, after a remarkable business career in the Sudan, went on to build in other African countries large international companies and manufacturing plants, particularly in Madagascar, where the textile industries and factories he created were extensive. He also expanded his activities in Europe, especially in Germany, where in Hamburg he has the headquarters of his textile industries and engineering companies. He maintains a home in Israel, a country he loves and admires, and where he has family, friends, and connections.

The Abboudi family of Yacoub, Eliaho, and Ibrahim, were shopkeepers and small importers in Omdurman. On leaving the Sudan with their children, they built successful businesses; Yacoub in the United States, Eliaho in London and Hong Kong, and Ibrahim in Israel.

Other members of the Jewish Community, shopkeepers and otherwise, had moderate successes or did not fare so well, but none were in need or really poor.

The Sudan Jewish Population and Its Origins

The Sudan Jewish Community at its peak reached eight hundred to one thousand residents living in Khartoum, Khartoum North, Omdurman, Wad Medani, and Port Sudan with one, Shaoul Eliaho, remaining in faraway Marawi in the Dongola Province up north, while most of his sons moved to Khartoum North and Khartoum and made their careers there. Marawi is the site of small pharaonic-era pyramids from the ancient Egyptians who had reached it. In recent times, it has been the country of the powerful Shaigiya tribe,[2] from which some of the recent

2. A warlike tribe living around Marawi. In the past, they were skilled horsemen and bandits preying on passing travelers and caravans; and the caravans carefully avoided going through their territories. The Shaigiya prided themselves on their fearlessness and love of war as a sport. Early explorers stated that they could muster 10,000 fierce warriors with 2,000 horsemen. Alan Morehead, in *The Blue Nile*, (New York: Dell, 1968), compares their skills in war to the legendary Mamelukes. They were the main obstacle to invaders from the North.

Sudan leaders have come. It is also the headquarters of Sir Sayed Ali El-Merghani Pasha, the religious leader of the Khatmiya tribe, who also maintained headquarters in Khartoum North and Khartoum.

The Community was 90 percent Sepahrdim, the name given to Jews who were expelled from Spain in 1492 and then found refuge in the North African countries of Morocco, Tunis, Algeria, and Egypt and in the Mediterranean countries of France, Italy, Greece, and Turkey. The Ashkenazim (German Jews) among us were completely integrated with the rest, followed our customs and synagogues, and many of their youth intermarried with Sephardic Jews in Khartoum and Cairo.

Despite the fact that many of the Jews in the Sudan came from families who had lived for decades in Egypt, they were often known by their origins. The Moghrabi, from the Maghreb (west), were those originally from Morocco and Tunis. The Spanioli were those from Salonika, Rhodes, and Corfu in Greece and from Izmir and Istanbul in Turkey, some of whom spoke Spanioli, a Spanish Ladino. The European Jews were those from Italy and France and those originally from Algeria who spoke French. The Boghdadi were those from Iraq (from the word for Baghdad). The Egyptians were those Jews who were completely Egyptianized in habits and language. The Halabi Jews were those originating in Aleppo, Syria; and the Ashkenazim (usually pronounced Ishkinazim) were those from Eastern Europe.

All spoke Arabic, the language of the people in the Sudan and Egypt. Many also wrote it and some were scholars in it. Most Sudan Jews were also fluent in English, which was the second language of the administration, higher education, and international commerce in the Sudan. Some also spoke French at home, which was then the language of the elite and of education in many nongovernmental schools in Egypt, including the schools of the "Alliance Israelite" in Egypt and North Africa. The small Jewish Community of the Sudan had members from all the origins mentioned above, and they all lived together in one Community and one synagogue in harmony and love.

9

❧

The Jewish Recreation Club

The Jewish Recreation Club originally began as a sports club by and for Jewish young men in their teens and early twenties when they started a soccer team. Soccer, or football, was and is the favorite sport in the Middle East and Europe and a subject of great adoration by its public.

Attracted and inspired by the name Maccabi, with its origin in the historic Maccabean heroes of old, and emulating the Maccabi Basketball Team of Cairo, which at that time had acquired considerable fame in the Middle East and Europe for its performances and victories and which held the basketball championship of Egypt and was its representative in European and international championships, we called our soccer team The Maccabi Football Team and our club The Maccabi Sports Club.

As the Maccabis, we entered the tournaments of the Khartoum Football League, which included many excellent nonprofessional teams, among them teams of the Greek and Syrian communities and the British team from the Khartoum British Club, who called themselves the Arabians.

The Maccabi soccer team was successful in reaching the finals of the Khartoum Football League after defeating the Arabians in the semifinals. The final cup game was set to be played between the Maccabi and the Greek team, but it was cancelled for reasons that were never made clear.

The founders and team players in the Maccabi soccer team were Suleiman Bassiouni, our unbeatable goalkeeper; David Bassiouni, the center halfback; I. Weiss and Suleiman Shaoul, our two strong fullbacks; Eliaho Malka, myself, as the swift right wing; Shalom Seroussi, the inside right; and Maurice Marcovitch, the inside left forward. The left wing was an excellent player whom we listed in our team roster as Mayer. His real name however was Maher, and he was a Muslim friend who had joined our Jewish team.

In 1928, we rented spacious grounds for the Maccabi Sports Club on prestigious Victoria Avenue and constructed on it a hard tennis court and a few small rooms, which became a meeting place for Jewish youth and later for Jewish families.

In the beginning, our elders were not too happy about the exposure of our Jewishness through the Maccabi name and our success in the Khartoum Football League and did not want to preside over us. So we convinced the young manager of the Khedival Mail Line in Khartoum, David Hornstein, then in his early thirties, to be our club president.

In the late 1930s, we lost our grounds, when the proprietors of the Cinema Circus in the Sudan, the Licos Brothers, bought our club grounds and constructed on it what was then the largest open-air cinema theater in Khartoum.[1] By then, we were fully matured and responsible men; and now with the support of our elders, the Community in the early 1940s bought spacious premises, two city blocks behind the Khartoum Synagogue, on which was established The Jewish Recreation Club. They equipped it with a very large open-air dance floor, meeting rooms, and a cafeteria kitchen, where every evening you could get served a light kosher snack with your drinks. Adjacent grounds were also rented, where the youth practiced basketball and other sports.

The club became the meeting place for all our Jewish families, many of whom frequented it every evening. Some played their favorite card games, which ranged from contract bridge, whist, ramé, and poker.

---

1. All cinemas in the Sudan were open-air theaters. In Khartoum, there was no rain at all for ten months of the year; and the rainy season was brief, lasting no more than two months. Elsewhere in the Sudan, the rainy season might extend as much as three months. When it did rain during the brief rainy season in Khartoum, it was not for long and the movie would soon resume after the short shower. There was no morning or afternoon show, it being much too hot then. Instead, there were two shows in the cool evening hours, one at 6:30 P.M. or 7:00 P.M. and another at 9:00 or 9:30 P.M.

The theaters were spacious, about the size of a football field, and arranged with "boxes" on stepped, elevated terraces in the rear one-third of the theater and rows of seats in the front. The boxes where square enclosures on the stepped terraces, with four to six lawn seats each and a table for snacks and drinks. The seats were not crowded, and it was easy to fit in another two or three chairs for additional guests. Most of the Europeans had permanent year-round reservations for a box, alternating in each of the different cinemas, which conveniently changed the movie shown on a three-day cycle. The open-air cinemas served the function in those days of our present-day television.

18. Guests at the annual dance of the Jewish Recreation Club. *Left to right,* Spiro Girigottis, Sol Shaoul, Mary Girigottis, Bertha Shaoul, Eli Malka.

Others enjoyed a Ping-Pong or backgammon game or socialized over a scotch or Coke with a snack, discussing both gossip and business deals. Many a Jewish visitor to Khartoum would spend his first night visiting the club to make acquaintances or connections.

Purim costumed parties, bar mitzvahs, and other parties were held around the dance floor, usually in the evenings to avoid the day's heat. Also held at the club was the Annual Jewish Community Ball, a fundraising event that was always both pleasant and successful. It is interesting to note that the ball was attended by members of the other foreign communities in the Sudan, as we did theirs.

The presidents of the Jewish Recreation Club were elected from the new Sudan-born generation of Jewish leaders, descendants of the early settlers. The first elected president of the club was Shalom Seroussi, the elder of the Seroussi family and firm. He was followed by Albert Gaon, the elder of the Gaon family and partner of the Albert and Nessim Gaon firm. He was succeeded respectively by Maurice Seroussi, partner of the Seroussi Brothers firm; by my brother David Malka, who was then manager of the Building Materials Company in Khartoum; and by Leon Tamman, a senior member of the Tammam family and firms. Before

19. Dancing at the Club.

becoming president of the club, my brother David served it as its honorary secretary for a period of eight years. David Malka is a person who
can best be described as "the life of the party" wherever he is. Very active,
irrepressible, and outgoing, he acted as master of ceremonies for most of
the club functions (and frequently at whatever event he attended) and
made the club a pleasant and enjoyable place for all Jews and their
friends.

10

⚜

Jewish Leaders' Visits
to Khartoum

During World War II, the Jewish Community in Khartoum was fortunate to receive occasional visits from Jewish world Zionist and religious leaders.

Nahum Sokolov, President of the
World Zionist Organization

Nahum Sokolov, then president of the World Zionist Organization, visited Khartoum in 1934. He was accompanied by his daughter, Dr. Celina Sokolov, whom I believe I recall was a physician and who took care of her father and his health needs during his world travels in service of the cause of Zionism and Eretz Israel.

Nahum Sokolov was one of Theodor Herzl's greatest admirers; and in 1906, he became the secretary general of the World Zionist Organization, founded by Herzl. In London, he was involved in efforts to obtain the Balfour Declaration (1917); and in Paris, he was the head of the Jewish Delegation to the Peace Conference (1919). Thereafter, he was chairman of the Jewish Agency and the president of the World Zionist Organization from 1931 to 1935. It was in that latter capacity that he visited Khartoum in 1934.

He and other Jewish world leaders frequently visited the Jews of South Africa, who were at the time among the wealthiest and most prominent supporters of the Zionist movement. In those days, the air trip from South Africa to Palestine was too long to be made in one direct nonstop flight; and so a night stop on the way was necessary. Khartoum was a

20. Reception for Nahum Sokolov, president of the World Zionist Organization. *Center,* Sokolov; *to his right,* Rabbi Malka and President Ibrahim Seroussi; *to his left,* Dr. Celina Sokolov, his daughter, and Mrs. Seroussi; *behind* Sokolov, my fiancée, Dora, and me.

common stop for Jewish leaders on the way back to Palestine and Eretz Israel and afforded them the opportunity to visit the small Jewish Community in the Sudan and meet its leaders. Madagascar was another frequent stopover choice.

We were very excited when we received advance word of the visit of Nahum Sokolov and his daughter. We organized a large reception in their honor on the grounds of the Maccabi Sports Club; and it was well attended by a good number of the Jewish Community, young and old. At the reception, they were received and welcomed by Rabbi Solomon Malka and President Ibrahim Seroussi, and we were enthusiastic and energized by Mr. Sokolov's words and encouragement.

As the evening came to an end around eleven o'clock, I vividly remember that, as we accompanied them to the waiting cars on Victoria Avenue that were to take them to their rooms for the night at the Grand Hotel on the banks of the Blue Nile, I led a small, spontaneous street demonstration for them and for Zion. A mere decade or two later, such expression of feelings on the streets of Khartoum would have been unthinkable and would have caused severe repercussions. But this was in June 1934, and I was then the honorary secretary of the Sudan Jewish Community. I remember the date well, as it occurred a few days after my engagement to my fiancée and future wife, Dora Goldenberg, may God rest her soul. Because Sokolov appeared in his white summer jacket, complete with tie despite the oppressive Khartoum June heat, and with his ribboned, flat, white cloth hat always by his side, we too felt obligated to appear in our white jackets and ties out of deference to him and the occasion.

Rabbi Isaac Halevi Herzog, Chief Rabbi of Israel

Another memorable visit of Jewish leaders to Khartoum was that of Chief Rabbi Isaac Halevi Herzog, the chief Ashkenazi rabbi of Israel. He was also on his way back from South Africa to Palestine.

This was sometime in 1942 during World War II, when travel was by seaplanes that landed on the River Nile at a place known as Gordon's Tree, 30 miles south of Khartoum. Gordon's Tree, named after General Sir Charles Gordon Pasha of Khartoum, was a small town on the White Nile with a river airport used by seaplanes stopping at Khartoum. A few miles farther south lay the Jebel Awlia Dam, which stores the waters of the White Nile before the river goes on to join the Blue Nile in Khartoum and then continues on its way to Egypt. Many of the Egyptian Irrigation Department workers and employees that ran the Jebel Awlia Dam did their daily shopping at Gordon's Tree markets.

We were quite excited when my father, received word that Rabbi Herzog was coming. As the rabbi's son and honorary secretary of the Community, I was delegated to meet Rabbi Herzog at the Gordon's Tree river airport and escort him to the Grand Hotel on the Blue Nile in Khartoum.

In the short time I had to make arrangements, I called I. Segal in his office and asked him to accompany me to the river airport, to which he gladly agreed. Segal, a young man in his thirties from Palestine, had been recruited by the British to serve as director or deputy director of the Sudan Government Passport Office in Khartoum. As an Ashkenazi Jew from Eretz Israel, I considered him the ideal person to go with me to meet the chief Ashkenazi rabbi of Eretz Israel; and with him as chief of the Passport Office at my side, Rabbi and Mrs. Herzog would go through customs with no questions or difficulties.

21. Rabbi Issac Halevi Herzog, chief Ashkenazi rabbi of Israel.

Rabbi Herzog's seaplane finally arrived, splashing into the quiet river waters with its propellers spraying a mist around the plane and partially obscuring it from view. The plane taxied to the river bank and was secured in place. After what seemed a long time, the plane doors opened. Then after another wait, the passengers started coming out.

We greeted Rabbi and Mrs. Herzog respectfully and accompanied them to the Grand Hotel in Khartoum, where they would be spending the night. There, the hotel staff greeted the guests and showed them to their room for a much-needed brief rest.

An hour or two later, refreshed and rested, the rabbi and his wife joined us for afternoon tea in the hotel lounge, where, as instructed, I vigilantly watched to ensure that nothing nonkosher was being served. During tea, Rabbi Herzog asked to attend evening services (*arbit* in the Sephardic tradition and *maariv* in the Ashkenazi tradition) and asked me to bring some children along. We had anticipated this request and gladly drove him to the Khartoum Synagogue. My father and a minian of leaders and some children were awaiting them and greeted them warmly at the synagogue. Rabbi Herzog was gracious, and I still recall feeling deeply moved when he gave a *bracha* (blessing) to the collected children and expressed his hopes for them and for Eretz Israel. Even after all these years, I can still recall the sight of him, with his impressive beard, sitting on a chair in the synagogue, by the side of the teba, and raising his hands over the children's heads as he blessed them.

After services, we went on to my father's home for dinner, where my mother had prepared a lavish spread in his honor. After *birkat hamazon* (grace after a meal), Rabbi Herzog and my father talked late into the night about a variety of topics. I do not recall the exact subjects but whether religious or political, whether Torah, Talmud, or Halakha, Community affairs or Zionism, the Sudan or Eretz Israel, they certainly had a lot to talk about. I sat patiently waiting until it was time to take Rabbi Herzog and his wife to their hotel. The next morning, they left Khartoum.

Rabbi Herzog was a rabbinic scholar and a prominent Jewish world leader. Before he went to Palestine as chief rabbi of Eretz Israel, he was the chief rabbi of the Irish Free State in Dublin from 1921 to 1936. His son Chaim Herzog, after serving as chief of intelligence in Israel during the 1949–1951 period and as the leading military commentator of the 1967 Six Day War, became the elected president of Israel for the decade 1983–1993.

When in 1993 I wrote to his grandson Isaac Herzog seeking a picture of his grandfather to use in this book and any available confirmation of his visit to Khartoum, I received the following reply from his father, President Chaim Herzog:

> My son Isaac has passed your letter dated June 28, 1993, concerning the visit of my late father Chief Rabbi Isaac Halevi Herzog to Khartoum, on his way back from South Africa during the World War.

I found your story a most fascinating one. I recall the problems they had on returning from South Africa to Palestine and their adventures on the seaplane which brought them back home.

Your description, as far as I can remember is a very accurate one, but I have unfortunately no written record.

Rabbi Israel Brodie

Another prominent rabbi who spent sometime in Khartoum before the war was Rabbi Israel Brodie. Rabbi Brodie was then the Jewish chaplain of the Khartoum British Garrison. Later, he became the chief Ashkenazi rabbi of Great Britain. While in Khartoum, Rabbi Brodie frequently went to the Khartoum Synagogue for the Shabbat evening services and from there he often went with my father for a home-cooked kosher Shabbat dinner at my father's house. I remember this well because, after dinner, I would have to accompany Rabbi Brodie as he walked the five or six miles back to his quarters in the British Barracks because he would obviously not ride on Shabbat.

Less prominent but also of interest was the presence of some Jewish soldiers within the British Garrison in Khartoum. These young boys were made welcome in the homes of many Khartoum Jewish families, who strove hard to make them feel at home. Khartoum had a roller-skating rink owned by Mathias Nahmias, a local Greek Jew. The Jewish soldiers seemed to be particularly fond of and were frequently seen at the skating rink, which they used as a distraction from their military duties. I had other interactions with these young Jews, some of which I will relate later.

11

⌒❦⌒

Ethiopian Jews and Their Leaders

Taamrat Emmanuel and Tadessa Yacoub

In the late nineteenth century and early twentieth, the Alliance Israélite of Paris was interested in the fate of the Falashas and their connection with Judaism. In 1867, they sent to Ethiopia Professor Joseph Halévy (1827–1917), the great French Orientalist, who was then teaching Amharic in the Ecole Pratique des Etudes in Paris, on a mission to study the conditions of the Falashas.

In January 1904, they sent Halevy's student, Jacques Faitlovitch, who also knew Amharic, on the same mission. Faitlovitch's mission lasted nineteen months (ending in August 1905), during which he visited all regions where the Falashas dwelt in Ethiopia, investigating their Jewish practices and living conditions. He concluded that the appurtenance of the Falashas to Judaism was incontestable, and he made every effort to educate them, supply them with books, and bring them back to rabbinic Judaism.

According to the writings of Louis Rappaport[1] the ethnic name *Falasha* (stranger, wanderer, or exile) may have originated in the decree of the fifteenth-century Ethiopian monarch Yeshaq, who apparently said "he who is baptized in the Christian religion may inherit the land of his father; otherwise let him be a *falasi*."

In November 1907, the Alliance Israélite Universelle also sent Rabbi Haim Nahum, the Sephardic rabbi and diplomat from Turkey, who later became chief rabbi of Turkey and then of Egypt, on a similar mission to

---

1. From articles by Louis Rappaport in the Jerusalem *Post*, International Edition, of 1 June 1991 and by Karen Bacon in Yeshiva Univ., *Torah U-Madda Journal*, 1991–1992.

Ethiopia. Rabbi Nahum's mission lasted about four months, from November 1907 to March 1908, during which in Addis Ababa he visited the emperor and the French ambassador to Ethiopia, who facilitated his mission. Thereafter, he visited the Falashas in their villages around Gondar and other regions.

In *Un Grand Rabbin Sepharade en Politique* (1990), Esther Benbassa of Paris states that Rabbi Nahum believed that the Falashas must have been converted to Mosaism by a group of "Judaisers" coming from Egypt in the second or third century B.C.E., probably during the Ptolemic period, on Greek expeditions that followed the Atbara river to the Falasha regions in Abyssinia. Rabbi Nahum said that the Falashas knew biblical history but were totally unaware of the post-biblical period and that their Jewish practices were rather external. He estimated their total number at the time to be at only six to seven thousand, and he concluded that he was not enthusiastic about saving them back to rabbinic Judaism. He recommended rather helping them to immigrate from their poor regions and conditions, some to the north in Asmara and other parts of Eritrea and some to the south to Addis Ababa and its surroundings in order to improve their material and economic conditions.

On 18 September 1940, my father, Rabbi Solomon Malka, brought his friend Taamrat Emmanuel to my home, introducing him as "Professor Emmanuel," a former cultural attaché of the Ethiopian Embassy in Paris. The occasion was the Brit Mila which he himself was performing on his grandson and my son, Jeffrey Solomon. That baby is now an orthopaedic surgeon, associate professor at Georgetown University, and chairman of the Department of Orthopaedic Surgery at Fairfax Hospital in Virginia, the teaching hospital for three orthopaedic residency programs.

Taamrat Emmanuel was in Khartoum in the company of Emperor Haile Selassie, who was then in exile in Khartoum. He had joined the emperor's government in Ethiopia and, in 1939, accompanied him in exile to London and then to Khartoum. In 1941, Emmanuel returned to Ethiopia with Haile Selassie for the liberation of their country from Italian rule. While in Khartoum, he was living with the emperor in the so-called Pink Palace, on the banks of the Blue Nile, about one mile south of the Blue Nile Cinema at the southern edge of Khartoum. The Pink Palace had been assigned to Emperor Haile Selassie by the Sudan government during his stay in Khartoum. While in Khartoum, Taamrat Emmanuel frequently visited my father. Of similar ages, they rapidly became fast friends and enjoyed each other's company. I recall their having long discussions about Jewish affairs in Ethiopia and elsewhere.

Simon D. Messing of Hamden, Connecticut, wrote about Taamrat Emmanuel and other Falasha leaders in *The Story of the Falashas: The "Black Jews" of Ethiopia.* Messing recounts that Taamrat Emmanuel was the son of Falasha parents who had accepted Christianity through the efforts of Protestant missionaries in their village. The missionaries recognized the intellectual qualities of the child Taamrat and sent him to the Swedish mission in Asmara, Eritrea.

While there, Taamrat Emmanuel was discovered by Professor Jacques Faitlovitch, whose lifework was to rescue the Falasha and bring them to rabbinic Judaism, the pattern known in Western Europe as *Torah Im Derekh Eretz* (Bible together with the way of the land). Professor Faitlovitch had been sent on his mission to Ethiopia by the Alliance Israelite Universelle of Paris and was supported by a small purse from Baron Edmond de Rothschild.

Jacques Faitlovitch got Taamrat Emmanuel released from the Swedish mission in Asmara and found him a brilliant student who was already fluent in Italian, Amharic, and the Eritrean local language Tigrinya. He took him to Paris, enrolled him with other Falasha students in the Ecole Normale of the Alliance Israélite at Auteuil, a suburb of Paris, where he became fluent in French. Then he transferred Emmanuel to the Collegio Rabbinico in Italy; and in the following year, he entrusted him to Herr Goldschmidt in Jerusalem, who supervised his further educational development. In 1920, Taamrat Emmanuel was installed by Faitlovitch as director of the Hebrew School at Addis Ababa with fifty students, which Emmanuel later transferred to Gondar.

Professor Faitlovitch also introduced Emmanuel to the then regent in Addis Ababa. The regent subsequently became Emperor Haile Selassie, who took Emmanuel into his diplomatic service in Addis Ababa and abroad.

I first met Tadessa Yacoub in the early 1960s. I was in Addis Ababa on business for my company, Gellatly Hankey, and had to see the director of customs. I was taken to the American advisor in his corner office in the Customs Department, with whom I discussed our business affairs. I was then taken to see the Ethiopian director of customs himself, in the other corner office of the department, who turned out to be Tadessa Yacoub, nephew of Taamrat Emmanuel. I told him about the meeting my father and I had had with his uncle in Khartoum. Other than the business at hand, we also talked about the Jews of Gondar and elsewhere; and I asked him to join me for dinner at the Ras Hotel, where I was staying. He politely declined, mentioning that it was not advisable for him to meet a businessman in public in those times.

Simon Messing relates that Tedessa Yacoub attended his uncle's Hebrew School in Addis Ababa, and acquired a good knowledge of French, the favorite foreign language of the emperor. After attending a university (which he told me was in Egypt), he joined the Civil Service of the emperor in the Department of Customs, where I met him. He also served in the Bureau of Mines, Ministry of Posts and Telegraphs, as vice-minister of finance, and at last was given the title of excellency in his post of vice-minister of agriculture.

After the two world wars, interest in Ethiopian Jews was renewed; and in 1973, Rabbi Ovadya Yosef, then the Sephardic chief rabbi of Israel, rendered that the Beta Israel, as the Ethiopian Jews called themselves, descended from the tribes of Israel and that it was therefore obligatory upon the Jewish Community to accelerate the immigration of this community to Israel. This pronouncement was subsequently supported by the Ashkenazi chief rabbi of Israel, Rabbi Shlomo Goren, and led to the Ethiopian Jews' being recognized under the Law of Return and the Israeli government's committing to restore them to their homeland and to airlifting thousands of them from Addis Ababa to Israel in 1984 and 1991.

When Ronald Reagan was president of the United States, Vice-President George Bush personally went to the Sudan; and with the consent of its president, Major General Jafaar Muhamed El-Nemeiri, arranged the secret airlift of thousands of Falasha refugees to Israel from their refugee camps outside the ancient Sudanese garrison town of Kassala on the Sudan-Ethiopian-Eritrean border. Most of the refugees had walked to Kassala from their Gondar-region villages.

For his help in airlifting the Ethiopian Jews to Israel, President El-Nemeiri was condemned to death by the Sudan regime that overthrew him while he was on a trip in the United States. He then went from the United States to Egypt and lived in exile in Alexandria under the protection of President Hosni Mubarak. Later, to escape an extradition request from the Sudan government, he left Egypt for the Bahamas.

In the fourteenth century, the national legend of Ethiopia, *Kebra Nagast* (glory of the kings), Menelik I, the alleged child of the Queen of Sheba and King Solomon, was identified as the ancestor of the Ethiopian ruling family. Tradition has it that Menelik returned to his homeland from Jerusalem accompanied by Israeli guards, and it is to these Jewish guards that the Beta Israel of Ethiopia trace their origins.[2] Other theories assert that the Beta Israel are descendants of the tribe of Dan, who immigrated either after the Exodus from Egypt, when some of them failed to cross the Red Sea and went South to Ethiopia, or after the destruction of the first Temple, as the lost tribe of Dan, one of the ten tribes carried away by the Assyrians in 722 B.C.E. Late in the fifteenth century, the renowned Egyptian halakahist, Rabbi David Ibn Abu Zimra, in one of his responses said that the Ethiopians were basically Jews from the tribe of Dan who had adopted strange customs. What all these theories have in common is that they all associate the Beta Israel with the Jewish people. In all my flights on Ethiopian Airways, between Khartoum and Addis Ababa, I noticed that the planes had a lion painted on them representing the Lion of Judah, a symbol of the Ethiopian royal family.

There is something highly appropriate in calling the return of the Ethiopian Jews to Israel "Operation Moses." According to Josephus, the first-century Jewish historian, Moses once ruled in Ethiopia, which he entered as head of an Egyptian army and married the daughter of the Ethiopian King, Taharbis, who, out of her affection for him, delivered the city to him. The tradition that Moses ruled in Ethiopia is also shared by the Ethiopians, and Ethiopian Jews have a particular reverence for Moses.

2. Ibid.

12

⚜

The Jews of Aden, Yemen, and Eritrea

On one of my business trips to Aden in the 1950s, I went to see the remains of the Aden Synagogue in the old town of Aden. I was told it had been burned by some local fanatics. All that was left of it were high smoke-filled walls, which show that there was once a fair-sized community of Jews in Aden. The "old town" of Aden was where the native Yemenites lived and had their shops. It is a few miles inland from the Aden harbor area where British, French, and other foreigners lived and worked in the port. In the harbor area, they had their offices and shops, partly managed by English-speaking Indians; and, I suspect, before them by English-speaking Adenese Jews.

Quite a number of the Adenese Jews crossed gradually to Eritrea after the British left Aden. They were found in large numbers in Asmara, the capital of Eritrea, where they formed the largest part of the Jewish Community. They were mostly westernized, European-dressed, English-educated, and spoke English, Italian, and Arabic. These Jews were in contrast to the Yemenite Jews from the interior of Yemen and around Sanaʿa, the capital, who represented the typical religious Yemenite Jew of the old culture, Arab in dress and Arab-speaking, with some of them well learned in biblical Hebrew and the Torah.

When in Asmara, I used to pay a visit to Yacoub Aharoni, the Adenese president of the Jewish Community of Asmara in his big textile shop. On Shabbat eve, I would attend the *Kabbalat Shabbat* (Welcoming of the Sabbath service) in the Asmara Synagogue, a fairly small but beautiful, well-attended synagogue, accompanied by my friends from the Sudan, David and Maurice Aeleon, who then worked and lived in Asmara. There, I very much enjoyed the chanting of *Lekha Dodi Lekrat Kalla, Peni Shabbat Negabillah* (Come my friend to meet the Bride, let us welcome the Shabbat) in the Yemenite Adenese melody, chanted by all together with vigor and enthusiasm. This poem, one of the finest of Hebrew religious poetry from the middle of the sixteenth century, is chanted on Shabbat eve in every synagogue in the world in a great number of melodies set to it by various composers, ranging from the East European melodies to various Sephardic melodies.

What amused me and interested me most was to see three Ashkenazi shohetim, ritual kosher slaughterers from Israel, in their long black caftans, joining enthusiastically in the chanting of the *Lekha Dodi* in the Adenese Yemenite melody, quite foreign to their Ashkenazi East European melodies and even to other popular Sephardic melodies. These three Ashkenazi Orthodox shohetim from Israel were the slaughterers of the kosher meat factory in Asmara, about which more later.

As is generally known, Haile Selassie, the emperor of Ethiopia, was favorable to the Jews and to Israel. During his rule of Eritrea, a nice, big kosher meat factory was erected in Asmara; and those three Ashkenazi shohetim from Israel were the slaughterers employed by the factory to slaughter the cattle and certify the meat kosher for export to Israel.

On another day, I had occasion to visit the factory with Boris Gwertzman,[1] the shipping manager of Gellatly Hankey in Asmara, whose wife's brother owned the factory. They were all escapees from the Nazis, arriving penniless; but with their intelligence and hard work, they prospered in Eritrea. In their escape from the Nazis and before coming to Eritrea, both Borris and his brother-in-law Harry Kahan went first to Palestine, where they acquired a good knowledge of Hebrew and made connections. When I visited their kosher meat factory in Asmara, they invited me to lunch at Harry Kahan's home, where I met Boris's wife, Lea, and their ten-year-old daughter Varda, a beautiful little girl with reddish brown, curly hair, who I understand later married and lived in Israel.

The kosher meat factory was known by its business name INCODE, which I suspect is an anagram of the initials of their Hebrew names. It exported canned kosher meat, which was certified, as marked on the cans,

---

1. My friend R. G. Gibson, who at the time was Gellatly's director in Asmara and therefore Boris Gwertzman's boss, told me that Boris was Gellatly's chief shipping manager in Eritrea and very good at it, too. Gibson added that Boris was a staunch Gellatly man but had a lot of other "odd" interests, to which they turned a blind eye.

by the three Ashkenazi shohetim I met at the Asmara Synagogue on Shabbat eve. Harry Kahan was known as the owner of the factory; but Boris was a part-owner, in that his wife, Lea, owned shares in the company. Boris Gwertzman was an enthusiastic Zionist who moved to Geneva, Switzerland, where he died in the early 1990s survived by his wife, Lea, who still lives in Geneva.

Asmara has a beautiful climate, being 7,000 feet in altitude and not far from the Red Sea in Massawa. The Italians had made it into a European-style city; and many of the Sudan Jews went for vacation, for work, and for settlement. My old friend David Aeleon, Sudan-born son of Yacoub Aeleon, one of the early settlers in Khartoum, settled in Asmara first as exchange manager of Barclays Bank and then as a successful businessman on his own account. His brother Maurice Aeleon, who later became the husband of my niece Claudette Goldenberg, practiced law in Asmara and Addis Ababa. Dr. Suleiman Bassiouni, son of Ben-Sion Coshti, on his retirement as chief surgeon of the Khartoum Hospital, moved to Asmara with his family, practiced medicine there for a while, and then retired from there with his family to Israel.

I myself visited Asmara for the first time in 1942 for a vacation with my wife, Dora, and our two-year-old-son, Jeffrey. It was then still under Italian rule; and coming from the Sudan, where the ruling British stood aloof from the general population, I was surprised to see that the cabman who took us for a ride around the city in his one-horse hackney carriage and the waiter who served us in the European coffee house were as Italian as the Italian governor of the territory. We soon noticed that, unlike the British, the Italians in their colonies mixed with all levels of the native population and many intermarried with them. In their long rule of Eritrea and their five-year rule of Ethiopia, almost every Eritrean and Ethiopian spoke Italian as their second language.

I went many times thereafter to Asmara and from there to the old Red Sea port of Massawa, where Gellatly had an old-established office. Unlike Asmara, the weather in Massawa, except during January and February, is oppressively hot with high humidity. During the months of July and August, in particular, it becomes intolerably hot and humid, reaching at times more than 105 degrees Fahrenheit during the day. During those months, I saw our office staff holding at all times little towels with which to wipe the constant sweat off their foreheads, hands, and bodies.

To Eritrea, the British deported Yitzhak Shamir from Palestine in 1946. His deportation followed a few weeks after the blowing up of the south wing of the Jerusalem King David Hotel, which housed the British administrative and military personnel, by the Irgun Zvi Leumi (H. National military organization), of which Yitzhak Shamir was the leader. This and other actions by the Irgun were in response to the British major action, using 100,000 British soldiers, plus 1,500 policemen, to crush the leaders of the Zionist movement, the Yishuv, and Kibbutzim in Palestine. In particular, it was to protest the refusal of the British government, under Ernest Bevin and later Clement Attlee, to allow a one-time mercy allocation of entry permits to Palestine for 100,000 displaced Jews from Germany and Austria, as requested by President Harry S Truman and recommended by a British-American commission.

Instead, the British tightened control, promised to hang every Jewish terrorist, and hunted for Jewish leaders. They placed 20,000 British soldiers in Tel Aviv alone and imposed on it a strict four-day curfew.

Yitzhak Shamir was on the wanted list, which was headed by Menahim Begin. He sought to avoid capture by disguising himself as a devout Jew, a black-coated perpetual student of the Torah. But he was identified by a British officer, captured, placed in solitary confinement in Jerusalem, and then flown by a British Halifax to Sambal camp in Eritrea, a few miles outside Asmara. There, he joined some of the 251 Palestinian Jews who, as early as 1944, had been dispatched to British camps in Eritrea and the Sudan. Yitzhak Shamir's wife, Shulamit, was also arrested and jailed in Jerusalem and was not allowed to take with her to jail her baby boy Yair, despite a hunger strike which she only ended on the twelfth day after persuasion of the man she always obeyed, her trusted Rabbi Arye Levin.

The above narrative is described in Yitzhak Shamir's 1994 autobiography *Summing Up*, dedicated to Shulamit. He also describes how he escaped from the Sambal camp, in one of the last sensational escapes from Africa, led and directed by Yacoub Meridor, then commander of the Irgun and later a partner of Menahim Begin in the Herut and Likud political parties and member of the Knesset; and presently minister of finance in the cabinet of Prime Minister Benjamin Netanyahu.

His escape from Sambal with five others was effected on 14 January 1947. They crawled at dusk through a tunnel dug under Sambal's fences and reached Asmara on foot. There, they took shelter with a young Italian family, a Jewish doctor and his Gentile wife, who gave them help. From there, they moved, doubled up, knees to chin, inside a coffin addition to an oil tanker car, which took three days and nights to reach Addis

Ababa. In Addis Ababa, it was decided that he and one of the other prisoners, his comrade Arieh, would try to go to Djibouti, then the harbor capital of French Somalia. They had the help of Jewish traders from Aden who owned a railway car that went weekly by rail to Djibouti carrying coffee beans. They were smuggled between coffee bags; and when they reached the vicinity of Djibouti, they were met by French police, who turned them over to the Djibouti rabbi's custody.

They appeared the next day at the Djibouti Police Headquarters and were informed that the British consul knew of their arrival and was requesting the French governor of Djibouti to turn them over to the British. However, a French lawyer came to their rescue and obtained for them the *droits d'asile* (right of asylum or refuge) as political prisoners. They remained in Djibouti for almost a year, detained in a villa with prisoners from the Vietcong, surrounded by French language and culture, which they learned and got to admire.

At last, the French arranged to have them picked up at Djibouti by a small French aircraft carrier that took them to Toulon, France. From there, they flew to Prague; and once there, took a direct flight to Haifa, where they landed on 20 May 1948, when the State of Israel was six days old. Yitzhak Shamir soon resumed his participation in the political movement of Israel.

Of the Yemenite Jews of Sana'a and the interior of Yemen, as distinct from the Adenese Jews, I remember that a few of them came from Yemen to Khartoum, in small groups of two, three, or four, partly on foot and allegedly on their way to Jerusalem. Although it did not seem to me that Khartoum was the right route to Jerusalem, we nevertheless had to take care of them. We housed them for a while in small rooms in the synagogue in Khartoum, then sent them by train to Port Sudan, where the good Isaac Pinto, husband of my niece Norma Sasson, may they both rest in peace, found them passage on a cargo boat or similar craft to Haifa.

13

❧

B'nai B'rith in the Sudan and Egypt

Ben-Sion Coshti Lodge of Khartoum, No. 1207

On 13 October 1843, twelve American Jews, most of whom were from Germany, met at Sinsheimer's Café, 60 Essex Street, New York City, and founded B'nai B'rith (Sons of the Covenant). Their purpose was to unite Jews of all origins and denominations in the work of promoting their highest interests and those of humanity,[1] and they adopted the motto Benevolence, Brotherly Love, and Harmony. They organized lodges and women's chapters in cities throughout the United States and in countries throughout the world, today numbering fifty-seven countries other than the United States. Before the Arab-Israeli conflict, B'nai B'rith was represented in many countries in the Middle East, including Egypt and the Sudan.

B'nai B'rith chose the menorah as the traditional symbol of its order. Its seven branches signify the noble ideals of B'nai B'rith: light, justice, peace, truth, benevolence, brotherly love, and harmony. The menorah was placed at the entry of the first tabernacle built by the children of Israel in the wilderness after their exodus from Egypt about 1200 B.C.E. (Ex. 25:8, 9, 31, 32).[2]

---

1. Constitution of B'nai B'rith International, Art. 2.
2. Exodus 25:8 and 9, "Let them make Me a sanctuary that I may dwell among them. According to all I show thee, the pattern of the Tabernacle, so shall ye make it." Exodus 25:31 and 32, "Thou shall make a candlestick of pure gold (H. Menorat Zahab) of beaten work shall the candlestick (H. Hamenorah) be made. There shall be six branches going out of the sides thereof: three branches of the candlestick out of the one side thereof, and three branches of the candlestick out of the other side thereof."

In 1934, Ezra Rodriguez, delegate and treasurer of the B'nai B'rith Grand District Lodge of Egypt in Cairo and later its president, was on a trip to Khartoum on business for the Singer Manufacturing Company, of which he was the managing director for the Middle East at its headquarters in Cairo. He approached me and Leon Ortasse, then respectively the honorary secretary and vice-president of the Sudan Jewish Community in Khartoum, proposing that we establish a B'nai B'rith lodge in Khartoum. This was to be part of the B'nai B'rith Grand District Lodge of Egypt and of the Grand District Lodge in Cincinnati, Ohio, in the United States, and for the defense of Jewish interests and the pursuit of Jewish philanthropy, unity, harmony, fraternal love, and peace.

We immediately arranged for a meeting with him and Jewish leaders at my home. I was newly married and had a nice new home. At this meeting, a decision was reached to establish a B'nai B'rith lodge in Khartoum, with the name of "B'nai B'rith Ben-Sion Coshti Lodge" in memory of Ben-Sion Coshti, the first Mahdiya Jew of the Sudan.

In December 1934,[3] brother Ezra Rodriguez installed the new lodge, its officers, and its twenty-two charter members in a solemn ceremony in the Khartoum Synagogue conducted in French and following all the practices and rituals of the B'nai B'rith. It was an impressive ceremony that imprinted on us the principles of the B'nai B'rith. In brother Ezra Rodriguez's presence, its first officers were elected: Ibrahim Seroussi, president of the Community, as its president; Rabbi Solomon Malka, as its mentor; Dr. Suleiman Bassiouni, son of Ben-Sion Coshti, as its vice-president; Eliaho Solomon Malka (myself), honorary secretary of the Community, as vice-president/honorary secretary; and Leon Ortasse, vice-president of the Community, as vice-president/honorary treasurer.

Later, I spent time translating the rituals and statutes of the B'nai B'rith supplied to us in French, the language of the B'nai B'rith lodges in Egypt, into Arabic, the main working language of our members, although many of them were acquainted with both English and French. On the local level, we supported Jewish education of our children, helped some of them to go to college, and when things became difficult, we helped with B'nai B'rith and other funds those of our youth who needed it to go Israel, often through Cyprus.[4]

---

3. The installation was ratified by B'nai B'rith International in Jan. 1935.

4. For obvious reasons, it was not possible to book passage from Khartoum to Israel. Travel was therefore arranged ostensibly to Cyprus and, once there, to Israel.

Of interest among our local efforts was the agreement we reached with the Comboni College of Khartoum,[5] a Canadian Catholic Brothers school attended by most of our boys for primary, secondary, and professional studies. We convinced the college officials to substitute the daily hour of study of Catholic scriptures for all children by a daily hour for the study of the Torah and Jewish prayers for our Jewish children, with us supplying our teacher, Farag Shoua, and them the school hour and classroom. This was a nice addition to the Hebrew classes our children were already attending twice weekly at the synagogue.

Also, when the British governor of Khartoum made it mandatory for shopkeepers to close their shops on Fridays or Sundays, at their option, to attend Muslim or Christian prayers, we requested and he agreed to extend the order to Saturdays as a third option, so that Jewish shopkeepers could attend Jewish Saturday services. This had the effect of increasing attendance at the Shabbat morning services in the Khartoum Synagogue and of proper observance of the Shabbat, its rest, and holiness.

On the international level, B'nai B'rith was our window to the outside Jewish world and our contact with it. Through the *B'nai B'rith Magazine*, which we received regularly from the United States, we had news of the Jewish world and of the suffering of the Jews in Nazi Germany. In the Sudan in 1942, we also heard the daily broadcasts from Berlin radio of the former mufti of Jerusalem, Hag Amin El-Husseini, with his message to the Arab world of hatred of the Jews and his call to "kill the Jews wherever you find them. It pleases Allah." At this time, we in B'nai B'rith went around collecting contributions from the Jewish shopkeepers and other Jews for the suffering Jews of Germany. Modest as they were, I sent them with a list of contributors to the *B'nai B'rith Magazine* in the United States, having no better way of reaching the German Jews and expressing our solidarity with them.

Our relations with the Egyptian lodges were pleasant and cordial; and

---

5. Bishop Comboni, after whom the Comboni College was named, was head of the Catholic Mission in the Sudan, before the Mahdiya rule. He died in Khartoum on 10 Oct. 1881. In his book *Fire and Sword in the Sudan: Fighting and Serving the Dervishes* (London: Greenhill, 1990), 35, Austrian-born General Sir Rudolph Slatin Pasha, then still the Egyptian governor of Darfur, mentions that Bishop Comboni traveled with him on 29 Mar. 1881 on his steamer from Khartoum to a point on the White Nile and then on a five-day march to El-Obeid. From El-Obeid, Bishop Comboni made a tour through Jebel Nuba in the Nuba Mountain District, which Slatin went on to El-Fasher, capital of Darfur Province.

on my yearly visits to Cairo, on vacation or business, brother Ezra Rodriguez, then president of the Grand District Lodge No. 16 of Egypt and the Sudan, would introduce me at a meeting of the Cairo Lodge, where I would give the fraternal greetings of the Khartoum Lodge and a report of our progress. Similarly, Rodriguez would join us and guide us whenever he was on a business visit to Khartoum. I recall a visit of brother Solomon Cicurel Bey, a leading member of the Cairo Lodge and later president of the Jewish Community of Cairo and owner of Les Grands Magasins Cicurel, well-known department stores in Cairo. He was visiting Khartoum as head of the delegation of the Egyptian Chamber of Commerce. I met him at a meeting of the Sudan Chamber of Commerce and shook his hand using the B'nai B'rith identification sign. He immediately recognized it; and knowing the weight his words carried, spoke very highly of me to my firm's British managing director, who was then president of the Sudan Chamber of Commerce.

Grand District Lodge of Egypt, the Sudan, No. 16, and the Cairo Lodge

While serving as president of the Grand District Lodge of Egypt and the Sudan No. 16, brother Ezra Rodriguez continued to establish lodges in other cities of Egypt. Among these, I particularly remember the "Tanta Lodge," whose honorary secretary was another Malka, whom I got to know through B'nai B'rith communications.

But most important of all was the foundation in Cairo in December 1938 of the first women's auxiliary of B'nai B'rith, under the name of the Deborah B'nai B'rith Women's Union Lodge, with sixty-eight charter members of the elite Jewish ladies who were then among the cream of Cairo society. It was granted Charter No. 242 by B'nai B'rith International and was founded under the auspices of brothers Ezra Rodriguez and Jack Blau, respectively president and honorary secretary of the Grand District Lodge of Egypt and the Sudan No. 16; Grand Rabbi Haim Nahum Effendi, Hakhambashi of Egypt; and brother Simon Mani, president of the Cairo Lodge.

In his letter of 3 April 1939 acknowledging the foundation of the Deborah B'nai B'rith Women's Lodge, brother Henry Monsky, grand president of the Supreme Lodge in Washington, D.C.—formerly the title of the president of B'nai B'rith International—wrote to brothers Rodriguez and Blau as follows:

In these hours of trial for our people we have need for courage and stoicism. To B'nai B'rith in Egypt has fallen the task of serving as the African outpost of our great order. You have served the cause of Israel and B'nai B'rith nobly for many years.

It is cause of great rejoicing to the Supreme Lodge that the first Women's Auxiliary of B'nai B'rith in Cairo has been formed under the auspices of the Grand Lodge of District No. 16 at a time when other Grand Lodges overseas are being crushed under the heel of tyrants who know not the harmony, benevolence and brotherly love that are the cardinal virtues not only of B'nai B'rith but of all humanity. It is inspiring to have a new link in the B'nai B'rith chain welded in Egypt at this time.

By the early 1950s and particularly by the time of the Israeli Sinai campaign in 1956 and the coordinated French-British-Israeli attack on the Suez Canal, things had become difficult for the Jews in the Sudan and Egypt. We all ended our open B'nai B'rith activities and declared our lodges "dormant," which they are to this day. After the difficult period of dispersion and readjustment, however, we all cropped up in other parts of the world, from the United States to France, from the United Kingdom to Switzerland and Israel, to continue our fraternal relations and efforts for Judaism and the Jewish people, with our fellow Jews, in B'nai B'rith and other Jewish organizations.

About B'nai B'rith in Egypt, Gudrun Krämer writes in *The Jews in Modern Egypt:*

The one communal association to have a countrywide organization were the lodges of the B'nai B'rith. In the 1920's a number of lodges were active among Egyptian Jews: the Ashkenazi "Maimonides" lodge and the Sephardi "Cairo" lodge in the capital (established in 1887 and 1911 respectively), the "Eliahu Ha-Nabi" lodge in Alexandria (1891), "Ohel Moshe" in Tanta (1921), "Maghen David" in al-Mansura (1923), "Israel" in Port Said (1924). In 1934 "The Grande Loge du District D'Egypte et du Soudan" united them and the "Ben Sion Coshti Lodge" in Khartoum (1934) under one organization which later established the women's lodges "Deborah" in Cairo and "Ruth" in Alexandria (both in 1939) as well as the youth lodge A.Z.A. (Aleph Zadek Aleph) in 1943. . . .

The B'nai B'rith adopted the ideals of humanism and philanthropy from the Freemasons but not their ritual and critical attitude towards religion. They defined themselves as a Jewish organization active on behalf of charity and communal reform, cultural revival and the defense of Jewish interests in general. By the turn of the century, the lodges of B'nai B'rith,

which were largely made up of members of the rising commercial and professional middle class, were actively working for democratic and social reform within the Jewish Community, establishing schools, workshops and
charitable institutions of all kinds. They also supported the movement of
spiritual and political Zionism. . . .

In Alexandria, around Easter/Passover 1925, teachers in the Catholic
Missionary school of Ste. Catherine, which was attended by a large number of Jewish students, shocked the Jewish Community by distributing
anti-semitic material repeating the traditional blood libel accusations.
B'nai B'rith immediately responded and established the "Union Juive pour
l'Enseignement" (The Jewish Union for Education) which the very same
year was able to open a Jewish Secondary School, the "Lycee de L'Union
Juive pour L'Enseignement" in the suburbs of Moharram Bey. By 1928 it
had about 450 students, most of them of rather modest backgrounds
(p. 72).

During the one hundred fiftieth anniversary of B'nai B'rith, I was grat-
ified to see that we had not been completely forgotten. In the special one
hundred fiftieth anniversary issue of the B'nai B'rith International *Jewish
Monthly*,[6] of October-November 1993, its chief editor, Jeff Rubin, wrote
under the heading "Near and Far":

In its 150 year history, B'nai B'rith has ridden the tides of history from
the Lower East Side of New York to such far lands as Sudan, Egypt, Iraq,
Lebanon and Japan.

B'nai B'rith opened its first lodge in the region in 1886 with the creation of the Maimonides Lodge in Cairo, Egypt. Oriental District 11, created in 1911, would eventually embrace a crescent shaped territory to
Belgrade, Serbia in the north, to Baghdad, Iraq in the east, to Khartoum,
Sudan in the south to Algiers, Algeria in the west. B'nai B'rith was particularly active in Egypt with lodges in four cities. These lodges joined with a
lodge in Khartoum to form District 16 in 1934.

At the one hundred fiftieth anniversary celebrations held 17 November 1993 on Ellis Island, New York, I was requested by the International
president, then Kent Schiner, to give an interview to the B'nai B'rith
press agent and photographer because of my distinction in being the only
member present who had belonged to B'nai B'rith in three different con-
tinents; Africa (Khartoum), Europe (Paris), and North America (White

6. *The Jewish Monthly* succeeded the *B'nai B'rith Magazine*.

Plains, New York). Part of that interview was included in the commemo-
rative video of the event.

By the Grace of God, at age eighty-seven in 1996, I am one of the last
surviving members of B'nai B'rith District No. 16 of Egypt and the Sudan
and the last of the Ben-Sion Coshti Lodge of Khartoum. I am still active
in B'nai B'rith in the United States, presently as chaplain of the Westchester-Putnam Council of B'nai B'rith, former president and member at
large of White Plains B'nai B'rith Unit 5249 of District 1, and Anniversary Club member.

Before Ezra Rodriguez became president of District 16 of Egypt and
Sudan, Salvator Abrabanel had been president of the Grand District
Lodge and the Cairo Lodge. It was this same Salvator Abrabanel who, in
1932, founded the first B'nai B'rith lodge in France, having been sur-
prised when he relocated to France from Egypt to find that there was no
B'nai B'rith presence in France.

Apart from the Abrabanel activities for B'nai B'rith in Egypt and
France, the Abrabanel name arouses in us Sephardim, who originated in
Spain, memories of the expulsion from Spain in 1492 and of the great
Don Isaac Abrabanel (1430–1508), who is said to have sought, using his
influence at court and a magnificent bribe, to convince Ferdinand and Isabella to reverse their decree of 31 March 1492 expelling all Jews from
their dominions. But he failed when Tomás de Torquemada, the grand inquisitor, exclaimed to the king and queen "Judah sold his master for
thirty pieces of silver, now you would sell him again."[7]

7. Cecil Roth, *A History of the Jews: From the Earliest Times Through the Six Day War*
(New York: Schocken, 1970), 226–27.

14

⚜

B'nai B'rith in France
Loge de France No. 1151

According to the records of Loge de France No. 1151 supplied to me by my old friend brother Jacques Bronsen, honorary secretary of the Loge de France, it was brother Salvator Abrabanel who founded this Loge de France in Paris. Arriving from Cairo, where he had been a B'nai B'rith leader, and finding no B'nai B'rith presence in France, he worked with local Jewish leaders and other B'nai B'rith immigrants from Egypt to found the first B'nai B'rith in France. He became its first president when the Loge de France No. 1151 was installed on 27 March 1932 by Judge Liberman, president of the Grand District Lodge of England, who had gone over from London for that purpose.

Brother Salvator Abrabanel followed his own installation by later installing the Alsace Lodge in Mulhouse and the Loge d'Algiers in the name of the Supreme B'nai B'rith Lodge in Cincinnati and its then president, brother Alfred Cohen, who just happened to be the grand B'nai B'rith president in Cincinnati when the Ben-Sion Coshti Lodge was installed in Khartoum in December 1934 by brother Ezra Rodriguez of the Grand District Lodge of Egypt. Brother Salvator Abrabanel died in Paris on 2 September 1935, and as reported in the *B'nai B'rith Magazine* of November 1935, his loss was mourned by the entire order and especially the European grand lodges.

The Loge de France and other French lodges found themselves obliged to suspend their activities during the World War II; but in October 1945, brother Saby Amon, with fifteen other B'nai B'rith survivors, recommenced the activities of Loge de France and elected brother Baron Edmond de Rothschild as president, brother Risenfeld as mentor, and brother Edgar Abrabanel as secretary general.

I joined the Loge de France during my residence in Paris from 1975 to 1981. I was attending the Shabbat morning service in the eighty-year-old synagogue of Edmond Rothschild, La Synagogue de Boulogne-Billancourt, and asked if I could meet a member of the B'nai B'rith. I was introduced to Claude Bloch, who was then president of the Boulogne-Billancourt Congregation as well as president of the Loge de France in Paris. I shook his hand using the old B'nai B'rith sign first shown to me in Khartoum in 1934 for identifying members of other B'nai B'rith lodges. He recognized it and embraced me as a fellow B'nai B'rith brother. We then became friends to this day, and he immediately involved me in the activities of the Loge de France.

I later noticed that when Claude Bloch installed new members of the Loge de France, he did this in a closed meeting (B'nai B'rith members only) giving them the very same signs and symbols given to me back in Khartoum and Cairo in 1934–1935. These included the transmission of the special grip and handshake for identifying other members of the B'nai B'rith and the three-finger hold on the chest when addressing a meeting, both intended to symbolize the B'nai B'rith motto Benevolence, Brotherly Love, and Harmony. There were also symbols and signs expressing the nature of the order given to it in 1843 to hear, to see, and to keep silent. These symbols and rituals are still used in France and, I believe, in other European lodges. They had the weight of their moral and emotional values and their impact on new members. They no longer seem to be in practice in the United States, although that is whence they undoubtedly emanated.

Joining the Loge de France gave me the opportunity of meeting one of the great French Jews and B'nai B'rith leaders in the person of brother Jean-Pierre Bloch. In my time, he was the honorary chairman of the Loge de France and frequently addressed us on Jewish subjects and concerns and was particularly vehement in his attacks on the anti-Semites, who were then recommencing their activities in the French press. From the time he was president of the Loge de France in the 1950s, he conducted conferences in defense of Jews and Jewish interests both in B'nai B'rith open meetings and in other circles. He was also a leader, president, and more recently chairman of LICRA—Ligue Internationale Contre le Racisme et Antisémitisme (International league against racism and anti-Semitism), which I also joined during my stay in Paris.

Jean-Pierre Bloch was a hero of the French underground resistance and was apparently condemned to death in 1943 by the Vichy government. He escaped, however, to London, after evading his prison guards. A lawyer and an imposing orator, he put his talents in the service of France, Judaism, and the most noble causes of humanity throughout his life. He was minister of the interior in the first government of Charles de Gaulle. On 27 April 1993, he was honored by France and decorated by President François Mitterand with the Grand Cross of the Légion d'Honneur with the title "Minister of Defense," its highest decoration, in a military ceremony in the Invalides. The ceremony was attended by his wife, Gaby Bloch, their children, and grandchildren; LICRA leaders Grand Rabbi Sirat (chief rabbi of France); Jean Kahn, president of the Consistoire Israélite de France; André Braunschweig, vice-president of the French Commission Nationale des Droits de L'Homme (Commission for Human Rights); Mme. de Gaulle; and French politicians and leaders, among others.[1]

The Loge de France was involved in establishing the European Anti-Defamation League, which is in constant touch with the American ADL. Every closed meeting of the Loge de France includes a report updating ADL activities and the political situation in Israel by chairmen of the respective commissions. Whenever I visit Paris, usually in May or June, I make it a point of accepting the courteous invitation of my friend brother Jacques Bronsen, of the Loge de France, to attend the last session of the season, to bring them greetings from their brothers in the United States, and to meet old and new friends.

---

1. *Revue de Droit de Vivre* (The right to live), May 1993.

15

B'nai B'rith in the United States

Honoring the Past, Building the Future
—B'nai B'rith motto on its one hundred fiftieth anniversary, 1993

From my involvement with B'nai B'rith in the Sudan, Egypt, and France, I found in B'nai B'rith my best channel to get involved with the Jewish people and their problems, in fraternizing with them and serving their youth, and in expressing by word and deed my attachment and love for Eretz Israel, its people, and its state. I adopted for myself the principle I learned in France, "once a B'nai B'rith, always a B'nai B'rith," something brother George M. Bloch, president of District 19 in Europe was fond of saying.

And so immediately on my arrival back in the United States and upon taking residence in White Plains, New York, in September 1981, I sought to join a B'nai B'rith lodge and to continue my adherence to the order and, through it, to implement my father's and Hillel's teaching not to separate myself from the Jewish Community wherever I went and to serve and defend my Jewish brethren wherever they are. In mid-September 1981, I was attending the Rosh Hashana (Jewish new year) services in the Conservative Temple Israel Center of White Plains, which I had joined fifteen days earlier, and asked Sol Shapiro, then president of the temple, whether I could meet a member of the B'nai B'rith. He directed me to Lawrence Metzger, a member and former president of the White Plains Lodge of B'nai B'rith. Brother Metzger did not recognize the B'nai B'rith handshake, and I realized that these symbols were no longer practiced in the United States. But he promptly took me to the meetings of

96

the White Plains B'nai B'rith Lodge No. 1749.[1] With him and his wife, Caroline, a former president of B'nai B'rith Women's Chapter, my wife, Bertha, and I attended our first convention of B'nai B'rith International in Washington, D.C., in 1984, with International President Gerald Kraft presiding. A powerful personality and orator and a committed B'nai B'rith leader, he worked tirelessly and full time for B'nai B'rith, just as did the international presidents who followed him, the formidable brother Seymour Reich, who presided over the International Convention in Baltimore in 1988, which I attended with my wife; and International President Kent Schiner, whom I met at the one hundred fiftieth anniversary of B'nai B'rith on Ellis Island, New York, in 1993. In 1996 at the convention of District One of B'nai B'rith, I met brother Tommy A. Baer, the international president of B'nai B'rith, who was reelected for a second term, 1996–1998.

At these international meetings, I saw the greatness of B'nai B'rith, its influence, tremendous organization, and breadth. I listened to presidents of the United States and presidential candidates who came to the international conventions to address our members and seek our support on behalf of their programs for the country, the Jewish people, and Israel. I also heard addresses by the likes of Prime Ministers Yitzhak Shamir and Shimon Peres.

These conventions were attended by about 1,500 delegates from B'nai B'rith lodges all over the world, from Australia, New Zealand, Western Europe, and North and South America. There were lively workshops and debates with panels of prominent leaders, discussions of present and future plans of the B'nai B'rith, elections of the international presidents, banquets, receptions, and celebrations. The effort and work it took to organize these events flawlessly was quite remarkable.

At these conventions, I met old and made new friends. Among them was William Waxler, the honorary president of B'nai B'rith International and a resident of Israel, who was the only one to remember that there was a B'nai B'rith Lodge in Khartoum and a District Lodge in Egypt. There I also met Brother Claude Bloch from Strassbourg, France, president of District 19 of Europe, and brother Charles Haim Musicant of the Loge de France.

1. By individual decision, some B'nai B'rith lodges now include women and are known as units. The White Plains Lodge No. 1749, established in 1948, became Unit No. 5249 in 1988.

22. Eli Malka, president of the White Plains Unit, presenting the B'nai B'rith award for Community service to the retiring Rabbi Morris Davis.

In 1985, I was elected president of the B'nai B'rith White Plains Unit 5249, and with the support, help, and guidance of outgoing President Sigmund Meyerowitz and former President Albert Steinhart, I went on to serve my two-year term with energy and enthusiasm.

I put all my experience and the lessons and examples I learned at the international conventions, district conventions, and board meetings into the service of my unit. I repeatedly said to our younger leaders that the more they got involved and the more they participated, the more they would learn and the better they would serve their B'nai B'rith goals and people, thus gaining satisfaction for themselves and appreciation and honor from others.

I tried to encourage old and new members into action directed at youth services, Jewish traditions, and support for Israel. I organized several general meetings for that purpose; and in view of my age, I appealed to younger leaders to come forward. Young attorney Herbert Kanarek responded, succeeding me as president and accomplishing much for B'nai

B'rith and Israel. He was succeeded by a still younger leader, Arnold Bernstein, who has also gone far in working for B'nai B'rith.

"Honoring the past, building the future" was the theme of B'nai B'rith at its one hundred fiftieth anniversary in 1993, a theme I followed at the fortieth anniversary of the White Plains B'nai B'rith, then known as Lodge 1749 and since 1988 as Unit 5249, with tributes to the past and hopes for the future and awards to recognize past presidents and other long service in B'nai B'rith.

In May 1986, I visited the B'nai B'rith International Archives in Washington, D.C., and with the help of Archival Consultant Mrs. Hannah Sinauer, I was able to find my 1936 article, "Jews in the Sudan," in the *B'nai B'rith Magazine*, telling of some of the events related in the early chapters of this book. I also found the registration of the B'nai B'rith Ben-Sion Coshti Lodge in B'nai B'rith Charter Book No. 1, listed under No. 1207, dated 28 January 1935, as well as 1939 correspondence between Ezra Rodriguez, president of the Grand District Lodge of Egypt and the Sudan No. 16, and Henry Monsky, president of B'nai B'rith International.

On 7 May 1989, I was honored by the White Plains B'nai B'rith Unit with their annual Youth Services Award for "Life long commitment to B'nai B'rith ideals and Jewish causes" attended by numerous friends and personalities.

With my friend Herbert Kanarek, then president of the White Plains Unit, myself as its chaplain, and my wife, Bertha, we left for Jerusalem in March 1989 as part of the U.S. B'nai B'rith delegation to the "Prime Minister's Conference on Jewish Solidarity with Israel." For me, the most impressive and emotional moment was when brother Seymour Reich stood on a high platform by the Western Wall, holding up his arms, flanked on one side by Yitzhak Shamir and on the other by Shimon Peres, and read out loud the Jerusalem declaration of Jewish solidarity with Israel. He declared that "we, the representatives of world Jewry assembled here in Jerusalem, the eternal and undivided capital of Israel, affirm our solidarity with the state and people of Israel. We support Israel's deep yearning in its 40 year quest for a just and lasting peace and are united in our commitment to Israel's continuing security."

16

❧

Egyptian Jews and
the Sudan

Almost all the Jews of the Sudan came from or through Egypt, and most had family connections in Egypt. As a result, they frequently traveled to Cairo and Alexandria, which were favored places for vacations, the education of their children, family and business visits, and eventual retirement.

In the 1920s and 1930s, it was a five-day and four-night journey from Khartoum to Cairo. The journey started on Sudan Railways from Khartoum to Wadi Halfa, connecting there with the Sudan government steamer service from Wadi Halfa to Shellal (Ar. cataract), the river port for the town of Aswan. From there, the Egyptian State Railways continued the last leg of the trip from Aswan to Cairo. The two-day and three-night voyage by river steamer from Wadi Halfa to Shellal was particularly pleasant and interesting. Steamers stopped on every outward sailing at Abu Simbel, the three-thousand-year-old Temple of Ramses II. There, the passengers would land and visit the beautiful ruins of the temple, with its four giant statues of Ramses II on the front wall, facing the Nile, and the elegant statues of the beautiful Nefertiti, the royal spouse. This is the same well-known Abu Simbel that was in danger of being submerged by the waters of Lake Nasser and was saved by being elevated and restored at the cost of millions of dollars, largely contributed by Americans in the 1940s and 1950s and through the United Nations Educational, Scientific, and Cultural Organization (UNESCO). Lake Nasser is the huge reservoir created by the Aswan Dam, which backs up the waters of the Nile.

At the end of the river voyage and just before stopping at Aswan's

23. Temple of Ramses II at Abu Simbel.

24. Elephantine Island, opposite present-day Aswan and on which a Jewish notable built his home at the site of the Jewish temple that had been destroyed in 410 B.C.E. Courtesy of Mémoires Juives—Patrimoine photographique, Paris.

river port of Shellal, the steamers passed Elephantine Island. The book *Juifs d'Egypte Images et Textes* recounts that a Jewish colony existed on Elephantine Island and that documents written in Aramaean were found referring to the "military Jewish colony of Elephantine."[1] Apparently, following the fall of Jerusalem, Judeans sought refuge on the banks of the Nile and set up a colony on Elephantine Island opposite the town of Seyene (present-day Aswan) and subsequently either became prisoners or mercenaries. In time, they built on the island a Jewish temple, which followed the ancient sacrificial cult practiced in Jerusalem with some incorporated elements from the local Aramaean cult practiced in Seyene. In 410 B.C.E. the Jewish temple of Elephantine was burned down by the local population. It has been postulated that the burning occurred because of the Jewish practice of ritually sacrificing sheep conflicted with the veneration of Khnemu, the ram-headed god in the neighboring Egyptian temple. On the high point of the island, atop the ruins of the ancient Jewish temple, is an imposing palatial residence, built by an Egyptian Jewish family as its country home.

As the steamer approached Shellal, it also passed by the historic Egyptian island of Philae (now submerged), and one could see from the ship's deck a beautiful view of the island and the great temple of the goddess Isis, described as the magician, source of life, and director of the rites of resurrection and commander of the stars. This temple was also saved from disappearing under the waters of Lake Nasser by dismantling it piece by piece and reconstructing it on the islet of Agilkia.

As a student in the 1920s, I made this journey between Khartoum and Cairo several times, traveling to and from my English boarding school, adjacent to the ancient Fostat (old Cairo). Like many others in the late 1930s and 1940s, I repeated the trip, this time with my family in first-class sleeping cars and steamer accommodations and in fairly good comfort. By 1942, we made the trip by seaplane, departing from Gordon's Tree river airport on the Nile, 30 miles south of Khartoum, and landing on the Nile at Rod El-Farag, a suburb of Cairo. Later still, we flew regular airlines from Khartoum to Cairo.

Jews have, of course, been in Egypt since ancient times; but we are here concerned with the Jews of Egypt and their connections with Sudan Jews in modern times. From 1925 to 1960, Haim Nahum Effendi

---

1. Les éditions du Scribes, *Juifs d'Egypte: Images et Textes* (Jews of Egypt: Pictures and texts), 2d. ed. (Paris: Les éditions du Scribes, 1984).

25. Hakhambashi Haim Nahum Effendi, grand
rabbin of Egypt. Courtesy of Mémoires Juives—
Patrimoine photographique, Paris.

(1872–1960) was the hakhambashi (grand rabbi of Egypt). He was born
in Manisa, Turkey, near Izmir, studied law in Istanbul, and made his rabbinic studies at the Yeshivot of Tiberias and the Rabbinical Seminary in
Paris while simultaneously studying Oriental languages. Before going to
Egypt, he served as chief rabbi of the Ottoman Empire in Istanbul; and at
the demand of Mustapha Kamal Atatürk, he also served in various diplo-
matic functions, such as a member of the armistice negotiations in the
Hague in 1918–1919, advisor to the Turkish delegation at the Treaty of
Lausanne in 1923, and as unofficial representative to the United States.
In *The Jews in Modern Egypt*, p. 96, Gudrun Krämer says of Rabbi Nahum

that he was a man of unusual erudition, culture, and political experience, who gained a reputation as a diplomat and Orientalist rather than spiritual guide to his flock. "The best rabbi of the diplomats and the best diplomat of the rabbis (p. 97)," as Krämer was later to say of him. The forces behind his appointment as grand rabbi of Egypt were, on the one hand, the president of the Jewish Community, Joseph Aslan Cattaoui Pasha, himself a former Egyptian minister of finance and minister of communications (the highest positions ever reached by a Jew in modern Egypt), who personally had much in common both in outlook and in career with Rabbi Nahum; and on the other, the B'nai B'rith Cairo Lodge, which he was soon to join.

In 1925, King Fu'ad, with whom Rabbi Nahum had excellent relations, appointed him by royal decree "Chief Rabbi of Egypt and the Sudan" and in 1929 granted him Egyptian nationality. The inclusion of the Sudan in his rabbinate was part of the customary Egyptian political effort to include everything in the Sudan as being part of Egypt and thus to maintain Egypt's influence over the Sudan's destiny and future, a position in direct opposition to the British policy to avoid that very end result. In 1931, the king made Rabbi Nahum a senator and, in 1933, a member of the Egyptian Academy of Arabic Language. Among the rabbi's works was a translation he made for King Fu'ad, from Turkish to French, of the Ottoman firmans addressed to "the walis and khedives of Egypt." Rabbi Nahum never visited the Sudan nor showed interest in its Community or its progress; yet whenever my father, Rabbi Malka, visited Cairo, he would call on Rabbi Nahum in the Cairo rabbinate, where they presumably discussed religious and other matters concerning the Sudan Jewish Community.

The Jewish Community in Cairo was always led by a Cattaoui as president and a Mosseri as vice-president, two of the oldest, wealthiest, and most influential families in Egyptian society. The first Cattaoui, Yacoub Menasse Qattawi (1801–1883), whose family name seems derived from Qatta, a village near Cairo, founded the banking and trading firm of J. M. Cattaoui e Figli (It. and sons) in Cairo, Alexandria, and Paris. Together with Yacoub Mosseri and Yacoub Levy Menasse, who followed him as sarraf pasha (chief cashier), he was one of the first Jews to leave Haret El-Yahoud (Lane of the Jews) behind Mouski and Hamzawi avenues, where most of the Arabic-speaking, poorer Egyptian Jews lived in meager conditions. Haret El-Yahoud would be the Cairo equivalent of the Lower East Side in early twentieth-century Manhattan. He was the first Jew to

26. Joseph Aslan Cattaoui Pasha, minister
of finance of Egypt and president of the Cairo
Jewish Community. Courtesy of Mémoires
Juives—Patrimoine photographique, Paris.

be granted the title of bey; and when in the early 1880s he was made a
baron of the Hapsburg Empire, and thus an Austro-Hungarian citizen
and aristocrat, the Cattawis took to calling themselves "von Cattawi"
and later "de Cattaoui."

Yacoub Menasse Cattaoui, the lifelong president of the Cairo Jewish
Community, was succeeded by his son Aslan Cattaoui Bey; then by
Moise de Cattaoui Pasha; Joseph Aslan Cattaoui Pasha; and in the 1940s,
by René Cattaoui Bey. In 1946, the Community presidency was assumed

by a member of the newly emerging elite, Salvator Cicurel Bey, head of the family that owned Les Grands Magasins Cicurel. The Community Council now included leaders like Ezra Rodriguez, president of the B'nai B'rith Grand District Lodge of Egypt; lawyer Leon Castro, president of the B'nai B'rith Cairo Lodge and leader of the Zionist movement in Egypt; and Joseph Picciotto Bey, member of the Egyptian Senate. I met President Salvator Cicurel Bey in Khartoum when he came as the leader of the Egyptian Chamber of Commerce delegation, Ezra Rodriguez when he established with me the B'nai B'rith Ben-Sion Coshti Lodge of Khartoum, and Leon Castro in a meeting of the Cairo Lodge on a visit from the Khartoum Lodge. I met Guido Mosseri in Geneva in the late 1960s after he left Egypt.

These Community leaders and most of the Jewish elite were educated in French and English universities and spoke French at home. Many of the middle class also spoke French at home, having attended either local French schools or Alliance Israélite schools. About half of them obtained a himaya, a foreign-government protection that also provided a passport from France, Great Britain, Italy, or Austro-Hungary, all of whom were pleased to bring these minorities under their protection and influence. As foreigners, they had extraordinary legal and economic privileges under the "capitulations" status then ruling Egypt; but foreign citizenship worked against them when Egyptianization of the economy, administration, and employment started. The other half were Arabic-speaking, Egyptianized Jews, some of whom were Arabic scholars, like the well-known Karaite poet, lawyer, and writer Murad Faraj.

In the 1930s and 1940s there were about 40,000 Jews in Cairo, of whom six to seven thousand were "Karaites" and five thousand were Ashkenazim, who kept a separate Ashkenazi synagogue and rabbi and a separate Ashkenazi Community Council in Darb El-Barabra (Lane of the barbarous, or foreign, tongue, in this case Yiddish), which was also located behind Mouski Avenue near Haret El-Yahoud.

In Alexandria, a cosmopolitan Mediterranean port, there were at that time 30,000 Jews. Of these, 10–15 percent were Ashkenazim; and about 30 percent were Arabic-speaking. Unlike the Jews in Cairo, they all maintained one Community Council, one president, and one chief rabbi. In Alexandria, as in Cairo, the Community was led by great old Jewish families, in this case the de Menasces,[2] Rolos, Aghions, Goars, and

---

2. The Alexandria Menasses used the French spelling of their name.

Tilches, who were in no way inferior to the Cairo elite in wealth, prestige, and influence. The first de Menasce, Yacoub, who followed Yacoub Cattaoui as sarraf pasha to Khedive Ismail and with him established many banking and trade companies, was, like Cattaoui, granted Austrian protection and made a baron of the Austro-Hungarian Empire. On moving from Cairo to Alexandria, he became the president of the Alexandria Jewish Community and was followed by two elected presidents, his eldest son, Behor David Levy de Menasce, and Behor Moshé Aghion; and later, by Behor David Levy's eldest son, Baron Behor Levy de Menasce, who was president of the Community until the outbreak of World War II, when, as an Austro-Hungarian citizen, he was treated as an enemy alien. Alfred Tilche was next elected president, followed by Robert J. Rolo, of British education and citizenship. The council of the Community included many other prominent Sephardim, such as Alfred Nessim Cohen and Ovadia Salem, and also some Ashkenazim, among whom were Herman Schlesinger and Marco Nadler, a wealthy industrialist. Lea, a member of the Nadler family, converted to the Coptic Orthodox faith and married Boutros Boutros Ghali, a scion of a well-known Egyptian Coptic family who later became secretary general of the United Nations.

The Cattaouis, Mosseris, de Menasces, and others established and supported many Jewish institutions in Cairo and Alexandria, including hospitals, schools, and synagogues and practiced charity toward their poorer brethren in the hara (street) in Cairo and Alexandria.

The Grand Synagogue of Cairo, Sha'ar Hashamaim (Gate of heaven), was built in 1903 by the family of Nessim Mosseri Bey at 17 Adli Pasha Street and was familiarly known as Keniset Al-Ismailia (Ismailia quarter synagogue). This imposing synagogue was recently renovated through a gift by Nessim Gaon[3] of U.S. $700,000. Though visited now by Jewish tourists from all over, it has difficulty having a minian because the Cairo Jewish population has dwindled to an estimated 150–300, mostly elderly Jews.

I attended High Holiday services at Sha'ar Hashamaim during its heyday in the mid 1920s while a student in Cairo. I was taken there by Rabbi Haim Hayon, a friend of my father's and a member of the Beth Din of the Cairo rabbinate with whom I was staying for the holidays. It was then packed tight with congregants from the Jewish elite and Cairo Commu-

3. Sudan-born president of the World Sephardic Federation and philanthropic businessman in Geneva, Switzerland.

27. General Muhamed Neguib, president of Egypt, visiting the Cairo Grand Synagogue in 1952. Courtesy of Mémoires Juives—Patrimoine photographique, Paris.

nity while Rabbi Nahum presided by the Ark alongside the Community president. As was the custom of the day, on the day of Yom Kippur, the governor of Cairo came to the synagogue to stand at the Heikhal (Ark) and present his greetings on behalf of himself and the government to the Jewish Community.

In 1952, General Muhamed Neguib, leader of the "free officers revolution" of July 1952, also visited the Grand Synagogue of Cairo as part of his efforts to reassure the minorities of Copts, Jews, and others; and he also paid special visits to Rabbi Nahum and other minority leaders for the same purpose.

While a student in Cairo, I also visited the ancient Ben-Ezra Synagogue in nearby Fostat, site of the discovery of the geniza, of which more later. Its teba (central prayer bima) bears the awe-inspiring inscription "The inhabitants of this town recount that in this place Moses, our Master, has invoked the name of the Lord." "In this place" implies that, at the site of the Ben-Ezra Synagogue, Moses delivered his prayer in Exodus

28. Ben-Ezra Synagogue, Cairo, interior, showing the teba. Courtesy of Mé-moires Juives—Patrimoine photographique, Paris.

29. Ancient Fostat (old Cairo) Cemetery.

9:30–33: "And Moses went out of the city from Pharaoh, and spread forth his hands unto the Lord; and the thunders and hail ceased." This prayer is reproduced in its original Hebrew text in an inscription on the Ben-Ezra teba, next to the first.

Another tradition also localizes the grave of the prophet Jeremiah, who was buried in Egypt near Giza, as being in the Ben-Ezra Synagogue in Fostat. The Ben-Ezra Synagogue is also being restored by donations from the Bronfman families.[4]

Fostat, that I mentioned above, was the great metropolis of Egypt in which most of the Jews lived before the period when the Fatimids, under Amr Ibn El-A'as, conquered Egypt in the year 969. Following the conquest, the Fatimids established their new capital a few miles north of Fostat, in what later became present-day Cairo, and called it El-Kahira, which remains Cairo's Arabic name to this day. The name originates from the Arabic El-Qahir (the conqueror or victorious). Over the next two to three centuries, the Jews and others gradually moved from Fostat to Cairo, with Fostat becoming known as Old Cairo.

Historic Ben-Ezra Synagogue was built in the year 862 C.E. on the ruins of a Coptic Church, and it is still surrounded by a number of historic Coptic churches. It was in Ben-Ezra Synagogue that the Jews of Fostat worshipped and where Maimonides and other Jewish scholars taught. In 1896, Solomon Schechter, then a biblical scholar in Cambridge, England, and later the founder and first president of the Jewish Theological Seminary of New York, received two Christian visitors who brought him Hebrew fragments they had purchased in Cairo. He recognized them as being from the Hebrew original of the Apocrypha book of Ben-Sira, the Ecclesiasticus that had been lost and known only in its Greek translation. That same year, he traveled to Cairo; and after several months of intensive effort, he extracted from the geniza of the Ben-Ezra Synagogue about 100,000 pages now known as the "Cairo geniza," which he took back to Cambridge for further study. Another 100,000 pages from the Cairo geniza were later discovered by other researchers and bibliophiles and deposited in libraries throughout the world.

4. Daniel J. Elazar, *The Other Jews: The Sephardim Today* (New York: Basic, 1988), 101.

17

❧

British Rule and the Status of Jews after 1899

Under the Anglo-Egyptian Condominium agreement of 1899, the Sudan was governed by a British governor general. This official was nominated by the British government and appointed by the khedive (later by the king) of Egypt and also held the title of sirdar, or commander in chief, of the Egyptian Army in the Sudan. The Union Jack shared the skies with the Egyptian flag over the Governor General's Palace in Khartoum, all governor's and district commissioner's headquarters in the provinces, and all Sudan government buildings. Egyptian officials shared some of the lower governing positions with the British.

But following the assassination of Sir Lee Stack, governor general of the Sudan, by an Egyptian in Cairo in November 1924, Lord Edmund Allenby, the British high commissioner in Cairo, issued an ultimatum to the Egyptian government demanding the evacuation of all Egyptian army troops from the Sudan. Egyptian Prime Minister Saad Zaglul Pasha, an Egyptian nationalist leader who earlier had been exiled by the British to the Seychelles islands in the Indian Ocean because of his resistance to the virtual British rule of Egypt exercised through the high commissioner, resigned. Lord Allenby, however, forced acquiescence of his ultimatum after going to see King Fuᶜad, accompanied by a contingent of British troops and tanks.

Following the evacuation of Egyptian troops from the Sudan, the Egyptian mamours (town or district sheriffs) of many Sudanese towns, including Khartoum and Omdurman, were relieved of their positions and replaced by Sudanese mamours under British district commissioners. Egyptian judges and other Egyptians in sensitive or semisenior positions were replaced by Lebanese Christians, imported from Egypt and Beirut, who were considered more loyal to the British. After these events, there was no doubt of the dominant, and even single British rule of the Sudan and the absence of Egyptian rule, except for the Egyptian flag's continuing to fly together with the British flag over the Khartoum palace, provincial headquarters, and districts.

Only the Egyptian Irrigation Department, with headquarters in Khartoum under direct control from Cairo, continued to function independently, with its Egyptian engineers and resident offices monitoring the waters of the Nile from its sources in Lake Victoria and Albert Falls through the Sudd in Southern Sudan at Malakal, the dam of Jebel Awlia south of Khartoum, and other dams along the Nile to its final pouring into the Mediterranean. On a business trip to Uganda and Kenya accompanied by my friend and co-director Sayed Makkawi Suleiman Akrat, a former permanent under secretary of the Sudan Ministry of the Interior, we traveled to visit one of the sources of the Nile at Albert Falls. In that beautiful but remote and lonely place, we were met by two Egyptian engineers whose job was to watch and measure the falls and to send their data onward. I recall how delighted they were to see us in the lonely location. After the Khartoum office, the Egyptian Irrigation Department was busiest at Malakal, where at the proper time they sent dredgers, engineers, and extra staff to clear passage through the Sudd swamps on the White Nile so that the waters could flow on to North Sudan and to Egypt.

Throughout this period of virtual sole British rule, the gradual transition of authority to Sudanese administrators, followed by self-government, the first meeting of Parliament in January 1954, and Sudanese Independence on 1 January 1956, the Jews were well regarded; and we had no complaints, either individually or as a Community, about our treatment by the British or the Sudanese. It was a period of unhindered progress, controlled inflation, and peaceful existence, during which we all made progress in our trades and professions, participated in the country's development, and cultivated friendships and connections among the Sudanese and other communities, many of whom we had grown alongside.

During the British administration of the Sudan government, we were all issued Sudan passports, which after Independence were replaced by Sudan Republic passports and Sudanese Nationality Certificates, by grant to all those who had arrived in the Sudan after 1898 and by domicile to those who were in the Sudan on or before 1898, as was the case for the

Bassiounis and the El-Einis. This rule applied equally to the other foreign communities, such as the Syrian, Lebanese, Greek, Armenian, and Italian residents, some of whom opted for their own nationalities and passports.

Similar to the case in Egypt, Jewish personal law was allowed to apply to us in the Sudan. In accordance with Jewish law, my father, Rabbi Malka, had to and did issue *Eilam Shar*ei* (Jewish legal information or declaration) in all inheritance, marital, and family matters, which the Sudanese courts then applied and enforced.

18

⚜

Harrassment of the Jews and Their Departure after 1956

During World War II, anxiety heightened about our situation as Jews because of the rising anti-Jewish propaganda on Egyptian radio and in
Egypt and the venomous anti-Jewish Arabic broadcasts from Berlin radio
by Hag Amin El-Husseini, the former mufti of Jerusalem. After escaping
to Berlin from Baghdad in 1941–1942, Hag Amin El-Husseini allied himself with Hitler in the goal of exterminating the Jews, expelling them
from Palestine, and establishing an all-Arab state in Palestine. His daily
broadcasts in Arabic on Berlin radio called upon all Arabs to "kill the
Jews wherever you find them. It pleases Allah."[1]

In Egypt, the advance of Field Marshal Erwin Rommel's Afrika Korps
toward Alexandria and the sympathy of the Egyptian nationalists, including King Farouk, toward the Germans gave Jews cause for concern.
Many Jews and non-Jews fled from Alexandria to Cairo and Upper Egypt
and some to the relative safety of the Sudan, bringing with them their
businesses. Joseph Nadler of the well-known Jewish family (now residing
in Geneva), manufacturers in Alexandria of Nadler confectioneries, was
one of those who moved to the Sudan and stayed for a few years in Khar-

---

1. In *The Dhimmi: Jews and Christians under Islam*, Bat Ye'or documented Hag Amin
El-Husseini's broadcasts by citing the following extract from the German radio records:
"On 1 March 1944 at 12.30 P.M., speaking on Berlin radio, the Mufti, after vilifying Jews,
Britain, and America, called on the Arabs to rise and fight, saying 'Arabs, rise as one man
and fight for your sacred rights. Kill the Jews wherever you find them. This pleases God,
history and religion. This saves your honour. God is with you.'" Because 12:30 P.M. in
Berlin is 7:30 A.M. in Khartoum, Cairo, and other Arab capitals, this call to kill Jews in-
cited the Arab people just as they were beginning their day (Bat Ye'or 1985, 389–90).

toum. While there, he established a partnership of his business with Bittar & Co., one of the leading firms in the Sudan. When the Germans were at El-Alamein, there was great turmoil and fear in the Sudan of their possible victory and push toward the Sudan and the Nile valley. In Khartoum, scores of empty railway sleeping cars lay idle on the railway side lines at the Moghren, where the Blue and White Niles meet near Khartoum, ready to evacuate senior government officials and others should the need arise. Fortunately, the Germans were routed by Field Marshal Lord Bernard Montgomery in the now-famous battle of El-Alamein, and we breathed a sigh of relief.

In 1948 at the height of the Arab-Israeli conflict and the Israeli War of Independence, committees of Sudanese merchants went around raising funds on behalf of the Palestinian cause and to fight the Jews in Palestine. One of these committees was headed by the twenty-four-year-old son of one of my best clients and friends. They were accustomed to receiving donations from my company and myself for their charities and religious funds. But when this committee visited me in my company's offices asking for contributions for their Palestinian cause, I refused to approve the giving of funds designed to kill fellow Jews. Unfortunately, as these committees went around in the Omdurman market and businesses, some of our Jewish shopkeepers succumbed to the pressure and made donations. This situation caused a great split and anger in the Jewish Community. In *The Jews in Modern Egypt*, Gudrun Krämer describes a similar series of events occurring there. He relates that the Wafdist newspaper *Sawt El-Umma* of Cairo published blacklists of Jewish businessmen who were urged to prove their loyalty and to expiate for their previous acts of exploitation by contributing to the Palestinian cause. But when Jewish contributions for the Palestinian cause amounting to E£ 40,000 were received in June 1948, *Sawt El-Umma* wrote that this ridiculously low sum was rejected by the Egyptian government.

Also in 1948, as a consequence of Israel's victory in its War of Independence, we were subjected to various harassments, particularly when passing through customs at the airports in Egypt. In one of these instances, I was flying from Khartoum to Rome with a night stop in Cairo with my family and our friends Ibrahim Mourad El-Eini and his family. When we passed through the Cairo airport, the Egyptian passport officers were holding two passenger lists, one for Jews and the other for non-Jews. The non-Jewish passengers were allowed into Cairo with their passports and baggage and were free to go anywhere they wanted. The

Jews, El-Eini, myself, and our families, were taken under police escort, without our passports and with only our hand baggage, to the Heliopolis Palace Hotel in the suburbs of Cairo, where a police constable was at the desk with instructions not to allow us to leave the hotel. In the morning, again under police escort, we were taken back to the airport. Our passports were handed back to us on boarding the plane and our baggage, though only in transit, had been searched thoroughly for any suspicious or incriminating objects.

In Khartoum, there were various occasional harassments. One of them was the amusing story of the matza (unleavened bread for Passover). In those days just before Passover, we imported matza from London in one shipment to cover the needs of the whole Community. When the matza shipment was unloaded at the custom's enclosure in Port Sudan, our Community agent, Isaac Pinto, may he rest in peace, who was the Port Sudan manager of the clearing house Trucco & Co., telephoned us in Khartoum to tell us that the custom's officer would not clear the matza shipment for entry because of the *Magen David* (Star of David) affixed on each box. The irony was that the identical emblem happened to be the symbol of the Sudan Customs Department and was worn on the uniforms of its officers.

On hearing of this occurrence, I telephoned the director general of Sudan Government Customs Department in Khartoum, Sayed Amin Farid, a great gentleman whom I knew. He granted me an interview the same day and quickly found a compromise solution, in which the boxes of matza would have the Star of David painted over with black paint. He telephoned instructions to the Port Sudan Customs office to allow clearance of the shipment after the necessary obliterations had been made. Someone in my office in turn telephoned our agent, Issac Pinto, who complied with the obliteration instructions and was then able to clear and dispatch the shipment to Khartoum, where it arrived 48 hours before Passover Eve. Our treasurer and gabbai, Albert Gabbai, may he rest in peace, quickly took over the shipment when it arrived in Khartoum and managed to distribute it in one day so that each family had its matza in time for Passover. Such harassments were however minor and did not much alter our ways, as we continued our normal activities and associations with Sudanese friends.

Our problems became more serious, however, in 1956, following Israel's foray into the Sinai and the British-French military action over the Suez Canal, and continued until after the 1967 Arab-Israeli Six Day War that resulted in the defeat of the Egyptian, Syrian, and Jordanian forces and their announced intentions to wipe Israel off the map.[2]

Around this time, the Sudanese newspapers started daily anti-Jewish attacks. I went to see Prime Minister Sayed Abdalla Khalil to complain about these attacks. His response was, "don't pay much attention to the press; they attack me every day," which did not do much to reassure me or appease my concerns.

In the meanwhile, the attacks intensified and then turned personal against the Malkas, when it was reported that my brother Edmond, who had left the Sudan in 1957, had gone to Israel and had spoken on Israeli radio, addressing the Sudanese and taking the side of Israel, even though in fact he never did. One newspaper attacking the Malkas urged, "if you cannot put them to death, then torture them and make them suffer." Simultaneously, a statement was circulated abroad and relayed to my brother Edmond, which he repeated in his book *Sephardi Jews—A Pageant of Spanish-Portuguese and Oriental Judaism Between the Cross and the Cresent* that we his brothers who were still in Khartoum (myself; Sam, may he rest in peace; and David) had been coerced into publishing in all Sudanese dailies a declaration stating in these unnatural terms, "Whereas our brother Edmond has proved a traitor to the motherland, we hereby disown him." In fact, I was never asked, nor were Sam and David, to issue any such declaration, nor did any such declaration appear in any Sudanese papers in Khartoum. To quote my brother David, "It never happened."

What did happen was that, on the day the attack on the Malkas appeared in the Umma newspaper, *El-Umma*, I requested and got an appointment for that same evening to see Sir Sayed Abdel Rahman El-Mahdi Pasha, the patron of the Umma Party, who was at that time the most influential Sudanese leader. I went to see him with my friend Daoud Ishag, who was then president of the Sudan Jewish Community. Sir Sayed Abdel Rahman El-Mahdi Pasha received us courteously; and when I explained what his newspaper and other Sudanese newspapers were writing about the Sudan Jews and the Malkas, he stated that he had nothing against his fellow citizens the Jews and promised to stop his newspaper from such writings. He kept his word, and his newspaper did not print any further attacks.

2. Benjamin Netanyahu, *A Place among Nations: Israel and the World* (New York: Bantam, 1993), 131–32.

At this time, a policeman was permanently placed at the corner of my home at 13 Sayed Abdel Rahman Street. I asked the reason for this action and was told it was for my protection. In addition, my sisters were panicking over the progression of events, and I spent time trying to comfort them.

Seeing what was now happening to us and even worse for the Jews in Egypt, it was becoming clear that there was no more life for us in the Sudan. Therefore, the exodus of the Jews from the Sudan started in 1957 and continued so that, by the late 1960s, almost the entire Jewish Community had left with their families and whatever they could salvage of their businesses and properties. Each man planned his departure in his own way and time and according to his personal circumstances. All left under their own power and without outside help. They went to more welcoming and hospitable countries, some to the United Kingdom, Switzerland, and the United States; some to Nigeria and France; and some to Israel via Cyprus or Europe. Again, it was not possible to travel directly from the Sudan, an Arab country, to Israel. Thus for those traveling to Israel, it was necessary ostensibly to travel to Cyprus or Europe and from there book safe passage to Israel.

In early 1960, exit permits were introduced and required before any travel abroad. These permits could be difficult to obtain, especially for Jews. By mid-1960, Sudanese nationality and Sudanese passports were withdrawn by the Sudanese government from most of the Jews who had left the Sudan. The daily *El-Rai El-Am* (Public opinion) published the names of those affected,[3] and others not on the list were contacted by Sudanese consulates abroad and were informed that their Sudanese passports were no longer valid and were asked to surrender them. *El-Rai El-Am* commented "these names of themselves need no further comment." The editor stated, "I could not believe that the bearers of such names could have been related by citizenship to the thirsty, hungry and oppressed of the West, East, North and South of the Sudan. Where are they now? Did they establish a new Israeli colony in the occupied land or

---

3. *El-Rai El-Am* reported the following list of those whose Sudanese passports were withdrawn: "Edward Abraham Dwek, Aslan Seroussi, Shalom Yacoub Ades, Esther Malka, David Aslan Cohen, Samuel Solomon Malka, Makhlouf Malka, Rahma Levy, Rachel Malka, Rahma Baroukh Israel, Shlomo Ishag ben-David, Victor Malka, Joseph Ades, Sarina Ades, Jeannette Malka, Sarina Gabriel Cohen, Flora Aslan Cohen, Ibrahim Massoud, Nessim David Gaon, Bertha Waldman Shaoul, David Solomon Malka, Max Gabriel, Albert Gabbai, Alice Joseph Tammam, Ashili Gabriel Cohen."

did they go to destroy places other than the Sudan?" In the same article, *El-Rai El-Am* repeated the previous accusation first made concerning my brother Edmond Malka. "We have heard that some of the Zionist Jews who have lived in the Sudan have returned to the "occupied land" with the wealth of our country and that some of them in Israel's broadcasting station, spread their venom and sometimes address our people as if they were one of them—our people who fed them and fattened them, not knowing they were feeding wolves." As far as I know, none of the Sudan Jews worked for or broadcast from the Israeli radio. The reader can imagine the terror and feeling of impending doom such words had on Jews still trapped in the Sudan.

In my case, I left the Sudan for the last time, hurriedly, in April 1964, when my first wife, Dora (may she rest in peace), mother of my children Jeffrey and Evelyne, was diagnosed in Khartoum with cancer. Dr. Abdel Halim Muhamed, the chief government physician who later became a member of the Supreme Council, decided we could leave quickly for London with referral to Dr. Harris, the Sudan government doctor in London, for radiation treatment, which was then not available in the Sudan.

We consequently left for London within two weeks, leaving everything behind in Khartoum, house and all. With us went our daughter, Evelyne, a student at the University of Geneva, who happened to be in Khartoum to spend the Passover with us. Our son, Jeffrey, was in the United States undergoing his medical residency training. I left Khartoum on the annual two months leave I was entitled to as executive director of Gellatly Trading Co. Ltd. in Khartoum. However, as the treatment of my wife prolonged, I asked for release of my job after expiration of a six months' unpaid leave of absence. Because I was in London, things were arranged there with R. Y. Rule, chairman of the Gellatly Group; Arthur F. J. Carter, managing director in London; and R. G. Gibson, the managing director in Khartoum, who was on his annual leave in London. The many letters of understanding, appreciation, and high regard from these gentlemen and others in the Sudan gave me much solace and encouragement during these difficult times.

While in London and with the introduction of Messrs. Rule and Carter to a company associated with Gellatly, I succeeded in getting appointed director of Rolls Produce Company in London. This company traded in produce commodities, one of my lines of expertise. Unfortunately, as my wife's condition worsened, I decided to give up this good job in London to move to Geneva, where my wife could continue her treatment and Evelyne, her studies at the University of Geneva.

When in Geneva, I tried to get a permit for an offshore trade office of my own for the sale of Sudan produce to Europe but failed in doing so. I therefore accepted an offer of a Geneva friend, Moshé Baroukh Soleiman, to become a partner and management consultant in his firm Mobaso S.A. of Geneva. This firm dealt in gemstones (rubies, emeralds, sapphires, etc.), in which he was a prominent authority and supplier in Europe. It served us both well. He was able to attend to the side of the business requiring expertise in gems and travel to the supply sources while I organized, managed, and consolidated the expansion of Mobaso interests in Europe from the Geneva office and was therefore able at the same time to attend to my wife and cover my heavy expenses for the period we were in Geneva.

My wife died in Geneva in January 1966. At this point, there was nothing left for me to go back to in the Sudan, despite my unsold house and real estate holdings there. I therefore waited for my daughter Evelyne to graduate with a master's (license) degree in political and economic sciences from the University of Geneva and then, accompanied by her and my son, Jeffrey, who had come from the United States to be with his ailing mother and to undergo training in orthopaedics at the University Hospital of Geneva, I immigrated in August 1966 to the United States of America.

19

✤

Independence of the Sudan and British and Egyptian Policies

As the Sudanese were struggling to gain independence from both British and Egyptian rule, the underlying policy of the British Sudan government officials was to stress the pro-British way of government leading eventually to a pro-British independent Sudan. On the other hand, a large segment of the population felt by culture, education, religion, and way of life more drawn toward an independent Sudan in union with Egypt.

The British policy targeted gaining over the religious leaders; the notables, sheikhs, and omdas, and their followers; and the Gordon College-educated government officials, who were trained and encouraged by their British senior officials to take over the higher posts of government when the British left. Among the Sudanese religious leaders, the two with the greatest religious and political influence were Sir Sayed Abdel Rahman El-Mahdi Pasha and Sir Sayed Ali El-Merghani Pasha.

Sir Sayed Abdel Rahman El-Mahdi Pasha was the son of Muhamed Ahmed Ibn Abdulla El-Mahdi, the Mahdi who had led the jihad and revolt against the Egyptian-Turkish government in 1881. He was the religious leader and the imam (leader of true Muslims) of the Ansar (helpers and supporters) and patron of his political party, the Umma Party. *Umma* can be translated as "the nation" but more correctly as "the Muslim community." All three terms, *imam, Ansar,* and *Umma* had been used by his father, the Mahdi, before him and by the prophet Muhamed and the caliphs before them.

Sayed Abdel Rahman El-Mahdi wanted an independent Sudan without any Egyptian influence, which concurred with the Sudan government British officials' aims and policies. The British conferred titles and afforded help to Sayed Abdel Rahman. He was made a knight of the British Empire with the title of sir, and the Egyptians followed with their highest honor by conferring the title of pasha. He thus became Sir Sayed Abdel Rahman El-Mahdi Pasha. He was given back all of Aba Island, from which his father had led his revolt, in the form of a 20,000-feddan cotton scheme. Because a feddan is about 4,200 square meters (about 1 acre), this scheme brought with it much wealth, particularly in the 1950s, when cotton prices were high. Other properties were also returned, and restrictions on the Mahdi family were rescinded. His political influence in the government and among his community and followers grew enormously. He was endowed with an imposing personality and adopted an almost royal attitude commanding respect.

Sir Sayed Ali El-Merghani was in favor of an independent Sudan allied to Egypt. He too was similarly decorated, and it was at this time that he became Sir Sayed Ali El-Merghani Pasha. Neither man however used the titles of sir or pasha and preferred their own title of sayed.[1]

The president of the Umma Party, the political arm of Sayed Abdel Rahman El-Mahdi, was his eldest son, Sayed Saddig El-Mahdi. He was also the director general of Dairat El-Mahdi, the administrative offices of the Mahdi's properties and his Aba Island plantations. I visited Sayed Saddig El-Mahdi (*Saddig* means righteous) in his Dairat offices several times in connection with his cotton and other businesses. In one of these visits, he introduced me to his then nineteen-year-old son, Sayed Sadig El-Mahdi (*Sadig* means truthful), who was studying at Oxford University and was on summer vacation in Khartoum. This son later became prime minister of the Sudan, as I will describe later.

The Umma Party was supported by many prominent Sudanese government officials, lawyers, doctors, and businessmen. Among them were Judge Muhamed Saleh El-Shingiti, who was to become speaker of the first Sudanese Parliament; advocate Sayed Muhamed Ahmed Mahjoub, future foreign minister and prime minister of the independent Sudan; Dr. Abdel Halim Muhamed, who became a member of the Sudan Supreme Council; and businessmen such as Osman Saleh, all of whom were personal friends of mine.

The Umma Party's popular support came from the people of the White Nile and Kordofan provinces. The Ansar served Sayed Abdel Rahman

1. As used here, *sayed* is a title of respect for a distinguished leader.

El-Mahdi loyally in his Aba Island plantations and elsewhere. In times of political turmoil, they would come from Aba Island, Omdurman, and the surrounding areas in huge demonstrations in his support that usually ended in the vast grounds of the Mahdi's Omdurman residence and his Dairat El-Mahdi office grounds. One of these demonstrations occurred when General Muhamed Neguib flew to Khartoum to represent Egypt at the official opening of the first Sudan Parliament. The Ansar came from all sides in the thousands to protest General Neguib's or any other Egyptian presence at the event. The disturbances caused several deaths, including that of the British police commissioner of Khartoum, upon which General Neguib had to return to Cairo, and the opening of the Parliament was postponed.

Sayed Ali El-Merghani, the other main religious leader, was the head of the Khatmiya sect. He was a highly respected and influential religious leader and had his followers throughout Northern Sudan, from Khartoum North to Wadi Halfa and in Dongola Province among the Shaigiya tribes. His headquarters and residences were in Dongola, Marawi, Khartoum North, and Khartoum. He too had many followers among government officials, notables, businessmen, and political leaders.

He preferred not to make himself politically conspicuous, but his followers founded the Ashigga Party. *Ashigga* means brothers and sisters from the same mother and father. The Ashigga Party worked for the complete independence of the Sudan in union or alliance with Egypt, the position favored by Sayed Ali El-Merghani.

The leader of the Ashigga Party was Sayed Ismail El-Azhari, graduate of the American University of Beirut and a mathematics teacher at Gordon College. Previously, he had been the secretary general of the Graduates Council, a group formed of all graduates of Gordon College and other intermediate and higher schools. The Graduates Congress, composed of councils from several schools eventually had its own constituency in the elections of the first Sudanese Parliament.

Neither Sayed Ali El-Merghani nor the Ashigga Party was looked on favorably by the British government officials, but both had a large following. I therefore saw no big cotton scheme given to their notables, except one to a former senior army officer, Sayed (formerly Bimbashi [lieutenant colonel]) Khalafalla Khaled, who later became minister of defense. Sayed Khaled would visit me in my office in Khartoum wearing his Egyptian tarbush to discuss my handling the sale of his cotton crop for him to the main cotton exporters, Rye Evans & Co., whom my company represented and whose managing director was my Jewish friend, Alexander Ben-Lassin, may he rest in peace.

The British treated Southern Sudan very differently. The South, consisting of Equatoria Province, with its capital at Juba; Bahr El-Ghazal Province, with its capital at Wau; and adjoining provinces had an indigenous non-Arab population, consisting of Nilotics, African blacks, and animists. These provinces were virtually separated from the Muslim North by the British governor's policy of designating them as "closed districts," to which travel from the North was not allowed without permits, which were not easy to obtain. Permits were however given to a large number of Christian missionaries, both Protestant and Catholic, who did a whale of a job in educating the southerners and converting them to Christianity. It was these Christian southerners who led the revolts and wars against the Muslim North when Sudanization of the South, mostly by Northern Muslim administrators, and its Islamization were activated. It was also these southerners and their leaders who conducted repeated negotiations, reconciliation attempts, and wars, the end of which are not yet in sight. It is also these same Southern Sudanese whom the Northern slave traders drove to the slave markets of Egypt and Arabia as late as the nineteenth century and who, when used in the Army of the Khedive of Egypt, proved to be loyal, disciplined, and effective soldiers. When the British reconquered the Sudan under Kitchener, they had great respect and confidence in the Sudanese battalions they used and considered them to be among their best and most loyal soldiers.

Southerners and their political parties participated and succeeded in electing some of their members to the first Parliament, and some of their leaders became ministers in future governments.

20

❦

The First Sudanese Parliament and Government

In preparation for Independence in 1956, elections for the first Sudanese Parliament were held in 1953, under the authority and rule of a five-member Electoral Commission, composed of one Egyptian; one Briton, and three Sudanese, who came one each from the Umma Party, the Unionists, and the South.

The Unionists, renamed the National Unionist Party (NUP) and who's leaders were from the former Ashigga Party, won a clear majority; and their leader, Sayed Ismail El-Azhari, formed the first Sudanese government. This first Parliament took office on 1 January 1954, with Azhari naming an all-NUP cabinet and himself as prime minister. In 1955, the Parliament passed a resolution demanding the evacuation of all Egyptian and British forces. The evacuation was completed later that year, and all British government officials relinquished their posts to Sudanese administrators. Prime Minister Azhari generously compensated the leaving British officials of the Sudan government and allowed the transfer of their gratuities and pensions in transferable pounds sterling. At that time, around 1956–1957, the Sudanese pound was fully equivalent to the pound sterling in transferable currency and was thus worth 4.8 U.S. dollars.

In those elections for the first Sudanese Parliament, I too did my duty as a Sudanese citizen and voted. I recall standing in a long line at the Khartoum Museum polling station, a stone's throw from the Nile embankment. In front of me in line was my friend Oxford-educated Sayed Mamoun Beheiry, then the governor of the Bank of Sudan and later the

125

Sudan minister of finance and even later governor of the Bank for African Development.

Late in 1955, Sayed Ali El-Merghani and Sayed Abdel Rahman El-Mahdi, meeting publicly for the first time in a decade, called for a united government after Independence. In December 1955, the Sudan was declared "The Sovereign Democratic Republic of the Sudan" and the powers of the governor general were invested in a five-man Supreme Commission, the last governor general having departed two weeks earlier. On 1 January 1956, the day of Independence, the flags of the Condominium, Britain and Egypt, were lowered; and the new Sudanese flag was raised on the Republican Palace by Sayed Ismail El-Azhari of the NUP, prime minister of the united government, with Sayed Muhamed Ahmed Mahjoub of the Umma Party its foreign minister.

The independent Sudan was soon recognized by foreign governments. It became a member of the Arab League and was admitted to the ranks of the United Nations. The Azhari government ended when leading members of its NUP Party broke off to form the People's Democratic Party (PDP) supported by Sayed Ali El-Merghani. The Umma Party and the PDP formed a parliamentary coalition, which elected Sayed Abdalla Khalil, secretary general of the Umma Party, as the new prime minister and formed a cabinet of Umma and PDP ministers that did not include Azhari.

Following continued rivalry between the political parties, the army stepped in; and Commander in Chief, Major General Ibrahim Abboud announced the military's assumption of power to "save the country from the politicians." He appointed a Supreme Council of military officers and a cabinet of military and civilian ministers and named himself council president and prime minister. Despite revolts by other military officers, Abboud consolidated his government and stayed in power from 1958 to 1964.

Sayed Abdel Rahman El-Mahdi died on 24 March 1959. P. M. Holt and M. W. Daly say of him, "the great sectarian and nationalist leader who dominated politics in the Sudan since the first World War and the Independence of the Sudan in 1956 was seen as the culmination of his life's work."[1] He did not however realize his ambition to become the

---

1. *A History of the Sudan: From the Coming of Islam to the Present Day* (New York: Longman, 4th ed., 1988).

monarch or president for life of the independent Sudan. His eldest son, Sayed Saddig El-Mahdi, succeeded him as head of the Ansar.

General Abboud leaned toward the nonallied countries, but he also maintained good relations with the United States and Britain. He and many of his ministers were of the Shaigiya tribe and allied with the Khatmiya sect, led by Sayed Ali El-Merghani. He succeeded in implementing many projects, including the establishment of the Sudan Central Bank and the Agricultural and Industrial Bank of the Sudan, but failed to reverse the deteriorating economic situation.

Although Abboud and the parliamentary governments that preceded him showed no special animosity toward Sudan Jews, it was in 1957, during his government, that Jews started leaving the country. The Arab-Israeli war of 1956 and Gamal Abdel Nasser's anti-Jewish and anti-Israeli propaganda and policies in Egypt made it difficult for Jews to feel secure in Arab countries.

At the end of General Abboud's rule, in 1964, a transition government was formed to return to parliamentary civil rule; and elections for an enlarged lower house of 173 members resulted in 76 members from the Umma Party, 54 from the NUP, 5 from the Islamic Front/Muslim Brotherhood, and 8 from the Communists. A coalition government of the Umma Party and the NUP was formed, with Sayed Muhamed Ahmed Mahjoub of the Umma as prime minister and Sayed Ismail El-Azhari of the NUP as president of the Supreme Council.

Sayed Saddig El-Mahdi died in September 1961. His brother Sayed El-Hadi El-Mahdi (*El-Hadi* means the guide) succeeded him as imam, and Saddig's son, Sayed Sadig El-Mahdi, grandson of Sayed Abdel Rahman El-Mahdi, became leader of the Umma Party.

21

❦

The Nemeiri Government

Nationalization, Confiscation, and Islamic Law

With political bickering continuing, an army coup of "the free officers," led by Colonel (later Major General) Muhamed Nemeiri, seized power in May 1969 in what became known as the May Revolution. Nemeiri outlawed all political parties and established a Revolutionary Command Council (RCC) of ten young army officers under his presidency and a cabinet of military officers, which included a civilian prime minister (Babikr Awdallah), two southerners, and members of leftist or Communist parties, though their parties had also been outlawed.

Sayed Sadig El-Mahdi was invited to join the government; and when he refused to join with the Communists, he was arrested, as were El-Azhari and Mahjoub. Imam El-Hadi El-Mahdi retreated to the Mahdi's stronghold on Aba Island; but after rioting by his Ansar in Omdurman, Nemeiri attacked him by air and by land on Aba Island with heavy loss of life. El-Hadi El-Mahdi was himself killed while attempting to escape to Ethiopia. Aba was occupied, and the extensive holdings of the Mahdi's family were confiscated. Azhari died in 1969 and was praised for his earlier role in the Independence of the Sudan.

Nemeiri's regime, during which he was prime minister and held all presidential powers, lasted from 1969 to 1985 and during this period underwent many changes in its composition and its loyalties and in its local and foreign policies. I will not attempt here to record the tremendous developments in this long and important period, except to mention a few events that relate to our subject.

In the early period of 1969–1970, the government started to organize the economy on a socialist basis and nationalized, with what was considered reasonable compensation, all foreign banks, insurance companies, some foreign-based Sudanese companies, and the major British companies dealing with international shipping, engineering, and trading, many of which had been in the Red Sea area since the turn of the century. These included the British Gellatly Hankey Group and the Gellatly Trading Co. Ltd. All their British and Sudanese directors were released, management was handed to other Sudanese managers, and Gellatly Trading Co. Ltd., was renamed the May Trading Company in honor of the May Revolution of Nemeiri and the "free officers."

In 1970, there followed the confiscation and take over of several Sudanese companies. Foremost among them was the major Sudanese group of Osman Saleh & Sons, who were accused of betraying the May Revolution by siding with and financing Sayed El-Hadi El-Mahdi in his refuge in Aba Island and in collaborating with the Sudan Zionist Jews who had left the Sudan by dealing in business with them and smuggling their money out of the country.

Others who were confiscated and their remaining properties expropriated included the Jewish firm of Muradsons; various old firms of Syrian origin such as G. N. Morhig and Sons and Malouf Sons; the Greek group of cinema chains, Licos Brothers; the well-known native firm of Hafiz El-Barbary of Port Sudan; and numerous others. All were accused of being capitalists, the Jews of being Zionists, all of selling their properties and receiving their proceeds abroad, and of leaving the country. A few of these confiscations were later reversed.

In 1975, my own Khartoum home, a large, two-story villa, was expropriated by presidential decree, transferring the ownership to El-Ittihad Al-Ishtiraki Al-Sudani (the Sudanese Socialist Union), none other than the political party of President Nemeiri. In the 1973 Constitution of the Sudan, it had been proclaimed the sole political organization in the Sudan and General Nemeiri its chairman. The party was liquidated in 1985. The decree listed S £62,400 to be paid to me in compensation. My Sudanese attorney, Sayed Abdel Aziz Shiddou, who at the time of my writing in 1996 is minister of justice in the Sudan, finally managed in 1980 to get this compensation paid to me, but after transfer, the compensation netted only U.S. $55,000, less than one-tenth the value of the property on the date it was expropriated. My advocate, Shiddou, appealed on my behalf the low compensation and got an order for another S £40,000 to be paid to me by the Sudanese Socialist Union. Despite numerous petitions through various channels to President Nemeiri, this sum was never paid.[1] At the time this sum was worth U.S. $32,000. With the decline in the value of the Sudanese pound, this is now worth about $85, not a misprint, but an example of the decline of the Sudanese economy.

After the early period of leaning toward the socialist bloc, Nemeiri was transformed into a close ally of the United States and, in return, obtained substantial American economic aid and support from the International Monetary Fund for his various projects. Relations were strained for a time when, in March 1973, the U.S. ambassador was among three diplomats killed by Palestinians in a reception at the Saudi Embassy in Khartoum and Nemeiri released the convicted murderers to the PLO. Nevertheless, relations with the United States continued and intensified.

Relations with Egypt were also close, and President Nemeiri stood out as the only Arab supporter of President Anwar Sadat's Camp David peace treaty with Israel. This alliance angered many and caused the resignation of Sayed Sadig El-Mahdi, who had accepted Nemeiri's appointing him to the Sudanese Socialist Union (the same El-Ittihad Al-Ishtiraki Al-Sudani that owned my home) after the two had reconciled. Nemeiri was also criticized and later indicted while in exile for his government's collaboration in transporting the Ethiopian Jews from Kassala in the Sudan to Israel, in which event Vice-President George Bush played a big part.

Finally, in 1983, Nemeiri declared his "Islamic Revolution" and decided that Sudanese law must be in accordance with the precepts of Islam, the Shari'a law, which was to apply to both Muslims and non-Muslims in the Sudan. He appointed Hassan Al-Turabi, a London- and Sorbonne-educated legal scholar and leader of the Muslim Brotherhood-led National Islamic Front (NIF) to be the attorney general of the Sudan. He set up special courts to pass judgments of floggings, amputations, and executions, which brought despair to some Muslims, the Christians of South Sudan, and other non-Muslims, as well as the concern of the United States and the International Human Rights Organization and

1. According to the CIA World Fact Book 1996/97, p. 398, the exchange rate of the Sudan pound in January 1995 was £434.8 to U.S. $1.00. Thus the S £40,000 approved as an extra compensation to me for confiscating my house but never paid is now worth U.S. $9.20 instead of the U.S. $32,000 I would have received had it been paid at the time it was approved.

the temporary freezing of U.S. aid. Thereafter, Nemeiri moderated his Islamization process.

In 1985, Nemeiri left the Sudan on his annual visit to Washington, D.C., to ensure the continuation of U.S. economic aid and for his annual medical checkup. In his absence, strikes and disturbances asking for his overthrow took place in Khartoum. He left immediately for the Sudan; but, upon learning en route of the army takeover of his government in April by the commander in chief, General Abdel Rahman Sewar El-Dahab, he decided to go into exile in Egypt.

22

◊✦◊

Sadig El-Mahdi and the Islamic Military Government of General Omar Al-Bashir

The military government of General Abdel Rahman Sewar El-Dahab returned democracy to the Sudan in 1986. Parliament was reconstituted and in a coalition government of the Umma Party and the Democratic Union Party (DUP), Sayed Sadig El-Mahdi became prime minister and Sayed Ahmed Uthman El-Merghani, head of the El-Merghani family, became president of the Supreme Council.

Although Sayed Sadig El-Mahdi moderated Nemeiri's Islamization, he was unable to resolve the issue of Islamic law, which remained the bone of contention between the rebels in the South and the government of the North. After three years of democracy under Sayed Sadig El-Mahdi, a militant Islamic government seized control in 1989 in an army coup under the leadership of General Omar Al-Bashir. Again, Islamic law proved an insurmountable problem; and the Sudan People's Liberation Movement of the Southern Sudan (SPLM) rejected General Bashir's decision to resolve the issue of implementation of Islamic law through a national referendum.

Although at the beginning General Bashir dissolved all political parties including the National Islamic Front, the regime proved to be strongly influenced ideologically by the Muslim Brotherhood-led National Islamic Front. In fact, since 1989, the NIF leader, Hassan Al-Turabi, has been considered the de-facto power behind General Bashir's regime. The regime is now an ally of Iran and follows its Islamic fundamentalist policies. The Sudan is believed to be a haven for terror and terrorists who strike against Mubarak's government and civilians in Egypt and for worldwide and armed militants who kill intellectuals, Egyptian Christians, soldiers, and tourists in Egypt.

Following a visit to the Sudan by Iran's president, Iran has been supplying the Sudan with armaments and petrol; and the Sudan has adopted the same foreign policy as Iran, which includes attacks against the Arab-Israeli peace process and Israel's peace agreements with the PLO and Jordan. Christian residents of the South and elsewhere have been leaving the Sudan in fear of the Islamic laws, the fundamentalist policies of the government, and the economic crisis and inflation. Their exodus started in the early 1970s and continued into the 1990s. Numerous Sudan Catholic Syrians and Italians, Armenian and Greek Orthodox, and Egyptian Copts immigrated to the United States, United Kingdom, and Canada. An Egyptian Copt, an old friend and former colleague recently wrote to me from Canada, where he and his children now live. "Since I left the Sudan in 1970, 95 percent of the Egyptians left the Sudan, immigrating to Australia, and a few to Canada and elsewhere." In an apparent step to improve its image abroad, the Sudan government recently delivered the international terrorist Carlos to France, and Hassan Al-Turabi has been lecturing in the United States, England, and France and granting interviews about Sudan's politics and regime to foreign journalists in the Sudan.

Nevertheless, the Sudan remains a haven and passageway for international and Arab fundamentalist terrorists. When a terrorist wanted by the United States for killing Americans in Beirut left his refuge in the Sudan, American intelligence agents were thwarted in their attempt to arrest him at his plane's next stop in Jedda because the Saudi government refused the plane permission to land to prevent his capture by Americans in Saudi territory.

More recently, Egyptian President Hosni Mubarak's car was sprayed with bullets while on his way to a meeting of the Organization of African Unity in Addis Ababa. Mubarak said he believed Sudanese fundamentalists were linked to the attack and that the men who committed the assassination attempt had sneaked into Ethiopia from the Sudan. Mubarak accused Hassan Al-Turabi, the real power behind the Sudanese military government of General Omar Al-Bashir, of being the principal force behind plots to undermine Egypt's government.

Mubarak is joined by officials in Saudi Arabia, Algeria, Tunisia, Jordan, and other countries in asserting that militant Arab fundamentalists are trained in the Sudan to bear arms against their governments, although little concrete proof has been revealed.

23

❦

Sudan Jews in the Diaspora and Israel

The Sudan Jewish Community, though small, produced several notable leaders in their new countries and in world organizations.

Nessim Gaon

Foremost among the former members of the Sudan Jewish Community is the Geneva-based philanthropist and business magnate Nessim Gaon, who is also president of the World Sephardic Federation. When he arrived in Geneva from the Sudan in 1957, he continued his business in oilseeds, grains, animal feeds, and a variety of other commodities; and after a few years, he had expanded his business interests worldwide. In Geneva, he also established his own shipping, financial, and construction companies and made a fortune in business and in real estate investments under the name of NOGA Companies, an anagram of his surname. He constructed and owns the finest modern shopping and office blocks in the center of Geneva, the NOGA Hiltons on the bank of Lake Geneva, and similar ones in Cannes, France. His real estate holdings also included luxury apartment buildings in Geneva and in Israel, the latest being the NOGA Tower in Tel Aviv, next to Harkayon Park.

Gaon has used his extensive wealth to shore and finance, usually in millions of dollars, Jewish education and institutions, especially the university education of Sephardic students throughout the world and in Israel. In the United States, he contributes generously and annually to the Yeshiva University of New York. In 1973, Yeshiva University awarded Gaon an honorary doctorate of humanities at a ceremony in the Plaza

30. Nessim Gaon, president of the World Sephardic Federation, and Menahim Begin.

31. Nessim and Renée Gaon with Yitzhak Rabin.

32. René Cassin, Hakham Solomon Gaon, and Nessim Gaon on the occasion of their being awarded honorary degrees by Yeshiva University, New York.

Hotel in New York with his brother Albert from Houston, my brother David from New Jersey, and myself at his side.[1]

He also supported the establishment of the Chair of Sephardic Studies, chaired by Hakham Solomon Gaon, the former Sephardic chief rabbi of Great Britain.[2] Its program director is Rabbi M. Mitchell Serels, the

1. At the same ceremony, an honorary doctorate in humanities was awarded to René Cassin (1887–1976), professor of international law, laureate of the Nobel Peace Prize in 1968, and one of the greatest French Sephardi Jews. He represented France at the League of Nations and later at the United Nations and was one of the drafters of the Universal Declaration of Human Rights. Severely wounded in World War I, he became very active in veteran affairs and the cause of peace and headed the Alliance Israélite Universelle for many years, beginning in 1943.

2. In its Honor Roll for 1996, Yeshiva Univ. mentioned Nessim Gaon among its "Guardians," those who contribute U.S. $100,000–$999,999 to its schools. Since the early 1970s, Nessim Gaon has contributed such an amount annually.

Sephardic rabbi of Magen David Synagogue—my own synagogue in New Rochelle, New York. Both rabbis accompanied him when he went to welcome King Juan Carlos of Spain on behalf of the world Sephardic Jewry[3] on the king's visit to the Madrid synagogue on 31 March 1992, the five hundredth anniversary of the expulsion of Jews from Spain in an important healing gesture.

As president of the World Sephardic Federation for the last twenty-two years, Nessim Gaon enlisted the support and participation of numerous Sephardic leaders in North, Central, and South America when he visited them in a 16,000-mile tour, which he called the Sephardic Caravan. He enrolled most of them in the World Sephardic Federation's Board of Governors, which later met in a symposium in Jerusalem, which was attended by the president and prime minister of Israel and by a cross section of rabbis from around the world. The far-reaching purpose of the symposium was to nourish knowledge and pride in Sephardic culture and heritage, maintain religious tolerance, extend educational activities for Sephardic students and youth, and assist with the economic growth of Sephardim in development towns in Israel.

I have been a member of the American Sephardic Federation (ASF) since my arrival in White Plains in 1981 and recall attending some of its celebrations in 1992 to commemorate the five hundredth anniversary of the expulsion of the Jews from Spain in 1492. These celebrations were held at the Yeshiva University in Manhattan, in the Bethel Synagogue in New Rochelle, New York, and at the State University of New York (SUNY) at Purchase.[4] They included commemorations of the philosophy, poetry, music, and science from the Jewish Golden Age in tenth- and eleventh-century Andalusia.

In January 1955, I attended the American Sephardi convention in Miami with 450 delegates and Sephardic leaders from all parts of the United States, South America, and Europe. We were led by Leon Levy,

3. The New York *Times*, in its edition of 23 Nov. 1996, announced in a long article that Rabbi Serels would be awarded the Order of Civil Merit of Spain with the honorific title of don, by command of King Juan Carlos. The presentation was made by the consul general of Spain in a ceremony held on 4 Dec. 1996 in recognition of Rabbi Serels's work at Yeshiva Univ. and his service to the Sephardic community in general.

4. At SUNY Purchase, there was a concert of Sephardic Spanish music and songs by the "Voice of the Turtle," whose name is derived from the verses of the Song of Songs. It was interesting that these musicians, using old instruments such as the Ud, Kanoun, and Daraboukka were not of Sephardic or Spanish origin but instead were Ashkenazi musicians who studied and played Sephardic music.

longtime president and Senior Presidium member of the American Sephardic Federation. In March 1995, Leon Levy was elected chairman of the Conference of Presidents of Major American Jewish Organizations, the first Sephardi Jew selected in a critical time to lead this politically powerful group of American Jewry.

To remind the reader, it was 31 March 1492 that King Ferdinand and Queen Isabella promulgated their expulsion decree ordering the 300,000 Jews of Spain to leave their dominions within four months. This was the final triumph of the Inquisition and long efforts by Tomás de Torquemada, the grand inquisitor, who incidentally was reputed to be himself of Jewish descent. Efforts by Jewish Community leaders Don Abraham Senor and Don Isaac Abrabanel to have the decree rescinded were unsuccessful. It was not until December 1968 that the Spanish government issued a statement revoking the edict of expulsion and granting full recognition to the six-hundred-member Hebrew Congregation of Madrid and its Beth Jacob Synagogue. In 1970, I visited the newly recognized Beth Jacob Synagogue and met with some of its members. The reader can imagine the emotions of the moment with the knowledge of the Malka family having left Spain in 1492, departing by sea from the port of Málaga on a ship sailing to the port of Tangier, Morocco.

In May 1978, ten years after that first recognition of the Madrid synagogue, the new Spanish government granted freedom of ideology, religion, and worship for individuals and communities. By 1992, the Spanish Jewish Community had swelled to 20,000 Jews in Madrid and Barcelona and consists mostly of Jews from North Africa and Europe.

Among the numerous projects in which Nessim Gaon and the World Sephardic Federation under his presidency have been involved are Project Renewal and the Leadership Educational Program, supplemented by his personal scholarships to thousands of disadvantaged Sephardic students in Israel's universities and vocational institutions.

Project Renewal is a massive effort by the Israeli government in partnership with Jews of the Diaspora to rehabilitate the disadvantaged neighborhoods of Israel and development towns. As much as 90 percent of the inhabitants of these neighborhoods are Sephardim from Arab countries, who, when they arrived, were designated "Oriental Jews" to differentiate them from Sephardim from European countries. They were placed there by the preexisting dominant Ashkenazi establishment when they fled in great numbers following the turmoil that occurred in Arab countries when the State of Israel was established in 1948 and after the 1956 Arab-Israeli War.

American Jewish communities have been twinned with many of these neighborhoods, and American Jewish leaders have taken an active role in their rehabilitation. In doing so, many affluent Jews in the United States and in other countries of the Diaspora have come in contact not only with Sephardim but also with Jews who are presently in the lowest socioeconomic stratum.[5]

The educational program, funded by the Jewish Agency, provides scholarship grants to young leaders from development towns who wish to continue their studies at various universities in Israel. So far, this program has benefited seven thousand students, of whom five thousand future Sephardi leaders were graduated in a ten-year period.

Nessim Gaon was elected chairman of the Board of Governors of Ben-Gurion University in the Negev, which, with an estimated 30 percent of its student corps being Sephardic, has the distinction of having more Sephardic students than any other Israeli university. A large number of these students are supported through scholarships from Nessim Gaon. Gaon has also served, sometimes simultaneously, as governor of the Hebrew University in Jerusalem and of Bar Ilan University and as vice-president of the World Jewish Congress. He has also headed the fund-raising activities for Keren Hayesod, Keren Kayemet, and Israeli Bonds in Geneva and French-speaking Switzerland (la Suisse romande).

In Geneva, he united the Ashkenazi and Sephardic communities under his presidency and constructed the beautiful Heikhal Haness Synagogue and Cultural Center and continues to support its activities.

Gaon was also active on the political scene in Israel. He was present during the 1977 meeting of Anwar Sadat and Menahim Begin in Israel. He has often said he would go to any extent to help the cause of peace with the Arabs and that the Sephardim could be very helpful in developing the dialog with them.

Leon Tamman

The other business magnate engaged in work for world Jewry and Israel was Leon Tamman of London. He left the Sudan in the early 1960s where among other activities he had constructed the only pharmaceuti-

5. Elazar, 54.

33. Leon Tamman.

cal factory in the Sudan. From his group companies, International Generics, in London, his business interests extended to the European continent and to the Far East. He too made a large fortune in both business
and real estate. In London, he established the Sephardi Federation of
Great Britain and the Commonwealth, of which he was president and

chairman. His son-in-law, Eddie Ishag, also from the Sudan, is the senior vice-president.

In Israel, Leon Tamman oversaw his charitable and political work from his Israeli headquarters in the Daniel Hotel in Herzlia, which he owned. From there, he established the Ta'ali world movement for a united Israel[6] aimed at eliminating discrimination between Ashkenazim and Sephardim and bringing on their unity for Israel. At Leon Tamman's invitation, I attended as U.S. representative one of its early meetings in July 1987 at the Herzlia Hotel, at which Leon Tamman was elected world chairman; David Silvera director general in Israel, and attorney Sidney Shipton executive director in London.

Tamman served as a leading member of the Board of Deputies of British Jews and as chairman of the Presidium of the World Organization of Jews from Arab Countries (WOJAC), representing the 700,000 Jewish refugees who fled to Israel from Arab countries. Knesset member and former minister Mordechai Ben-Porat, chairman of the world executive committee of WOJAC, has urged the world to recognize that the flight of 590,000 Palestinian Arabs from Israel at the time of Israel's creation constituted one of the many such population exchanges in the world in past generations. The properties and wealth left by Jews in Arab countries and confiscated by their governments amount to billions of dollars, some details of which have been gathered by WOJAC.

Leon Tamman also served as a member of the boards of the World Jewish Congress, Hebrew University, and Ben-Gurion University. In 1989, B'nai B'rith granted him the B'nai B'rith International Humanitarian Award, some of whose previous awardees were such world personalities as Lord Sieff, Queen Juliana, Harry Truman, and Henry Kissinger. Alexander Coren included him as a leading personality in his book *Personalities from Jewish Communities in Europe*.[7] Leon sent me a copy of Coren's book with his handwritten inscription, "To my dear friend Eli Malka, a personality I have always respected and admired." Leon Tamman restored a number of Sephardic synagogues in Israel. I visited one of them, the Sephardic Synagogue of Salonica Jews in Tel Aviv, and found it to be a beautiful, thriving, and well-attended synagogue.

As I was readying this book for publication, I received the sad news that Leon Tamman had passed away in Jerusalem on 9 Sivan 5755

6. In Hebrew, Hatenua Haolamit le'ahdot Israel.
7. (Ramat Gan, Israel: Royal Printing, 1989), 30.

(7 June 1995). For two years, he had battled cancer courageously. After treatment and operations in London, he came, a few weeks before Passover 1995, for an operation at the Sloan-Kettering Center, Memorial Hospital for Cancer and Allied Diseases in New York City, where I visited him a few times. In expressing my good wishes for his recovery with a Jewish prayer blessing for recovery, he smiled and said hopefully, "Eliaho Hannabi visited me," referring to my name and relating my visit to that of my namesake, Elijah the prophet, the performer of miracles. May he rest in peace and may the Lord favor him with love and compassion for his good deeds and love of the Torah and Israel, Amen. Leon Tamman died at age sixty-seven at Haddassah University Hospital and was buried in Har Hazeitim (Mount of olives), in Jerusalem. His investments in Israel were estimated at the time to be close to $100 million.

The other Tammans are based in Geneva, Switzerland. Gabriel Tamman made his fortune in business, which he started in the Sudan and Nigeria and continued in Europe and the Far East. He is owner of an ultra-modern shopping arcade on Rue de la Confédération in Geneva and contributes heavily to the arts and culture in Switzerland, both directly and through his Gabriel Tamman Foundation. He is the publisher of a book about Geneva, detailing and depicting its history and development. On our last visit to Geneva in 1993, he and his wife, Lina, entertained me and my wife, Bertha, with a magnificent dinner at their Geneva home. On that occasion, we met their children and grandchildren and their in-laws, Ibrahim and Lola El-Eini, old friends from the Sudan. We spent the evening reminiscing about our Sudan days and thereafter.

On that same visit to Geneva, his brother Albert Tamman and his wife, Mathilde, took us out for Sunday brunch, with their children and grandchildren, at the President Hotel, which they own and which is one of the prestigious hotels on the bank of Lake Geneva. It reminded me that it had been in this President Hotel that many years ago I had had a meeting with Sayed El-Hadi El-Mahdi, who was the son of Sayed Abdel Rahman El-Mahdi. He was the imam of the Ansar sect after the death of his father and his older brother Sayed Saddig El-Mahdi. Aware that I was in Geneva, Sayed El-Hadi El-Mahdi had called and asked me to bring to him one of the "good Swiss watchmakers." He wanted one hundred gold pocket watches made, with his picture on the dial plate. His intention was to give these watches as presents to the notables, sheikhs, and omdas[8] who supported him, just as his father used to do with the Robes of Honor, which were beautiful woolen djibbahs that the British governor general in Khartoum, and the British governors of provinces, used to give at Palace levees or at Muslim ceremonial feasts to Sudanese notables, sheikhs, and omdas in recognition of their loyalty and services.

David Malka

My brother David Malka head-started the immigration of Jews from the Sudan to the United States in 1957, nine years before my own immigration. He quickly became the center in New Jersey around which Jewish immigrants from the Sudan (and later non-Jewish friends, too) gathered and, with his help, solved their difficulties in settling in the United States. With his rapid rise in commercial circles, first as vice-president and later as president and chairman of Borneo Sumatra USA Co., part of the International Borneo Sumatra Company, he provided many of them, family and nonfamily alike, with affidavits and guarantees where needed and jobs in his companies or other companies he had connections with, and all of them have remained close friends to this day.

David got involved in local Jewish matters, became a leader and benefactor of the Clifton, New Jersey, Jewish Center; member of the Clifton B'nai B'rith Lodge, solver and peacemaker whether in family matters or otherwise. Like Aharon (Aaron), our first high priest, he has pursued and has made peace. I am always proud of him and of his frequently saying that he has emulated me in my long path and endeavors for my fellow Jews and brethren in humanity.

When Father Augustin Baroni (later Archbishop Baroni) the former principal of his alma mater, Comboni College of Khartoum, came to the United States, David Malka, true to form, organized for him a large meeting and celebration of Comboni graduates in the United States. They came from all parts of the United States to pay their respects to their former principal and headmaster. Albert Gaon from Houston, Victor Shamis from New York, the Sassons and Malkas from New Jersey, and many others from the Sudan-born second and third generations came and made substantial contributions to benefit Comboni College.

8. Omdas are village headmen, or native town "mayors."

Others Sudan Jews in the Diaspora

There are many other Sudan Jews who excelled in the Diaspora: the Dweks, Ishags, and Seroussis in the United Kingdom and Israel; and the Shouas, Malkas, Adeses, Dannons, Benous, Baroukhs, and the Kudsis in the United States and Israel. There is also the third generation of Jews born in the Sudan and educated partly in Europe and the United States who have excelled in their professions and careers and are now in their forties and fifties. Of these in the United States, I would mention the grandchildren of Farag Shoua, one of the early settlers and first merchants in Khartoum. His grandson, son of Daoud Shoua, Joshua D. Salvator, is president and chief of surgery of the Heart Lung and Vascular Institute of Chicago.

Another grandson of Farag Shoua is Morris Sasson Levy, son of Sasson Smouha Levy and Farag Shoua's daughter Rahma. After graduating from Gordon College in Khartoum, he was sent to England for a three-year engineering course, following which he worked in London for a while and became a fellow of the Royal College of Engineers. On his return to Khartoum, he soon became the municipal engineer of Khartoum City. In 1959, Morris left Khartoum for the United States, where he joined Parsons, Brinkerhoff Engineering Company in New York City and, in the early 1980s, became one of their senior engineers in their headquarters in Boston, where he still is.

Also, if you will indulge an old man's prerogative, I am particularly proud of my own children, nephews, and nieces. My son, Jeffrey Malka, is now at the top of his profession. He is chairman of the Department of Orthopaedic Surgery at Fairfax Hospital in Northern Virginia, a tertiary care center and teaching hospital for three university orthopaedic programs in the Washington, D.C., area, and is an associate professor at the Georgetown University Medical Center in Washington, D.C. My daughter, Evelyne Klein, is a noted professional international banker and senior vice-president of the Republic National Bank of New York (part of the Edmond Safra Group) in charge of private international banking throughout Europe and the Far East. She visits and serves her multimillion-dollar accounts in all the capital markets of the world—London, Paris, Brussels, Geneva, Athens, Lisbon, Madrid, Hong Kong, Taiwan, Singapore, and Bangkok. Both Jeffrey and Evelyne are active leaders and benefactors in their respective synagogues. They have raised their children in the Jewish faith and are proud of their mixed Sephardic and Ashkenazi heritage and ancestry.

My niece Diana Ackman, daughter of my brother David, is a prominent American educator, director of the Social Studies Program of the U.S. Department of Education, and has headed several education missions on behalf of the U.S. Department of Education to places such as China, the Phillipines, Indonesia, and Russia. She is a former mayor of her town, Reston, Virginia, and quite a lady and mother.

My grandniece Nomi Levy, granddaughter of my sister Vicky Braunstein, has authored two most interesting and insightful works on the Sudan: her senior thesis at Colombia University in 1991, "The Mangled Mask of Empire: Ceremony and Political Motive in the Anglo-Egyptian Sudan, 1925–1937," and her master's thesis at Cambridge University in 1993, "American Diplomatic Relations with Sudan, 1977–1985."

My nephew Solomon Edmond Malka, son of my brother Edmond, is a CPA and business executive who came to the United States after business careers in Israel, Ireland, and South Africa. He is a successful, caring, and loving parent and family man. His sons, already American university graduates and executives, and his parents, brothers, and sister are all subjects of his love and care.

My nephews Raymond and Solomon Sasson, sons of my sister Allegra Sasson, are successful businessmen and strictly observant, shomer Shabbat, Jewish leaders. Solomon Sasson, whose wife, Lulu, is a Syrian Jew he helped come to the United States, is a leading participant in organizations for saving the Jews of Syria; and he has himself saved several Jewish men and women by helping them to get settled and by giving them a new start and good life in Brooklyn, New York. Their sister Jeannette Toledano is a kosher, knowledgeable humanitarian, who is always there to help the sick and disabled. She is married to Aaron Toledano, nephew of Rabbi Yacoub Moshé Toledano, the former chief rabbi of Alexandria (1930–1940), former Sephardic chief rabbi of Tel Aviv–Jaffa (1942–1950), and minister of religious affairs in Israel from 1958 to his death in 1959.

I am also proud of my grandchildren, who are following in the steps of their parents in education and loyalty to the Jewish faith. First among them is Jennifer Malka, Jeffrey and Susan's daughter, who at age twenty-three is already a graduate of George Washington University with a double bachelor's degree in education and Judaic studies and simultaneously has risen through the executive ranks to become the assistant to the district manager of Hechingers, a large chain of stores. In addition, in her "spare time," she has for the past four years been a teacher of Hebrew and Judaica at her temple's Sunday school and is involved and past vice-president of B'nai B'rith Youth, continuing the chain of B'nai B'rith workers going back to her great grandfather. Her sister Deborah was graduated recently from Barnard College, Columbia University. Their sisters, Dorothy and Judy, are still in high school. Of my daughter, Evelyne, and her husband, David Klein's two children, Alex is starting college with a special interest in environmental studies and his sister, Lauren, is in high school.

There are many other success stories of this generation in their newly adopted countries, but I cannot include all of them in this chapter. Their children, who have become entirely American, European, or Israeli may find a glimpse of their origins in this book.

Sudan Jews in the Israel Defense Forces

I would be remiss in my duty if I did not pay hommage to the hundreds of children, grandchildren, and great-grandchildren of Sudan Jews in Israel who have served honorably in the Israel Defense Forces (IDF). These young men and women fought for Israel with patriotism and zeal in all Arab-Israeli wars and conflicts, from the October 1973 Yom Kippur war against the Egyptian and Syrian surprise attacks, to their present-day defense against terrorists, Hizbullah fundamentalists attacks, Palestinian riots and disturbances, Hamas, and Syrian threats. Many have been wounded and some have been killed. Dozens of them are direct descendants of Rabbi Solomon Malka, the religious and spiritual leader of all Sudan Jews. I would like to cite especially two of his family who got killed when they and their IDF tanks were blown up, as they were going out of Lebanon in 1982, after the IDF expelled the PLO terrorists and their leader, Yasir Arafat. They were IDF officers Reuven Tueta, son of my niece Giselle Tueta of Haifa (three of whose seven grandchildren are now serving in the Israeli Army and whose eldest grandson, Shai, is a pilot in the Israeli Air Force and two others are in the IDF), and grandson of my sister the late Fortunée Goldring; and Yehuda Tuval, the husband of Esther Malka of Jerusalem, granddaughter of my sister, the late Esther Malka. May their memory be a blessing to the young children they left, and for the peace and security of Israel.

PART TWO

Eighty-seven Years from Omdurman to New York

According to its root the tree will grow;
What and who a man is appears in his works.
—Santob de Carrión,
fourteenth-century Spanish rabbi

24

◦✻◦

My Childhood and
Jewish Sites in Cairo

Train up a child in the way he should go:
and when he is old he will not depart from it.
—Proverbs 22:6

I was born on 7 November 1909 to Rabbi Solomon Ben-Yehuda Malka
and Hanna Bat David Assouline Malka in the synagogue compound that
included the living quarters of my parents in the City of Omdurman.
Omdurman is one of the largest indigenous cities in the Sudan and in it
lived most of the Jews who came from Egypt in the early 1900s. It is located across the Nile from Khartoum, the capital of the Sudan, and is
located close to the confluence of the Blue Nile and the White Nile as
they meet and flow north toward Egypt as the main Nile. My birth certificate, which was prepared in Arabic, most probably from information provided by the attending Sudanese midwife, gives my nationality as
"Israeli," presumably meaning an Israelite, and my religion as "Mousawi,"
literally meaning of the religion of Moussa, or Moses.

At the age of four, I was taken to the kindergarten of the Church Missionary Society (CMS.) Girls School, where the kindergarten teacher
was my eldest sister, Esther. At age six, I was sent to the Catholic Mission
Boys School in Omdurman; and when we moved to Khartoum, I continued at the Catholic Mission School in Khartoum. At age twelve, I graduated with the Primary School Certificate, equivalent to the eighth grade
in the United States. Officials at Gordon College of Khartoum considered me too young to be admitted to their secondary school because they
apparently required an admission age of fifteen or sixteen, and I was

34. Eli S. Malka as a young man.

therefore sent for my secondary school education to the Church Missionary Society English Boys Boarding School in Cairo. This school was locally known as Al-Madrassa Al-Ingilizia, (the English school). From there, I graduated at age sixteen with the Egyptian Secondary Certificate and with the English Matriculation and was thus already well advanced in both the classic Arabic and English languages in addition to the usual sciences and mathematics of the day.

From then on, I continued to educate myself by attending courses and studying and reading every subject that caught my interest throughout my life, earning a diploma in accounting and auditing from the Finance Department, Khartoum; a Bsc. in commerce from Comboni College, Khartoum; and a degree in mercantile law from Wolsey Hall, Oxford University. In Khartoum, I joined the Sudan Cultural Center, founded by the British officials and with a large library on all sorts of subjects. I remember from those days a lecture by Sir John Carmichael, then the secretary of the interior, in which he said "You be like the camel in the bush, he chews from every tree and then settles on the one he likes best. So you go into the library and read from all books and then settle on the ones you like most." It was his use of the metaphor of comparing us to the camel, we poor Sudanese locals who would not otherwise understand without the example of the camel, that amused me and caused me always to remember his comparison. I nevertheless took his advice and finally settled mostly on topics of history, economics, religion, and politics.

In my parents home where I grew up, living according to the Torah laws and Jewish traditions and customs was the normal way of life, automatically acquired and learned by the children. The celebrations at home of the kiddush and dinners of the Sabbath, Jewish festivals, and the Passover seders were great feasts to look forward to and enjoy with all the family, friends, and out-of-town visitors. I continued these celebrations and customs in my own homes in Khartoum, Geneva, Paris, and White Plains, always inviting other than my family, friends, and out-of-town visitors who could not celebrate them in their own homes.

In Khartoum, the Passover seder was always in my father's home. He wanted all his children to be there with their wives and children. He invited with them every Jewish visitor in town and brought home with him from the synagogue everyone who had no place to go for the seder. My mother never knew how many people my father would bring in, but she was always prepared for the forty to fifty people she knew she should expect. She could rely on the help of her Sudanese cook, whom she had trained and brought up since his teens. He knew all about the kasher, Pessah seder, and Shabbat. For extra help, she could count on her six daughters and her Sudanese suffragi (waiter).

With my father leading the seder we would chant the first songs "Kaddish Wurhaz, Karpas Yahas," recite the kiddush, wash our hands, eat parsley, break the middle matza, and so forth, singing to ancient Salonica or Casablanca melodies and even an Egyptian-Moroccan one at the very end. When my father died, it fell on me to invite the family, friends, and visitors to my home seder; and at times, I also had thirty to forty guests and their families over. On one Passover eve in the early 1960s, I received a call from Mr. Rolo, an important Jewish cotton exporter from Alexandria. I do not recall Mr. Rolo's first name, but I think he was Robert Rolo, a future president of the Jewish Community of Alexandria. He said he had just arrived at the Grand Hotel and asked if he could attend my seder, of which he had been told by my friend Alexander Ben-Lassin. I welcomed him warmly and immediately sent my car to bring him to my home.

On 26 April 1986, in White Plains, Gannett Westchester staff reporter Gerald Ragan wrote:

> Malka grew up in a rich Jewish tradition as the son of the former Chief Rabbi of the Sudan. The Seder in Khartoum was always in Hebrew, Malka recalled in an interview in the White Plains Hotel following a meeting of the B'nai B'rith executive committee on which he serves. The Seder he said is about 75% in Hebrew with translations read out, he said. Otherwise there is nothing different from the one his father led many years ago. He and his wife Bertha were to play host to 16 for this year's Seder. "I used to invite people who could not make the Seder. I am doing the same here." Does he think back to the Sudan at this time of the year? Malka answered nonchalantly "Jews are the same all over the world. I can tell you one thing, we are thanking God we are not there at this moment" he said.

An old Sephardic custom I learned at my father's home and have continued in my seders in the United States bears describing. When my young grandchildren chanted, "Why is this night different from all other nights?" I would make each one in turn wrap three matzahs in a napkin, and swing it on her shoulder in the way that the Jews' carried their unleavened dough on their backs when fleeing the Egyptians, and I would ask each one in turn:

"Where are you coming from?" And they would answer, "From Egypt."

"Where are you going?" "To Jerusalem." I would then respond "Hashana Habaa Beroushalaim" (next year in Jerusalem) and bless them individually.

From all this ritual, I gained knowledge and strength in my faith and pride in my Jewishness. I practiced the Jewish customs and traditions with the Sephardic moderation and tolerance that set the Sephardi apart from the extreme practices and habits of some of the Ultra Orthodox East European Jews. In school and thereafter in society and business life, I mixed liberally with my many Christian and Muslim friends and always with mutual respect and understanding in our shared English and Arabic cultures as well as our multinational and international modes of life.

Cairo Sites

During my boarding missionary school days in Cairo, my father arranged to have me spend the Jewish festivals in the homes of his Jewish friends in Cairo. Memorable among them was a week at the home of Rabbi Haim Hayon, member of the Bath Din of the Cairo rabbinate and a colleague of my father's from their Tiberias days. He took me for the High Holidays to the Sha'ar Hashamaim (Gate of heaven) Synagogue,[1] the most beautiful in Cairo, where Rabbi Haim Nahum Effendi, the hakhambashi of Egypt, was officiating; where the famous hazzan (cantor) Hamawi was conducting prayers; and where the Jewish elite of Cairo were attending services. It was then called the Ismailia Synagogue, after the name of the Ismailia quarter, in which it was located. This beautiful synagogue was restored in 1981 at a cost of $700,000.[2] To the many Jewish tourists from all over the world who visit it when they are in Cairo, this synagogue is known as the Adli Synagogue, after the name of the street on which it is located. Sometimes, a Jewish Sephardic service is

---

1. Sha'ar Hashamaim is the name that the patriarch Jacob gave to the place in which he slept when he went out from Beer-sheba and went toward Haran. "And he dreamed and behold a ladder set up on the earth, and the top of it reached to heaven, and behold the angels of God ascending and descending on it" (Gn. 28:10–12). "And Jacob awaked out of his sleep, and he said, 'How full of awe is this place, this is none other than the house of God, and this is the gate of heaven [H. Sha'ar Hashamaim]" (Gn. 28:16–17).

2. By the Sudan-born philanthropist Nessim Gaon of Geneva, president of the World Sephardic Federation.

given for the tourists when a minian[3] is available. Cairo now has no more than 500 Jewish residents, down from the 40,000 it had before the regime of Gamal Abdel Nasser.

Sha⁼ar Hashamaim, or Adli Synagogue as it is now known, was built in 1903 by the family of Mosseri Bey, noted bankers of their time. In the late 1950s and 1960s, after the exodus of Jews from Egypt, I met in Geneva Guido Mosseri, a member of the same Mosseri family of bankers and his wife, daughter of another noted family of British Sephardic Jews, the Smouhas[4] of Alexandria. We became friends, a friendship continued by our children.

In those days, there was one or more synagogues in almost every quarter of Cairo where Jews lived. Most of them followed the Sephardic ritual or minhagim.[5] There were quite a few synagogues in Haret El-Yahoud, located behind the shop-filled Mouski Street of Cairo. Haret El-Yahoud was where most of the Egyptian Jews lived, though later it was only the less privileged who stayed there. There I visited Haret El-Yahoud Maimonides Synagogue, known as Kenesseth Rab Moshé after the great Jewish scholar and physician Rabbeinou Moshé Ben-Maimoun. In a small hall in the basement of this synagogue, Maimonides taught and prayed in the twelfth century when he was a physician in Cairo and physician to Saladin (Salah El-Din El-Ayoubi) and his court. When Maimonides died, his corpse was rested in this part of the synagogue for seven days before it was transferred to its final burial place in Tiberias, which many people visit in pilgrimage and which I visit every time I am in Tiberias.

In this same lower part of the synagogue, Jews, Muslims, and Christians come and sleep the night on the floor or on mattresses placed in alcoves dug in the wall to implore healing of their diseases. In *Juifs D'Egypte Images et Textes,* it is stated that there is still in that synagogue a plaque placed by King Fu⁼ad I, who in his illness exposed his royal attire

3. A minian is a quorum of ten adult Jewish males, required for a Kaddish (the Jewish memorial prayer for the departed) and for Jewish congregational prayers.

4. The vast properties of the Smouha family in Alexandria, including the famous Smouha Sporting Club and the horse-racing courses of Alexandria, were confiscated by Nasser after the British-French-Israeli attack on the Suez Canal in 1956. After long negotiations, the British government secured for the Smouhas compensation from the Egyptian government amounting to £14.5 million Sterling, a small faction of the value of their properties.

5. *Minhagim* is the plural of *minhaq* (H. custom), in this case the synagogal custom of ritual prayers and chants.

in that place and was healed. The last chief rabbi of Cairo, Rabbi Haim Douek, supervised the restoration of this synagogue in 1967.

Behind Mouski Street, there was also Darb El-Barabra, where many of the Ashkenazi Jews of Egypt lived and where the big Ashkenazi Synagogue of Cairo was located, a very impressive building in its time. It was the synagogue to which my future brother-in-law, Pascal Goldenberg, a prominent optician in Cairo and eldest brother of my deceased wife, Dora, may they both rest in peace, belonged. The Ashkenazi Synagogue was the only synagogue to suffer damage during the disturbances in Cairo in 1948 that followed the first Arab-Israeli conflict. It was reconstructed soon thereafter with funds contributed by the then prosperous Ashkenazi and Sephardic communities of Cairo and with the help of the Egyptian government.

During my school summer holidays I once lived for two months in Darb El-Barabra in the home of the mother of my Ashkenazi brother-in-law Bernard Goldring, husband of my elder sister Fortunée (the Sephardic Spanish form of her Hebrew name, Mazzal, or fortune in English). There I befriended the son of my age Maurice Goldring, who became my guide to the many Ashkenazi Jewish shops in Darb El-Barabra and where one could best buy goose meat, a then much-favored Ashkenazi food delicacy.

At another time during my early student days in Cairo, I was for the festivals at the home of Nessim Shalom, one of the Mahdiya Jews in Omdurman. His widow and sons took me to their Neveh Shalom "Sakakini" Synagogue, known locally as the Kenisah El-Kebira (big synagogue), so named because it was bigger in area than the Sha²ar Hashamaim Synagogue in the Ismailia quarter.

During another of the Jewish festivals, I left my Cairo boarding school to stay at the home of Shabtai Dwek, a former manager of Giulio Padova & Co. in Omdurman. There I became friends with his son of my age, Nessim Shabtai Dwek, whom I visited forty years later in his shop in Geneva, Switzerland. The Dweks took me to their Daher quarter synagogue. Sakakini and Daher were the quarters in which the wealthier Jews lived in those days.

It was in my Cairo boarding school that I learned and practiced the sports that I loved and played during the rest of my life, soccer (known as football there and in Europe) and tennis. In soccer, I made the second team of my school as right wing but managed to get put on the first team as a linesman, which was enough to allow me to travel with the first team to the major games they played and thus to participate in the tea parties that followed the games. One of these trips was to the city of Helwân, home of the Helwân Portland Cement Co. of Egypt, with whom I was to be associated in business many years later. I recall that, during that visit, we beat the city of Helwân's soccer team; and while on the side line as linesman, I could hear the Helwân public threatening revenge. I was afraid they intended to beat us up after the game, not an unusual event even now in Europe. Fortunately, nothing of the sort happened, and we enjoyed the tea party given by the city of Helwân in honor of the two games thereafter.

At school, I was taught tennis by Mr. Cooper, who allowed me plenty of opportunity to practice and to participate in games two or three times a week on our school's hard courts. When I was back in Khartoum, I joined some of the local soccer teams and tennis clubs and then founded, with other Jewish youth, the Maccabi Football Team and the Maccabi Sports Club, where we built our own tennis hard court.

I celebrated my bar mitzvah in the Khartoum Synagogue on my return from Cairo during one of the school summer holidays. On that Saturday, I went to the teba (reader's desk or bima) to read my Torah portion from the Torah scroll. The Thursday before, I had put on for the first time my Tefilin, or phylacteries, under the direction and benediction of my father.

25

Business Career and Trade Development in the Sudan

My first job was in the Shipping Department of Gellatly Hankey, the leading British company, in the Sudan, at a starting salary of E £8 a month (roughly equivalent to U.K. 8 gns.). In a matter of months, I resigned to take a better-paying job of E £10 a month in the Supply Department of the Sudan Defense Force. I later rejoined Gellatly and ascended its corporate ladder to the top.

Within the Supply Department of the Sudan Defense Force, I was assigned to the Audit Department. This happened to be located in the same building as the Sudan Government Finance Department, where we were given an intense accounting and auditing course by senior Finance Department inspectors. One of those was Shokeir, a then well-known Lebanese. I graduated from the course at the top of the class, amid much older and experienced accountants; and I have always felt that this particular course was of great benefit to me in my later business career because of the early understanding it gave me of finance and report analysis.

In the Audit Department, working under the supervision of a British auditor with the rank of staff sergeant, I soon discovered and reported serious discrepancies in the accounts of certain supply depots; and these reports were taken to higher levels. Toward the end of the year, I requested a raise in salary to the level of the older audit clerks who did the same job as I. Despite support and recommendation by the British director of the Audit Department, a bimbashi (lieutenant colonel) in the Sudan Defense Force, I did not get the raise; and so I resigned. I believe my youth and government regulations were the obstacles in my getting the higher pay.

Gellatly Hankey heard of my resignation and asked me back. I accepted rejoining the firm at a monthly salary of E £12 at that time a fantastic salary for a boy of nineteen and a salary usually not reached by a man until the mature age of thirty. It was then, in the 1925–1935 decade, enough money for a family of four to live on in Khartoum. I gave most of it to my father so as to participate in meeting my father's home expenses, where I was still living, and kept some for my own hobbies and private expenses.

This was a time when local office functionaries were in short supply; and the government, foreign banks, and commercial companies needed to import employees from Egypt for middle-level positions, usually of Lebanese or Jewish extraction. The reason for this shortage was that the few graduates from Gordon College, then the only local secondary and professional school, were, for a long time, hardly sufficient to fill the government jobs, for which they were trained and destined.

When I rejoined Gellatly Hankey, I was assigned to their Merchandise Department in Khartoum. It was a small import-export department with an executive head clerk, called a *bashkatib*,[1] who under a British manager, was responsible for all local buying and selling. I liked the job, worked hard at it, and caught the attention and liking of Gellatly's directors. In less than three years, I had become the bashkatib of the department; and before long, I was to replace the British manager and become manager of the Merchandise Department and responsible for developing all Gellatly's import, export, and trading activities.

Thus I started a thirty-year business career, during which I built up the Merchandise Department into Gellatly Trading Co. Ltd., one of the most important import-export and trading companies in the Sudan, with several import-export departments covering every aspect of Sudan trade. All along, I was encouraged and supported by John Allan Smith and Arthur F. J. Carter, the managing director and financial director respectively of the Gellatly Group in Khartoum. They were instrumental in the decision in Khartoum and London to transfer the departments and business activities I developed into a separate company of the Group, the Gellatly Trading Co. Ltd., with myself at its head. From its inception in 1953, I

---

1. *Bashkatib* is the combination of *pasha* and *katib* (Ar. clerk). It was the title given to the head clerk of an office in the government or commercial organization. Bashkatib El-Mudiria was the head clerk of the governor or director (mudir), through whom all messages or petitions had to pass to get to the governor.

35. Board of Directors, Gellatly Hankey & Co. Ltd., 1961. *Left to right*, L. C. Lyon, secretary; C. S. Robinson; A. F. J. Carter; J. A. Smith, M. C.; R. Y. Rule, chairman; J. St. C. Robinson; E. N. Bendell; T. Stileman. *Inset*, H. C. Garrod, secretary, (1935–1960). Courtesy of Gellatly Hankey.

was the director and chief executive officer of the Gellatly Trading Co. Ltd., the marketing advisor of the Sudan Soap Factory of the Gellatly Group, and the commercial advisor to Gellatly's branches and offices in Ethiopia, Eritrea, and Egypt.

E. N. Bendell was the first to inform me of the Board of Directors' decision to form the Gellatly Trading Co. with me at its head. Bendell served as director at Port Sudan and Addis Ababa and organized the endeavors of the Ethiopian Motor Transport Company to construct, through very difficult terrain, a motor road linking the coffee-growing district in western Abyssinia to Gambeila. Gambeila is an Ethiopian river port on the Blue Nile, from which the coffee could be transported by river to the Sudan.

Many attempts were made by other firms to entice me from the Gellatly Group and build up similar business for them. I stuck loyally to the Gellatly Group, however, which compensated me well in the end. I recall Smith's telling me that, like him, I worked on a commission basis on the profits I made for the Group and Carter encouraged me by continually increasing the percentage of commission I earned. My compensation pack-

age consisted of the salary of a British director; his privileges of a fur-
nished house (and because I owned my own house, a fair rental for living
in it); plus company-paid, first-class air travel for me and my wife to the
United Kingdom; and best of all, an agreed percentage of all gross profits
made for Gellatly Trading Co. before any expense or tax deductions. In
each of the last fifteen years of my service, I earned significant commissions that enabled me to keep two houses, one in Khartoum and another
in Geneva, Switzerland; to raise my family and educate my children in
the best schools and universities in Europe; and to accumulate capital
that helped me in future years.

Smith and Carter succeeded each other as managing directors, first in
Khartoum and then in London. R. Y. Rule, a major shareholder of Gellatly, was chairman of the Group. He regularly met with us once a year in
Khartoum and we with him in London. All three and the senior directors
who followed them (Arthur Frederick Day, Hugh Miles, Robert Geddes
Gibson [Gibby]) and the financial directors (Richard D. Campbell [Dick]
and Alexander Niven) and their wives naturally became personal friends
to both me and my wife, Dora. We socialized in each other's homes, and
they were frequent guests at the many dinners my wife arranged in our
Khartoum home when we invited prominent Sudanese in our business
circle.

In the mid-1950s and following the national effort aimed at the Sudanization of senior posts, we succeeded in attracting some prominent
Sudanese officials to join our Boards of Directors and work with us as active directors. The first to do so was Sayed Makkawi Suleiman Akrat,
whose last job before joining us was managing director of the Sudan
Gezira Board and before it, the permanent under secretary of the Ministry of the Interior. He too became a personal friend, and the two of us
had an interesting time together when traveling to our Sudan branches
and business connections in Uganda and Kenya.

Along with the growth of the Gellatly Trading Co. was the growth of
the Gellatly Engineering Co. Ltd., which dealt in all engineering products and had its own engineers, engineering workshops, and services.
Among others, members of the staff were the agents and importers of and
serviced British Morris and Austin cars (Nuffield); Dodge and other
trucks and vans; Firestone tires; Caterpillar tractors; Morris Harris agricultural machinery earth equipment, and air-conditioners; and Phillips
radios and appliances.

In 1972, the whole Gellatly Group was nationalized. Both their Su-

36. Gellatly's tea party for its retiring managing director, A. F. J. Carter. *Sitting center*, A. F. J. Carter; *to his right*, Eli Malka, Dorothy Carter, Dick Campbell Adele Romy, Joseph Soriano; *to his left*, Nashid Ghali, Betty Campbell, Hugh Miles, Dora Malka, Henry Romy, Nina Soriano, Fawzi Mikhail. Courtesy of Gellatly Hankey.

danese and British directors were relieved of their posts; and the management was turned over to other Sudanese managers, in some cases merging certain companies and lines with others. Because of its prominent position, the Gellatly Trading Co. Ltd., which I had built and headed, had the distinction of being renamed the May Trading Company, in commemoration of the May Revolution that, in 1969, had swept President Muhamed Nemeiri and his Revolutionary Command Council of ten young military officers into power. Unfortunately in due course, the May Trading Company lost the prominent position gained by Gellatly Trading Co. Many of its parts were merged or taken over by competitors, and its activities dwindled significantly.

In 1992, the London parent company, Gellatly Hankey & Co. Ltd. and its group of companies was taken over by the Inchcape London Group and became The Inchcape Shipping and Services. It was very sad for all of us who identified ourselves and our careers with the Gellatly name, but it is not an uncommon fate for large private companies that go public on the London Stock Exchange. The name Gellatly Hankey and Co. Ltd. was retained by the Eritrean and Ethiopian companies, though they are also part of the Inchcape Group.

During my career with Gellatly, I traveled the Sudan from one end to the other as well as other parts of Africa, the Middle East, and Europe, making many connections and friends along the way and becoming a

37. Gellatly Hankey staff in Khartoum: *Center*, Hugh Miles, retiring senior director; *to his right*, Eli Malka, Alexander Niven, George Shuggi; *to his left*, Adeeb Sabba, Robert Geddes Gibson, Aziz Galdas, Burwood Taylor, Fawzi Mikhail.

leader and president of the Sudan Jewish Community. Gellatly Hankey and Co. Ltd. was established in London in 1862 by Edward Gellatly and James Alers Hankey, who were the successors of Duncan Dunbar II, a Scotsman who was an important figure in the marine world and as a shipowner. They became leading agents for the cargo and passenger ships of many British and international lines, other than their own, providing all shipping services in ports and capital cities in the United Kingdom, Europe, and the Red Sea. In the United Kingdom, they had offices in

38. Gellatly Headquarters, Khartoum.

London, Liverpool, Glasgow, and Manchester. In Europe, they were in Antwerp, Rotterdam, Hamburg, and Marseilles.

Gellatly Hankey came to the Red Sea area around 1884–1886, with offices in Suakin on the Sudan side and Jedda on the Arabian side. The two ports were then developing as coaling stations for passing ships, and there was also the business of handling supplies for British forces and the traffic in Muslim pilgrims going to Jedda on the Arabian side. Suakin was also an African Red Sea port on the route to India, which was of vital strategic importance to the British. It was ferociously held and never fell to the Mahdi, despite repeated attacks by Osman Digna, his credited representative, a Suaknese of partial Beja descent. Throughout the Mahdiya, Suakin always remained in Egyptian hands, reinforced by British troops and commanded by British officers. For a time in 1888 when Osman Digna's attacks were fiercest and Suakin was in danger of falling to him, Gellatly's offices in the town became the military headquarters; and Sir Reginald Wingate planned his campaign there.

Osman Digna, supported by four thousand Hadandawa tribesmen,

39. Gellatly's office building in Port Sudan.

(known as fuzzy wuzzies because of their Albert Einstein hairstyles), laid siege to Suakin for more than three months. Kitchener almost captured Osman Digna on one occasion, and Digna's narrow escape did not dissuade Kitchner from his ambition to capture Suakin and thus dominate the Red Sea coast. At one time, he occupied a fortress a mere 2,000 yards away; but a raiding force drove him off.[2]

I visited Suakin in the 1950s in the company of my friend Ahmed Gadalla, who was then in charge of Gellatly's Merchandise Department in Port Sudan. I found the old Gellatly's "Suakin" house and offices, maintained as a historic site under the care of a Suaknese office manager. By then, there was hardly any business of importance to be done from that office.

My good friend R. G. Gibson, a former managing director of Gellatly Hankey in the Sudan and in London, named his house on the English Channel coast in West Bosham, West Sussex, "Suakin," in tribute to his-

2. George Blake, *Gellatly 1862–1962* (Glasgow: Blackie & Son, Ltd., 1962), iii.

toric Suakin and Gellatly's role there. He was kind enough to provide me with historic information I needed from the book by George Blake on Gellatly, a copy of which he later found and sent to me, although it was out of print for a long time.

From Suakin, Gellatly extended its offices and services to all parts of the Sudan and the Red Sea area. In 1905, immediately after the modern harbor and docks were completed, Gellatly opened offices in Port Sudan, which is now the only Sudanese port. Khartoum offices were opened in 1911 and later became the head office of Gellatly Hankey & Co. (Sudan) Ltd. The Massawa offices were opened in 1915; Asmara, about 1952; Addis Ababa and Djibouti, a year later; and Cairo, in the mid-1950s.

In all these ports, Gellatly extended complete cargo and ship-handling services, including warehousing, superintending, insurance, clearing and forwarding, stevedoring, bunkering, and ship chandlers. These services were later to grow into specialized companies of the group: the Sudan Warehousing Co. Ltd.; the Red Sea Stevedoring Co. Ltd.; and the Sudan Shipping and General Stores. For many years, Gellatly Hankey companies were handling over 50 percent of the Sudan export and import cargo.

Gellatly Trading Co. Ltd. established a Merchandise Department in each of the Sudan branches of Gellatly Hankey: Port Sudan, Wadi Halfa, Wad Medani, El-Obeid, Kosti, and Juba and also secured agents and clients throughout the country. These departments served as outlets for the sale of its imports, and those located in produce centers purchased produce for its export trade.

The manner in which purchases were made in the produce centers is interesting to relate. There were daily auctions, conducted and controlled by government agents and supervisors. Each day, as the produce of Sudan crops was brought in, it was arranged in designated lots, each owned by a different local farmer who had brought it to the auction grounds. Exporters' agents and dealers in produce then bid for each lot competitively, thus guaranteeing a fair market price for each farmer and lot. The purchased lots were then weighed and paid for in silver coins (florins and Egyptian rials) through government agents. The produce ran the gamut of all Sudan produce and varied by area. In Kordofan stations, there were daily arrivals of gum arabic, sesame seed, and groundnuts (peanuts); and in the Gedaref District stations, the produce was sesame seed, durra (dari or sorghum), and gum arabic. In Khartoum, produce dealers sold forward contracts[3] of their produce to exporters through local produce brokers.

Within the Gellatly Trading Khartoum head office, the Import Department A, which was the first established, handled the import and sale of wheat flour, tea in bulk, coffee, rice, and soap (initially from Egypt and later from Gellatly's own Sudan Soap Factory in the Khartoum North industrial area). The manager of this department was Fawzi Mikhail, one of my very first assistants in the original Merchandise Department. After Gellatly's nationalization, he left to become the manager of Aboulela Trading Company, one of the largest Sudan firms, and then retired to live in Cairo. Another early assistant was Aziz Galdas, who became the manager and then the director of the Sudan Soap Factory.

During World War II, the import of the main consumer products, especially tea, coffee, and sugar, had to be organized, controlled, and sometimes rationed. Sir Sarsfield Hall, then governor of Khartoum Province, appointed me to the War Supply Board and after the war wrote me a kind letter thanking me for my service on it. This board was composed of some of the major importers, some Sudanese wholesalers and retailers, representatives of the government sugar monopoly, and the Department of Economy and Trade, and was chaired by R. Beer, the Khartoum district commissioner. Simultaneously, I was also a member of the Sudan Chamber of Commerce committee and, at times, its chair, whose function was to regulate the allowable profit margin on all imports. Because of world shortages and difficulties in obtaining supplies during the war, we formed pools for unified purchasing, financing, and distribution of some principal commodities. Thus there was the wheat-flour pool, the tea pool, and the gray sheetings pool. Every pool was composed of the previous importers of the commodity in proportion to their import history, with a percentage reserved for newcomers. In each of these pools, Gellatly Trading was elected the pool agent; therefore, I and my staff conducted all the actual purchasing, distribution, and accounting and had a major role in policy decisions. Using these methods, the country was well served and the Sudan was one of the cheapest and most fairly supplied countries during the war.

In the Import Department B within Gellatly Trading, we handled the import and sale of gray sheeting used for menswear; gunny and jute bags

3. Contracts to deliver produce at a future date.

40. Soap stamping at Sudan Soap Factory, Khartoum North.

41. Unloading heavy vehicles in Port Sudan.

for the packing of all grains, oilseeds, pulses, and gum arabic; hessian cloth for cotton bales, fertilizers, insecticides, and sugar for the Sudan Government Customs Department monopoly. Cotton production was then at its peak, but it was reduced in later years in favor of other schemes and products. Therefore, the Sudan Gezira Board and the Ministry of Agriculture were large buyers of hessian cloth for their cotton bales, jute bags for their cottonseed packing, and fertilizers and insecticides for their cultivation. Gellatly Trading succeeded in securing by tender a substantial part of their purchases of all these items.

The Sudan Gezira Board produced Egyptian-type, long-staple cotton in the Gezira (Ar. Island), which is located between the Blue and the White Nile and is irrigated with water from the Blue Nile. The same type of long-staple cotton was produced by private cotton scheme owners using irrigation from the water of the White Nile and in the Tokar area in the Gash delta. The Ministry of Agriculture, on the other hand, produced American-type short-staple cotton irrigated by rainfall in the Nuba Mountains district and in the South.

Sugar was a government monopoly administered by the Sudan Government Customs Department. At that time, the total of Sudan's enormous requirements of sugar were imported and purchased via periodic tenders. Again, Gellatly succeeded in securing a high percentage of these tenders and in supplying a good part of the Sudan sugar requirements. In the early 1960s, huge schemes for sugarcane cultivation and production were started in the Kenana District, as were the necessary sugar refineries, with the result that by now the Sudan is almost self-sufficient in sugar and is exporting any sugar surplus. Through Gellatly, I handled all this business myself, with help from the Export and the Agencies departments.

Our Agencies Department handled a large number of agencies, extending from Allen and Hanbury pharmaceuticals to Nestle's products; from Catarello Egyptian cigarettes to Benson and Hedges Virginia cigarettes; from calico textiles from Manchester to raw materials for the growing local industries, such as aluminum circles for aluminum pots and polyethylene and other chemicals for the local plastics industry, and hard oils and resins for the soap industry.

Included in the Shell agency were the insecticides and chemicals for controlling cotton-plant diseases, including, among others, those for white ant and ball worm infestations. To control diseases, the cotton fields were sprayed from the air by using small low-flying Piper Cub

42. Gellatly Trading staff at the Sudanese Ministry of Agriculture. *Third from right*, minister of agriculture; *On his right*, Eli Malka, Mrs. and Mr. B. Taylor, George Shuggi; *on his left*, G. Aziz and an aide to the minister.

planes loaded with the appropriate chemical. As part of our service to the cotton growers, we employed an agricultural chemist, Ahmed Abdel Razik, who toured the cotton fields and reported on diseases. At the appropriate times the Piper Cubs and their pilots were brought over from Belgium for the actual spraying, using chemicals we also supplied. Because the chemicals used were harmful and dangerous, great care was taken to empty the fields before the actual spraying; and I am glad to say that no harm to humans was ever reported, although I do remember an occasional strayed donkey was harmed.

The last manager of the Agencies Department was George Shuggi, an old and trusted hand at Gellatly. He progressed to assist me in other departments and, when I left Gellatly, he was asked to replace me as executive director of Gellatly Trading. George Shuggi left the Sudan and retired in the United States, where he had been preceded by his sons Gabby and Camille. He kept in touch with me, and as we were going to press, I was sad to hear of his death in Ontario, Canada.

The Office Machines and Supplies Department and its workshop was another of Gellatly Trading's import departments. With Ahmed Abdel Fatah as its manager, it was the agent of Imperial Typewriter, Gestetner Duplicating Machines, and the like, making available the equipment, its supplies, and the necessary mechanical support service.

Finally, among the import departments of Gellatly Trading was the Buildings Materials Department, with its main depots in the Khartoum industrial area. It imported and stocked every kind of construction steel and material from reinforcing bars, iron beams, expanded metal, wire netting, and aluminum galvanized corrugated sheets to whitewood, red-wood, hardboard, batch and sanitary equipment, paints, cement, and the rest. Its warehouse manager was my old friend Joseph Soriano, a former senior accountant and branch manager; and its import manager, Edmond Kasparian, worked with me at the head office.

One of the major items the Buildings Materials Department dealt with was cement. For a time, we were importing from the British Portland Cement Co. and from the Helwân Portland Cement Co. of Egypt, who were themselves part of the Tiger Cement Group, headquartered in Denmark. I recall that Nyegaard, chairman of the Danish group, came to Khartoum to discuss with A. F. Day, then a senior director of Gellatly's Group, and me the possibility of a cement company in the Sudan. Nyegaard sent in his prospectors from Denmark and Egypt; and based in our Khartoum office, they fanned out throughout the Sudan to find suitable cement deposits. One of them was an Egyptian chemist, Ahmed Effendi, who set up his laboratories in a specially prepared room in our Khartoum office and spent long hours there analyzing samples from deposits sent in from all over the Sudan in an attempt to determine their potential.

In the end, Nyegaard's staff found in the Atbara region of the Northern Province large cement deposits of sufficient quality and size to last a great many years. There, the Sudan Portland Cement Company plants were founded, with their headquarters in the town of Atbara, which also was the headquarters of the Sudan Government Railways. The Sudan Portland Cement Company supplied most of the Sudan's cement requirements, and Gellatly Trading provided all of its marketing agents and distributors throughout the Sudan.

A. F. Day was one of those Britishers who took an interest in trade and commerce and grew with me in business experience. I remember our going together to government land auctions and successfully bidding for vast plots of land in the Khartoum North industrial area for our soap fac-

43. Group of importers. *Third from left*, Abdel Salam Aboulela, president of the Sudan Chamber of Commerce; *fifth from left*, Eli Malka.

tory and oil mills and in the Khartoum industrial area for our building materials depots. We became good friends; and it was a pleasant coincidence that, at one time, the wives of the three directors of Gellatly Trading Co., Dora Malka, Dorothy Carter, and Dorothy Day, all had the same first name.

The Export Department was a very important unit of Gellatly Trading Co. It developed the export of much of the Sudan's produce and established connections for it in the world buying markets. We exported cottonseed from the Sudan Gezira Board project, the Mahdi's Aba Island cotton plantations, and other cotton growers to such world oil mills as Unilever Brothers, whose buying headquarters were in Rotterdam, and to Shemen Oil Mills in Haifa before trade with Israel was stopped in the 1950s. We also participated in the export of Sudan sesame seed to Egypt, Europe, and Japan; groundnuts (peanuts, for which we had our own groundnut decorticating machinery in El-Obeid); oilcakes of all kinds for animal feed; and at one time durra. To Egypt and the Middle East, we exported, other than sesame, melonseed from Kordofan and white haricot beans and horsebeans from the Northern Province. Horsebeans, a variety of fava beans, known commercially as fool masri (Egyptian beans) are also grown in Egypt and are a staple food in both Egypt and the Sudan. They are rich in protein and can be deliciously prepared with spices and various other accompaniments, such as tomatoes and cucumbers, for breakfast or other meals. There are horsebean specialty restaurants in Khartoum, Cairo, Alexandria, and elsewhere, some of which are of wide repute, such as Benyamin in Alexandria and Muhamed El-Fawal[4] in Khartoum. Melonseed is roasted and used in Egypt much as peanuts and popcorn are in the United States.

Gellatly Hankey's staff at the branch in Cairo were the agents for the sale of Sudan produce from our Export Department to Egypt. It was managed by Zaki Fanous, an Egyptian former police officer. That office was sequestered by the Egyptian government after the British, French, and Israeli attack on the Suez Canal in 1956.

Today, I understand that all or most of the Sudan cottonseed and groundnuts are used locally for the production of oil for local consumption. The onetime hope for the Sudan's becoming the food basket for the Middle East has not materialized. Instead, the Sudan, beset by years of drought and famine, now sometimes has to import part of its own food requirements.

Gum arabic and cotton were two important and highly specialized exports from the Sudan whose exporters were very important clients of Gellatly's shipping lines. Gellatly Trading therefore elected not to compete with them in its export. Export of gum arabic is now under the control of a government board. Though electing not to compete in cotton export, we did bid for lots of Gezira Board cotton auctioned in the Sudan Chamber of Commerce in Khartoum on behalf of Rye Evans & Co., one of the largest exporters of Egyptian and Sudan cotton, whose chairman was my friend Alexander Ben-Lassin. I sometimes also negotiated on behalf of Rye Evans for purchases directly from the cotton growers.

One of the first managers of the Export Department was my nephew Mayer Malka. He later joined Rye Evans and Co. as director of their Import Division in Khartoum. Later still, he immigrated to the United States and lives in New Jersey, where he has had a successful business career. Izzat Sami Zakhari succeeded Mayer as manager of the Export Department. After nationalization of Gellatly Hankey, he founded his own

4. Literally, Muhamed the "fool-maker."

Arizona Trading Company in Khartoum and handled on an agency basis many of the same lines formerly handled by Gellatly Trading. In recent years, he has been running it from the Samzuk Trading Co. Ltd., the off-shore company he established in Limassol, Cyprus. Izzat and his companies have kept in close touch with me both in France and in the United States, and he has proved to be an active businessman and loyal associate and friend. I assisted him and his companies in sourcing their Sudan business in Europe and the United States and through him have kept in touch with Sudan affairs.

The last manager of the Export Department was Gamal Aziz Tadros. There, he acquired expertise in Sudan produce and exports; and after nationalization of Gellatly, he also established his own export company in Khartoum, in which I understand he achieved great success.

After nationalization of Gellatly Hankey, all directors were released and all managers of Gellatly departments left. Their departure undoubtedly contributed to the decline of its previous business activities as it continued under its nationalized name, The May Trading Company.

Gellatly Trading was a good training ground for many. When my daughter, Evelyne, was on summer vacation from school at the Faculty of Political and Economic Sciences at Geneva University, she spent a little time in Gellatly Trading departments to see commerce in real action. My son, Jeffrey, on the other hand, when on vacation from medical school, preferred to tour places in the Sudan of historical or cultural interest, such as the Sennar Dam on the Blue Nile in the Sennar district, Wad Medani and its province, and the Gezira Board plantations.

26

✣

Travels in the Sudan and Nearby

Over the years, I had occasion to travel on business to every important city and market in the Sudan and in neighboring countries. My business travels took me from Wadi Halfa, Berber, Atbara, Shendi, Marawi, and Dongola in the North to the Juba region in the South. From Port Sudan, Gedaref, and Kassala in the east to El-Obeid and Dilling in the Nuba Mountains in the west and further on to el-Fasher in Darfur and the furthest end of el-Geneina. I traveled from Wad Medani and Sennar on the Blue Nile to Kosti and Malakal on the White Nile. From Juba by car to Paulis, the center of coffee and palm oil in what used to be the Northern Belgian Congo (now Zaire), and by air to Entebbe and Kampala in Uganda and Nairobi in Kenya.

Traveling in the area was arduous and sometimes required a variety of means to reach the needed destination. From Khartoum, I would travel by air to Asmara in Eritrea and then by car to the Massawa area. Or, from Addis Ababa in Ethiopia by both train and car to Dirdawa and Harrar, the Ethiopian coffee centers. Eager to escape the Khartoum heat, my wife, Dora, accompanied me on some of my voyages to Asmara and Addis Ababa, where owing to their altitude, the weather was cool and pleasant. But that same altitude of 7,000 and 8,000 feet respectively made the air thin and difficult to breath and would make it unpleasant for her first few days there. Although I traveled to these places mainly on business, they were the occasion of many pleasant experiences.

On a trip to Juba, the main town in Southern Sudan, I would rise in the predawn hours and go the bank of the Nile to watch the crocodiles and hippopotamuses, who in these early hours would swim very close to

the banks of the river. I was told of a lion who was in the habit of standing at night on a section of the road about an hour out of Juba. Apparently, he would just stand there and quietly move off to the bush when
occasional car lights would shine in his eyes. On two nights, at midnight,
I was therefore driven out to that section of the road; but someone forgot
to tell the lion, and he did not appear. I complained about this to his
cousins when I saw them running free in the Nairobi National Park,
though what came of it I do not know.

On another visit, my friend George Haggar of Juba drove me an hour
or so out of town and up the mountains to an altitude of 4,000 feet to see
his coffee plantations. It is only at high altitudes that coffee grows, and
these were the first coffee plantations in the Sudan. When a few years
later, Haggar coffee reached the Khartoum market, he built a fine, large
house, where he and his family would visit from time to time from Juba.

In Juba, most of the shopkeepers were Northern Sudanese Muslim
Arabs, but the population in and around Juba was primarily African
Negro blacks. One could see them everywhere, some in their late fifties,
walking around naked or wearing only a small loincloth and surviving on
next to nothing except *bafra,* a flour ground from the bulk of certain
trees. Beautiful mangoes and papayas grew on not-much-tended trees and
could be purchased for very little. Our then Juba manager, Joseph Inglizi,
used to send me packages of these delicious fruits in Khartoum, and the
cost was mostly that of the air freight.

The way to Paulis, a town near Juba in the former Belgian Congo,
passes through elephant country; and once on a car trip there, a dangerous moment occurred when we nearly collided with an elephant protrud-
ing on the road. We were saved only by the quick swerve of our Southern
driver, who was accustomed to such events. In that same area, there was
an elephant's camp run by Belgians, who trained elephants and prepared
them for export to many of the world's zoos. On a visit to their camp,
they showed us around; and we got to ride on some of their elephants.

Once in Paulis, the hotel in which I stayed was filled with Belgian
men, all of whom were either government workers or in business, and
their young wives. A few miles out of town, I visited large Belgian owned
and managed plots where red coffee berries were laid out to dry in the sun
and where palm oil was extracted from trees.

One of my very last trips to Juba was in the company of our new Sudanese director, Sayed Makkawi Suleiman Akrat, so that I could introduce him to some of our branch offices. When finished with our visit to

Juba, we proceeded on by air to Entebbe and from there later to Nairobi. While in Entebbe, we visited the breathtakingly beautiful Lake Victoria, the largest body of sweet water I ever saw. Fascinated by the sight, we stayed for three days in an American hotel on its bank and visited the thunderous foam of Albert Falls, one of the sources of the White Nile. In 1976, this same Entebbe would be the site of the Air France airbus hijacking by Arab terrorists and their German accomplices at the airport. Their treacherous treatment of its mainly Jewish passengers, the theatrical performance of the infamous Idi Amin, and the heroic and spectacular rescue by the Israeli Air Force has been recorded in numerous books. The Israeli commander and hero of that rescue raid was Jonathan Netanyahu, the only Israeli to lose his life in that brave action and the brother of Prime Minister Benjamin Netanyahu.[1]

While in Kampala, the Sudanese ambassador to Uganda, who was a friend of Sayed Akrat, invited us to a dinner party at his home at which many Sudanese officials and friends were present. Early in the evening, I noticed that Captain Sharfi, the Sudanese military attaché in Kampala, quietly left. I subsequently learned that his early depature was on account of a skirmish that had occurred between Sudanese troops and Southern rebel soldiers on the Sudanese-Uganda border.

Later, in Nairobi, a beautiful tropical city with streets lined with flowering plants, we were met by Sir R. S. Campbell, chairman of R. S. Campbell, our Kenyan coffee supplier, who took us to visit well-known Mount Kilimanjaro. Though we did not climb it and only viewed it from the bottom, it was a remarkable sight not easily forgotten. Also from Nairobi, we took a side trip to the world-famous National Park, where animals roam free. We traveled by car on a paved road that ran all through the park and with the wild animals and park guards on all sides. As soon as we entered the park proper, a group of baboons, true to their nature, jumped on top of our car and rode along with us. On either side were herds of zebras, giraffes, and other animals sauntering freely along. We spent hours watching several families of lions, sleeping in threes and fours under their trees. Told that they would usually walk around in the

---

1. I had occasion to meet Benjamin Netanyahu in New York when he was Israel's ambassador to the United Nations, at the historic Spanish Portuguese Synagogue. This event was a party given by the American Sephardic Federation on the occasion of Spain's establishing diplomatic relations with Israel. Both Netanyahu and the Spanish ambassador were present and spoke knowingly of the Sephardic Jewish history in Spain.

afternoon, we waited for hours in our car; but they never rose from their lazy stupor while we were there.

In the Sudan, I recall an interesting visit to El-Fasher, capital of Darfur Province, once an autonomous sultanate under Sultan Ali Dinar. Ali Dinar ruled Darfur from El-Fasher for a time after the Mahdi state had been overthrown. He in turn was overthrown; and El-Fasher was annexed by the Sudan government in 1916, under the then governor general of the Sudan, Sir Reginald Wingate. I visited Ali Dinar's palace in El-Fasher. It was the most impressive building in the town, a tropical, two-story building that later became the Sudan Government Darfur Province Headquarters.

Earlier in history, El-Fasher and Darfur were first conquered in 1874 by El-Zubayr Rahma Pasha for the Egyptian government, under the Khedive Ismail. El-Zubayr Rahma was a notorious slave raider, slave trader, and merchant prince who controlled the caravan routes and slave trade in Bahr El-Ghazal and its surroundings. His power and influence was such that Khedive Ismail made him governor of Bahr El-Ghazal. Later, he was authorized to invade El-Fasher on behalf of the Egyptian government; and when he successfully accomplished this feat, he was granted the title of pasha and became known thereafter as El-Zubayr Rahma Pasha. Between 1881 and 1883, Darfur was administered for the Egyptian government by Austrian-born Rudolf Slatin Pasha, who had been named governor of Darfur. Darfur was subsequently conquered by the Mahdi, and Slatin Pasha became the well-known, long-time prisoner of the Mahdi.

Dilling, the capital of Nuba Mountains Province, provided another interesting trip. In 1933, I was in El-Obeid for a couple of months to replace Gellatly's El-Obeid manager, who was on his annual leave. While there, I received a telegram from Khartoum that my managing director, D. McFarlane, and his wife were coming to El-Obeid to visit the Nuba General Assembly in Dilling and requesting me to make the necessary arrangements.

Dilling and the Nuba Mountains, like the other Southern provinces whose native populations were mostly non-Arab, non-Muslim pagans, was a "closed district" to Northern traders and Muslim influence; and visitors from the North were only allowed in by special permit. I therefore telephoned the British district commissioner in El-Obeid, who granted me and the Greek driver I engaged for the car trip from El-Obeid to Dilling the necessary permits to accompany the McFarlanes. On arriving at Dilling, we went to the Dilling home of our Gellatly agent, Mr. Shami, and his wonderful wife, a native of the Nuba Mountains who had attended the Christian missionary schools. There, we found a representative of the British district commissioner with instructions to whisk the McFarlanes off to the British District House for the night and next morning's General Assembly celebrations. They left us to enjoy alone the sumptuous dinner and excellent quarters Mrs. Shami had prepared for all of us.

In classic British style, the next morning we were excluded from the Nuba General Assembly, which was held early in the morning entirely for the benefit of the British Community. After the ceremonies were over, we saw groups of Nuba participants roaming about in Dilling, both men and women completely naked, or almost, except for grass ornaments, spears, and the like. Later that morning, I retrieved the McFarlanes from the Dilling British commissioner's office; and when I went in to meet the commissioner, was saluted at the door of his office by a Nuba soldier personal guard, again essentially naked, except for a small wraparound. It still amazes me that the whole place was governed in 1933 by a single Britisher, whom the natives held in respect and awe.

27

⚜

Marriage, Family, and Children

I was married in the Khartoum Synagogue in November 1934 to Dora Goldenberg. She was twenty and I was twenty-five. Her brother Maurice Goldenberg in Khartoum had already married my sister Rachel two years earlier; and while visiting his brother Pascal in Cairo in 1933, I met her at her brother Bernard's home. She and her sister Ida were part of a group of five young ladies whom I recall spent long hours listening to opera and classical music recordings. She had been orphaned at a young age and had been brought up by her elder married brother Pascal, who was the main optician in Cairo. We went out dancing, and I became enamored of her. I did not however feel that I was ready for marriage at the time and returned to Khartoum.

Early in 1934, Dora and her younger sister Ida came to spend some-time with their brother Maurice Goldenberg in Khartoum and fre-quented the Jewish Recreation Club, where most Jews congregated nightly. There these young, fashionably attired, attractive red heads were a great hit and were swarmed by the local young Jewish men, who likened them to movie starlets. I quickly realized that I had better make a move or risk losing Dora to the competition, and I therefore courted my red-headed future bride and asked her to marry me. When she agreed, I asked for her hand in marriage from her guardian and elder brother Pascal Goldenberg. We were engaged on 10 June, just days before Nahum Sokolov, the president of the World Zionist Organization, visited Khar-toum, the preparation for which we worked on together.

We were of very different backgrounds. She had been brought up in French Catholic boarding schools (Mère de Dieu) of Rumanian ancestry. French and Italian were her mother tongues; and like many Europeans in Egypt, she spoke no Arabic. She loved opera and classical music and

179

would spend hours listening and discussing them with her friends. I, on the other hand, was brought up in the English and Arabic cultures, both of which she knew little; and my tastes went more towards light dance music and Sephardic and Arabic tunes. Love and youth soon bridged our differences; and we had a very happy marriage, experiencing life in its fullest and expanding our cultural horizons in our many travels and adventures.

We had three children. The first, Jenny, died at age six in Khartoum in 1942. She was the victim of an accidental burn while in the care of a babysitter. The anguish and grief for her loss remained with us for a long time. Our son, Jeffrey Solomon, then one and a half years old, and the coming of his sister Evelyne five years later helped us go on with our lives. Dora's attachment, love, and care of these two children was so intense she could not bear to have them out of her sight. From infancy, she spoke to them in French, and they grew up French-speaking at home. As toddlers, they were sent to private nurseries and kindergarten run by British ladies for the British children of Khartoum, and there they learned English. From then on, they learned to address me only in English, their mother only in French, and their Sudanese nannies and our servants in Arabic, which they picked up from them.

Dora always wanted the children to have a European education and orientation. Because they were little kids, we took them with us on our two- to three-month summer vacations in Europe, spending some of the time in Swiss mountain "children's homes" (similar to our summer camps in the United States), usually in and around Villars sur Ollon and later in Swiss finishing schools in and around Lausanne, where they enjoyed beautiful outings, sports, and points of finer education.

When Evelyne was six and Jeffrey eleven, we sent them to study at the English-French classes of the International School of Geneva, accompanied by their mother. At the end of that school year, however, we decided it was too hard for us and too early for them to start on their own in Europe. We therefore took them back to Khartoum, where Evelyne was enrolled in the Unity High School for girls and Jeffrey at Comboni College. Both of these schools followed the model of English schools and prepared students for the English General Certificate of Education (similar to the American High School diploma).

During the year that Jeffrey was at the International School of Geneva, he started his bar mitzvah studies with Professor Danielli of Geneva University. Back in Khartoum, he was bar-miztvahed in the

Khartoum Synagogue in 1953; and the evening celebrations were held in the open air at the Jewish Recreation Club, with a large party of music, dancing, food, and drink. It was a great event, attended by about three hundred fifty of our Jewish and non-Jewish friends and lasted far into the night as the band played on.

After Jeffrey finished his secondary schooling and obtained his Oxford Certificate of Education, we sent them both to England for their further education. Evelyne was enrolled at Wycombe Abbey at High Wycombe, one of the finer private English boarding schools, where she was sur-rounded by daughters of British aristocracy and nobility. Jeffrey went to Whittingham College in Brighton for his pre-med studies. Because Whit-tingham was a private English Jewish school, he met and made friends with children of prominent Jewish families, such as the Safras, Jamals, and Zilkas, as well as some Saudi Arabian boys, who were enrolled there to ensure they would not be fed pork. During both the short and longer school holidays, Evelyne and Jeffrey came home to Khartoum or joined us on our summer vacations touring Europe.

To achieve schooling abroad, it was necessary to be able to exchange Sudanese currency into European funds. My good friend, Oxford-educated Sayed Mamoun Beheiry, a co-member of the Rotary Club of Khartoum and a former governor of the Bank of Sudan, who was then minister of finance of the Sudan, helped me to achieve this by approving the transfer in foreign currency with adequate annual allowances for the education of my two children abroad and for my wife's and my travels abroad. This facility was also approved for other Sudanese subjects edu-cating their children abroad.

When Jeffrey finished his pre-med studies in England, we took both children to Geneva, where Jeffrey entered the School of Medicine of Geneva University and Evelyne enrolled at the International School of Geneva to finish her high school studies. After that, she enrolled in the Faculty of Political and Economic Studies of the University of Geneva. During this stage of our lives, I bought a six-room apartment in Geneva, where Dora lived and cared for our two children while they continued their studies. We usually arranged to spend our Passover holidays in our Khartoum home and other Jewish holidays in our Geneva home. We be-came members of the Maison Juive (Jewish house) of Geneva and the Geneva Sephardic Synagogue. There, we resumed our friendship and as-sociation with the Khartoum Jews who had established themselves in Geneva, families such as the Gaons, the Tammans, and the El-Einis.

In the early years of our marriage, we would vacation in Cairo, Alexandria, or Lebanon. The trip to Cairo by rail and steamer is a fascinating one, which I described earlier and which I well recall. Later, the trip was undertaken on seaplanes landing on the river Nile, and later yet on planes from regular airports. In Cairo, a very cosmopolitan place at the time, we would hit the town, visiting such popular spots as "Gropie's" famous pastry and tea shop, the Alfie street brasseries, and of course the pyramids and sphinx. We would also visit with my sister Fortunée Goldring and Dora's brother Pascal Goldenberg and their families. In Alexandria were the glorious beaches of Sporting, Stanley Bey, and Sidi Bishr; the restaurants and hotels on the beach; and the evening rides in horse-driven carriages along the corniche. By 1951, the date of our last visit to Egypt, the atmosphere had changed; and the anti-Jewish and anti-European attitude of the population was palpable. That year, we continued our vacation by boarding a ship of the Castle Union Line to Genoa and Marseilles and on to Rome and other parts of Europe. On following years, we skipped Egypt, flying straight through to London or Rome to start our vacations in various parts of Europe, such as the French Riviera.

28

⟡

Life in Khartoum

Thanks to the opportunities and achievements I had in the Sudan, we led an average upper-middle-class life in Khartoum. Despite the politics surrounding Jews, Arabs, and Israel that separated our paths, I still feel a great love for the Sudan and its people and remember with affection the years we grew and lived there and the many good friends, both Sudanese and non-Sudanese that we made.

We lived in a two-story villa that was designed and built to our specifications in 1942 by the Greek architect Stephanides, then a very prominent architect in Khartoum who was responsible for beautifying many of Khartoum's private houses. Our house, like most of the modern houses constructed in the 1940s and 1950s, was located in Khartoum's East Side. Later, more were built in the new Khartoum suburban extensions called Khartoum Nos. 1 and 2.

In the summer, which was the major part of the year, we slept in a large open terrace on the second floor. It was surrounded by a low cornice wall embedded with colorful, fragrant plantings and was in direct proximity to our indoor bedrooms. A little after sundown, which was always around 6:30 P.M., there was a cool, dry desert breeze that made for a pleasant night's sleep and was preferable to sleeping indoors, even with ceiling fans and air-conditioning. My son, who was at the time greatly interested in astronomy, delighted in observing the night sky studded with a myriad of sparkling stars in that unpolluted, cloudless, crystal-clear, desert sky.

It was always ten degrees cooler out on our lawn, surrounded by the bougainvilleas, than on the adjoining covered verandas that surrounded the house. It was therefore on this lawn, installed with armchairs and the necessary electrical equipment, that we spent many of our early evenings and received our friends. For our cocktail and dinner parties, we used the

44. My family.

garden lawn, the verandas, and the large 45-foot-long dining and sitting room, which we called the salon. The salon was fitted with ceiling fans and desert coolers on the open windows to bring in fresh, cool air. During formal parties when, after greeting the guests, the children had been sent to bed on the terrace, they would stay up late into the night, peaking over the terrace wall at the activities on the lawn below and rushing back to bed pretending deep sleep when my wife and I would intermittently check on them.

In the winter, which was from about mid-December to the end of February, the weather was beautiful, dry, and sometimes just cool enough to require a sweater or jacket, but mild enough to have evening parties on a grass lawn or dances on an open dance floor. Overcoats were never needed, and most people did not even own them. This was the busy social season, crowded with the annual balls at various clubs; Christmas and New Year's Eve parties; and cocktail parties given by embassies, banks, companies, and social friends.

During this social season, we were invited to many parties given by our Sudanese, British, and other communities social and business friends. One of these bears describing. It was the three nights of celebrations given by Sayed Mustapha Abou El-Ela on the occasion of the wedding of his British college-educated son to the first Sudanese female medical doc-

45. Annual Community ball at the Jewish Recreation Club. *Left to right*, Habib Cohen, Eli S. Malka, Solomon Shaoul, Bertha Shaoul, Esther Kaminsky, Dora Malka, Israel Kaminsky, Jeannette Cohen.

46. At the wedding of Saʾad, son of Sayed Mustapha Abou El-Ela, a friend and prominent businessman in the Sudan. *Left to right*, Mustapha Abou el-Ela welcoming Dora Malka, Mrs. Hakim, and Eli Malka.

tor in the Sudan. One of these nights of celebration, which my wife and I attended, was specifically for European friends and their wives and was held in the vast Abou El-Ela mansion and gardens in Omdurman. After dinner, served in grand European style, our wives were invited to the women's quarter of the house, where they were entertained to an all-women Sudanese dance party. As is traditional at these parties, the bride, in this case a substitute native dancer, attired in a sheer scarf and with her hair in a long African-style braid hanging down her back, danced for the group. The only man allowed was the bridegroom; and while the entourage clapped their hands in time with rhythmic native music, the bride "substitute" greeted the guest of honor with a traditional *shabbal* (swinging her hair over the groom).

My wife, Dora, and the other guests with her who had never seen this tradition before came out of the private party enchanted and with the souvenir of a lifetime. We, the men, were not that lucky and were left on the lawn to our conversations and entertainment.

Of the other two nights of entertainment, one was reserved for Sudanese men; and it was at these celebrations that the actual marriage contract was usually celebrated by the bride and bridegroom's agents or representatives and verses from the Qur'an were recited. There then followed food, dinner, and rejoicing. The third night was reserved for Sudanese native women friends alone and involved native dancing and entertainment.

In this pre-TV era, we had a box, twice a week throughout the year, permanently reserved for us and our children in the two large open-air cinemas of Khartoum. These were the Blue Nile Cinema on the Blue Nile embankment, converted from the previous British army cinema, and the Coliseum Cinema on Victoria Avenue in the center of Khartoum, on the site that had previously been our Maccabi Sports Club. These huge open-air cinemas had several rows of elevated boxes in the rear, enclosing seats and a table for snacks, and an orchestra seating area in the front half for individual seats. They showed the latest western films, both American and European, preceded by a Movietone or similar roundup of world news and usually a cartoon feature. Occasionally, we would go with our children to the Watania (National) Cinema, which would also show in addition Egyptian Arabic films, quite a few of which were entertaining.

Other times, we would spend an evening at the Jewish Recreation Club, where we would socialize with our Jewish friends, or visit each other at our homes. Sometimes, we would go out with friends on a dinner outing either at the Grand Hotel or at two or three other European restaurants or simply spend an afternoon on the veranda of the Grand Hotel, facing the Blue Nile. The children favored going to the large well-stocked zoo, also on the bank of the Blue Nile, or to the Moghren, the treed park located at the junction of the Blue and White Niles, where a delicious Sunday brunch of well-seasoned foul medames (stewed fava beans), felafels, and similar dishes could be had, after which the children had great fun playing in the park and along the bank of the Blue Nile with their friends.

Our cocktail and dinner parties were rather special if I may say so. Our cook was a European-style chef with a vast repertoire of elegant French and European dishes and the envy of many. Before coming into our employ, he had been trained and served as the cook of the British director of the National Bank of Egypt in Alexandria. Our children loved him and called him *Ammy Hassan* (Uncle Hassan), and he spoiled them whenever they came home on vacation from school in Europe. He used to meet them at the Khartoum airport on their arrival at two o'clock in the morning, the hour at which international flights arrived at Khartoum and when the heat was at its lowest. Both he and our two *suffragis* (waiters) were *barabra* (speakers of foreign languages), the plural of *barbari*, the name given to the tribes from around Dongola and the Sudan-Egyptian border north of Wadi Halfa. They were called barabra because, among themselves, they spoke a Nubian language foreign to Arabic in the same manner that the quarter where Yiddish-speaking Ashkenazi Jews living in Cairo was called Darb El-Barabra, the quarter of foreigners. My wife, Dora, was herself an excellent cook and contributed her own specialties and delicious pastries to our dinners and parties, though I much preferred that she remain away from the kitchen heat, despite the fans I installed in both the kitchen and the pantry.

Around 1934–1935, when we were newly married, we lived in a rented, one-story house and had one man, who served as cook and general servant, and a maid, who helped and kept company with my young wife, Dora. She later became the first nanny of our children. My next-door neighbor at the time was Joseph Tammam and his then young children, Leon (now in London), Albert, Gabriel (now in Geneva), and his daughter Renée, now the wife of Nessim Gaon, the Sephardic philanthropist in Geneva. Our terraces were separated by a mere wall, over which Joseph and I would converse and exchange the news of the day.

The hottest months in Khartoum were April to June, at which time the temperature would reach 100 degrees Fahrenheit but could reach 110 to 115 degrees Fahrenheit. Because of the dryness, 100 degrees Fahrenheit was uncomfortable but tolerable; but when the thermometer reached 110 degrees Fahrenheit or more, it became very trying. Fortunately, it did not stay at these high levels for too many consecutive days. This was also the sandstorm season. These *haboubs,* as they were locally called, could last for hours, during which the furious gusts of thick, fine dust would darken the air, turning day into night and with loss of visibility beyond a few inches. The gusts were powerful enough to blow over a person or object caught in their path; and the fine dust penetrated eyes, noses, and homes. During a haboub, all doors and windows were tightly shut, as we huddled indoors with the ceiling fans on. Despite pads to render all doors and windows as airtight as possible, the sand would still penetrate the shuttered houses, requiring a massive cleanup effort once the storm was over. For these reasons, we always tried to take our vacations in May and June to escape the heat and sandstorms, spending them sometimes in the cool, refreshing Swiss mountain stations in Villars sur Ollon or Crans sur Sierre, where the greenery alone was reinvigorating after the desert sands, and other times on the beaches of Cannes and Nice in France.

In the Sudan, there was a hill station on the Red Sea near Port Sudan called Erkawit, with a 3,000-foot mountain called Gebel Seila (mountain of Seila). The Sudan Railways built a small hotel camp there with full "grand hotel" service and offered a ten-day vacation package, including sleeping car accommodation from and to Khartoum at a reasonable price. My wife, Dora, and I and our six-year-old son, Jeffrey, went there once in the company of our friends and family physician Dr. and Mrs. John Papadam. Sayed Abdel Rahman El-Mahdi had his summer retreat in Erkawit; and when he heard that Dr. John Papadam, son of a Greek from the time of his father's Mahdiya, was there, he invited us and our wives to his camp for tea. There, following the familiar pattern he used everywhere, a Khalifa, or agent received us, made us welcome, and seated us, after which Sayed Abdel Rahman walked in, causing us to stand up for him and then continue our visit, which was of course enjoyed and appreciated.

In those early years before 1939, we would spend part of our vacations in the beautiful mountain stations of Alai, Dhour El-Shewir, and Bhamdoun in Lebanon; and in the 1940s, on the Mediterranean shores of Alexandria in its well-developed beaches of Sporting, Ibrahimia, Stanley

Bey, and Sidi Bishr. In all my life, I can honestly say that I have never encountered more beautiful shores with miles and miles of continuous white sand and well-developed beaches than those along the coast of Alexandria at that time. What has now become of these beautiful beaches I, unfortunately, cannot tell.

In July and August, the heat in Khartoum would be cooled down by the seasonal rainfall that occurred at that time, and the weather became pleasant again. But by mid-August, September, and sometimes into October, the heat would return, this time worse because of the humidity from the rainy season. This was the time of mosquitoes; biting flies; and from the banks of the Nile nemetti, very small flying insects attracted by light, which were a real nuisance and hard to avoid. We simply had to put up with these pests until November, with its better weather followed by the beautiful winter months.

29

ᕕᕕ

Life in the United States
and France

On 5 January 1966, my dear wife, Dora, succumbed to her cancer after two years of struggle in London and Geneva. She was buried on a cloudy, rainy day at the Jewish Cemetery of Geneva,[1] which was actually located in Veyrier, France, a village just across the Swiss border. This was because of the Swiss regulations preventing religiously separated cemeteries in Switzerland or the burial of the dead body directly in the soil, as required by Jewish law. Likewise, slaughtering for kosher meat was not allowed in Geneva. We therefore ordered our meat kosher meat from French Basle or from Zurich. More recently, kosher meat has been brought into Geneva from the nearer French border.

After Dora's passing, the dream of renewing our lives in the United States was revived. There was considerable urgency in proceeding with this decision because our Sudanese passports were rapidly expiring, Evelyne's having only six months left, and were not likely to be renewed by the Sudanese authorities. In this effort, the American consul in Geneva was truly helpful and sympathetic. She facilitated the immigration process by waiving such time-consuming or impossible-to-obtain requirements as police certificates from our previous residence in the Sudan and by expediting the process of granting immigration visas for the three of us, my two children and myself, enabling us to proceed to the United States before the pending expiration of my daughter's passport.

Before her passport expired, Evelyne and I first flew to New York on immigrant visas during the three-week Easter vacation of the University

---

1. Grave No. 508.

190

Monday

Call
 x Dave
 Punch a guy
 Delta return Aug.
 x Deb

write
 David Beasley

9 Concha Penny

Marriott

HOTELS · RESORTS · SUITES

of Geneva, to which she would return with her American "green card" to complete the last semester of her studies to obtain her License degree (master's) in political and economic sciences. In the United States, we were warmly welcomed by my brothers Sam and David and sister Allegra Sasson and their families, who had immigrated ten years earlier. They competed in taking us to their New Jersey homes and helped us in every way possible.

In the three weeks we spent in New Jersey and New York, we obtained our green cards; I rented a three-bedroom apartment on the seventeenth floor of the then newly built Mediterranean Towers in Fort Lee, New Jersey, with a glorious view overlooking the George Washington Bridge and Manhattan Island; and rented office space on the twelfth floor of the Business Office Building at 580 Fifth Avenue, located at the corner of Forty-seventh Street in Manhattan. During those same three weeks, I registered my American company, The Malka Mobaso Corporation of New York, in partnership with my Geneva partner Moshé Baroukh Soleiman, using the services of New York attorney the late Arthur Levitt, to whom my brother Sam, may he rest in peace, had introduced me.

When all three of us returned to the United States in August 1966 as permanent residents, our home in Fort Lee and my business office in Manhattan were ready for our immediate occupation. Jeffrey went straight into his orthopaedic residency at Mount Sinai Hospital in New York City, in which he had been accepted before his arrival.

Within three years of entering the United States as immigrants, our lives and careers took a new turn. My son Jeffrey married Susan Gelfand, daughter of Dr. and Mrs. Morris Gelfand of Philadelphia, in November 1967. Seven months later, he was drafted into the U.S. Army during the height of the Vietnam War and became Major Jeffrey Malka, assistant chief of orthopaedics at the 106th General Hospital, U.S. Army, in Japan, where the more severely wounded were evacuated from the Vietnam arena for their care.

Evelyne landed her first job in the United Nations Association of the United States in New York as program assistant, then joined the American Express Company as correspondent in the Foreign Remittance Department. In 1969, she joined the Chase Manhattan Bank, N.A., New York. After extensive postgraduate courses and training, she ascended the corporate ladder from the Credit Policy Division to become the credit and marketing officer for U.S. Regions and, by 1982, the vice-president for International Private Banking, responsible for Global Asset Management for European, Asian, Canadian, and Caribbean clients of high net worth. In 1974, she married David Klein, then of Peat, Marwick, Mitchell and Co. International Accounting firm, now director of finance and controller of Sarah Lawrence College, New York. Since January 1988, Evelyne Klein has been serving as senior vice-president of the Republic National Bank of New York in charge of international private banking throughout Europe and the Far East in recognition of her considerable professional banking capabilities. In the meantime, I dissolved my partnership in Malka Mobaso Corporation of New York and joined the prestigious firm of Phillip Brothers Division of Engelhards Minerals and Chemicals Corporation as the export sales manager of their steel department in New York, where my Sudan experience in international and steel businesses was of great benefit. There, I met the chairman and founder of Phillip Brothers, the righteous Jewish philanthropist Ludwig Jesselson, may he rest in peace. He counted me among his near business associates; and by his strict Jewish conduct in office and home and leadership in all Jewish efforts whether in the United States or Israel, gave me and many others an example of business leadership combined with proper Jewish conduct and endeavor. He died in Jerusalem in Sha'ar Zedek Hospital, which he had founded and generously supported, just as he had supported Yeshiva University in New York and many other institutions in the United States and Israel.

Life in France

In 1973, I retired from my job at Phillip Brothers and left for Paris, France, where I married in December 1973 my present wife, Bertha, and established my Paris office, the Malka Trading Company. Bertha was the widow of my Sudan friend Suleiman Shaoul, who died of cancer in Athens in 1968, two years after my own wife, Dora, had passed away from cancer in Geneva. Bertha, whom we fondly call Bettina, was warmly welcomed by my brothers and sisters, all of whom were friends from the Sudan, and by my children, whom she knew from their childhood in Khartoum. My grandchildren adopted her as their grandma, and she loves them, enjoys them, and spoils them with me.

Bettina and I found in our marriage a new life and new happiness. Together, we renewed our lives with revived energy, high spirits, and hopes. She continued with her Paris job in Cojasor, the Comité Juif d'Action Sociale et de Reconstruction, that helped the Jewish refugees from Egypt,

Lebanon, and Syria to reestablish themselves in France; the Jewish poor to reconstruct their lives; and the old to find comfort and care in their several Jewish homes in many parts of France. I established my Malka Trading Company in Rue Amsterdam in Paris; and we lived in Bettina's apartment, which she had purchased ten years earlier, located in the Paris suburb of Boulogne-Billancourt,[2] next to her French sister and nieces.

I joined the Synagogue de Boulogne, built in 1912 by Baron Edmond de Rothschild (1854–1934), for his own use and the use of the Jewish congregation of Boulogne-Billancourt. He commissioned the then famous Italian architect Emmanuel-Elisée Pontremoli (1865–1956) to design and construct it. It came out a beautiful edifice that faced the baron's own residence and spacious gardens across the street, since donated for public use and now know as Rothschild Parc. It is a spacious synagogue, with a four-hundred-person capacity and a traditional women's gallery all around on the second floor facing the Heikhal, and is filled to capacity on most Shabbats. In the first half of the twentieth century, Baron Rothschild gave this synagogue away to the *Consistoire de Paris* (Consistory of Paris) for the use of the Boulogne-Billancourt congregation, which today is mostly constituted of French Jews from Algeria and Morocco and a small minority of old French Jews from Alsace. I met there my friend Claude Bloch, then the president of the Boulogne-Billancourt congregation and the B'nai B'rith Loge de France in Paris. I immediately joined the Loge de France and continued my active participation in its work for the benefit of the Jewish people.

The Malka Trading Company soon did a fairly substantial business in French and European exports to the Sudan, usually on an exclusive export agency basis. My Khartoum connections, mostly the Arizona Trading Company, whose principal, Izzat Sami Zakhari, was my former associate at Gellatly, Khartoum, supplied the clients and enquiries; and I sourced them from such powerful French companies as Rhone Poulenc Polymeres and C. D. F. Chimie for plastic raw materials for the Sudan plastic industry, Cegedur-Pechiney for aluminum circles for the aluminum pots and pans industry in the Sudan, USINOR Steel for constructional steel, Société Générale de Fonderies for sanitary ware and

2. Boulogne-Billancourt, which borders the Bois de Boulogne on the outskirts of Paris, is the nearest suburb of Paris. By the Metro, it is 5 minutes to the 16th arrondisement (Paris ward) and 15 minutes to the Champs Elysées, the center of Paris.

bathrooms. I supplied them also with cement from Spain, yeast from Greece and France, and other commodities from Germany, France, and Italy.

While in Paris, we had the pleasure of enjoying Bettina's French family as well as many old and new friends from France, Egypt, and the Sudan. We purchased a French Peugeot car, which we used on weekends and holidays to tour throughout France, and we also visited London, Belgium, Italy, and Switzerland. Once a year, we would go to the United States for a month's vacation, visiting family and friends, my children and their families, Evelyne in White Plains, New York, and Jeffrey in Vienna and McLean, Virginia. The last week or ten days, we would reserve for a little vacation for ourselves in an American resort in places such as Hawaii, California, or the Virginia beaches.

In 1980, we decided it was time to relocate to the United States to be closer to our American children and their families. Bettina retired from her Paris job in Cojasor, and I liquidated the Malka Trading Company of Paris. By September 1981, we had returned to settle in the United States, Bettina entering as an immigrant and obtaining her American citizenship three years later. I purchased a condominium duplex apartment in White Plains within fifteen minutes drive from our daughter Evelyne's home and six hours drive from Jeffrey in the Northern Virginia suburbs of Washington, D.C. An hour's drive from our home were my brothers and sisters in New Jersey.

In September 1981, during the first month of our arrival in White Plains, we joined Temple Israel Center of Conservative Judaism and the Bʾnai Bʾrith Unit in White Plains, thus continuing our identification with the Jewish Community wherever we went and the observance of our Jewish laws and traditions. In Bʾnai Bʾrith, I continued my life commitment to Bʾnai Bʾrith principles and service to the Jewish people, Jewish causes, and support of Israel. This was the way of life I had adopted for myself since I served Bʾnai Bʾrith in the Khartoum Lodge from 1934 to 1950, the Loge de France in Paris from 1973 to 1981, and in the United States from 1981 to this day.

In 1986, I was elected president of the White Plains Bʾnai Bʾrith unit. During my two-year term, I energized it, multiplied its activities and public meetings, and encouraged the younger members to come and take over our offices so as to ensure renewal and continuity. In 1988, I celebrated the fortieth anniversary of the White Plains Lodge No. 1749 (later Unit 5249) by publicly honoring the ten presidents who had served it from 1959 to 1988 and two charter members who had remained with it since its founding in 1948. In recognition of their service and commitment to B'nai B'rith, I presented each of them with a bust of our master Moses, our lawmaker and liberator.

With the problems and worries of emigration from an Arab country and resettlement now behind us, I started fully to enjoy the religious liberty, equality of rights and opportunity, and freedom of political expression so precious and valued by those who have not lived with them previously.

I went on to join the organizations around me concerned with Jewish causes and the support of Israel. I joined the Westchester Jewish Conference and served on its Israel Action Committee. I became a member of the American Israel Political Action Committee (AIPAC) and participated in debates and campaigns to urge members of the U.S. Congress to support strong U.S.–Israel relations, strategic cooperation, military and economic aid to Israel, and loan guarantees to ease the settlement of Soviet and Ethiopian Jewish immigrants to Israel.

I also enrolled for the following eight semesters in classes on Jewish studies at nearby SUNY, Purchase. It was there that I had the privilege of getting to know and studying under Professor Roberta Barkan, the coordinator of Jewish Studies Programs at the University. Through her, I improved my knowledge of Hebrew Jewish literature and history and discussed many of the existing Jewish problems. Like many in the Westchester Jewish Community, I have a high regard for this lady, who participates in every Jewish endeavor in the area and has helped us in our B'nai B'rith programs for the benefit of Jewish college students. In her, I gained a friend and a teacher; and through her classes, I made many interesting friends, young and old.

Visits to Israel

Once in the United States, I was able to resume my regular visits to Israel. In 1967, a year after we immigrated, I flew to Israel accompanied by my daughter, Evelyne, and traveled to Israel almost yearly thereafter. Before that, my last visit to Israel from the Sudan was in 1951, after which all travel from Arab countries to Israel was banned.

My first visit to Eretz Israel from the Sudan was in 1928 at the age of nineteen. My father persuaded me to use the first two months' vacation I had from my Gellatly Hankey to make my first pilgrimage to the Holy

Land and visit his sister Alia in their native town of Tiberias. I traveled from Khartoum, second class (which was not so comfortable, but who cares at nineteen?), on a five-day rail and river journey to Cairo, thence by railway to Palestine through Qantara, El-Arish, and Refah on to Jerusalem. In Jerusalem, I had to go and pay my respects and present my father's greetings to Rabbi Ouziel Ben-Zion Meir, chief rabbi of Tel Aviv and thereafter rishon le Zion (chief rabbi of Israel). I was in awe of him, but he made me feel comfortable.

In Tel Aviv, I joined a group of youths led by a young man named Abraham, to whom I had an introduction from his brother-in-law, Israel Maller, in Khartoum. Abraham included me in a group of some ten Jewish boys and girls of our age, and together every evening we made the rounds of the Tel Aviv nightspots. Thereafter, a Sabra named Shoshana and a Lithuanian-born girl named Rifka corresponded with me for a long time.

In Haifa, I explored the Carmel and Hadar Hacarmel with its cafés and one evening even ventured to go down and see the Arab belly dancers and singers in the Arab cafés on the shore. I had a great time and nothing bad happened to me.

To reach Tiberias, I took a seat in a sherut (shared) taxi. Once there, I stayed for ten piasters a night in an old hotel built of beautiful Palestinian stone right on the bank of Lake Tiberias. On later visits, I looked for it and, in the 1980s, finally found it hidden by trees and having become a restaurant and bar.

In Tiberias, I was taken to the Shabbat morning service at the big synagogue and was introduced to the Hakham, Rabbi Raphael Bibas, a friend and colleague of my father since their Morocco days. He made me sit on his wooden bench behind the teba and gave me an *alia*[3] to the Sepher Torah. Following the Shabbat service, I was taken to my aunt Alia Malka's home in old Tiberias, where some thirty acquaintances and relatives gathered to see and make the acquaintance of Rabbi Shlomo Malka's son. Aunt Alia's son, Salim, had brought a damajan (a demijohn, or 2-gallon jar) of arrak, the strong anise-based drink similar to the Greek ouzo; and we had a good time, though I never saw most of them again. In the afternoon, we went to the house in modern Tiberias of my cousin Rachel Battan, the charming and intelligent daughter of my aunt Alia. In the evening, she and her husband and two sons took me to the just

3. An alia means being called to read from the Torah scrolls during the Torah service.

starting Kiriat Shamuel, a beautiful, newly built, modern development on the hilly heights of old Tiberias. In later years Kiriat Shamuel became a large town in its own right. As happens so often to good people, Rachel died of cancer at the early age of fifty.

On my last trip from the Sudan in 1951, I was on a business trip to Haifa. My business agents in Haifa, Steel Brothers, lodged me in their director's house on the French Carmel and entertained me at the still-exclusive British Club in Haifa. One evening, I took the opportunity to visit my own beautiful niece Giselle, daughter of my sister Fortunée Goldring. She and her husband, David Tueta, had fled Egypt to Israel and had been placed in a large absorption camp outside Haifa. It was a huge place, and I had a hard time finding them. I finally did locate them. Like the others, they had been placed in a small wooden shack and had a hard time of it; but they seemed quite happy to get away from Egypt and to be in Israel. Aware of my niece's husband's experience in shipping matters, I gave him a letter of recommendation to Shemen Oil Mills in Haifa, a client and the largest Israeli producer of vegetable oils to which I sold Sudan cottonseed. They soon placed him in the Haifa office of Zim's Shipping Company, where I believe he served till his death in Haifa.

In one of our more recent visits to Haifa, this time with my wife, Bertha, in the mid-1980s, my niece Giselle came to visit us in our hotel. We were staying at the Dan Carmel of Haifa. From the hotel, the view of the blue Mediterranean filled the horizon, framed by the sky which, in the evening, took on glorious reddish hues as the invigorating cool sea breeze drifted in toward land. Giselle, still stunningly beautiful and in good form at age sixty, was then widowed and with two married sons. Her son Shai later died as a victim of a bomb while on his way out of Lebanon with the Israeli Army.

Bettina and I have had many other visits from the United States to all parts of Israel, sometimes on our way to our vacation home in France; and each time they have never failed to have an emotional impact and increased our love and devotion to Israel. In addition to my own many nieces, nephews, and friends in Israel, Bettina also has many relatives and friends who welcome us.

47. Behind Eli Malka's seventy-fifth birthday cake. *Left to right*, our late sister Victorine Braunstein; our late brother, Samuel; and brothers Eli, Edmond, and David.

Left to right, Jeffrey, Evelyne, Eli, and Bertha.

Seventy-fifth and Eightieth Birthdays

On 11 November 1984, my daughter, Evelyne, and my son, Jeffrey, organized an affair at the Tarrytown Hilton in Westchester, where they celebrated my seventy-fifth birthday with great pomp, music, champagne, and food. There were speeches and dancing with family and friends. Among the guests were friends from B'nai B'rith and the Jewish Westchester Community with their rabbi, Rabbi Arnold Turetsky; my brothers and sisters and their spouses; my children and grandchildren; twenty-eight of my nieces, nephews, and their spouses; and many friends from the Sudan and the United States. They came from all parts of the United States, traveling from all the boroughs of New York City; from Gloversville and other parts of Westchester County in upstate New York, from Ft. Lee, Clifton, and elsewhere in New Jersey; from Highland Park and Chicago in Illinois; from Philadelphia; from Vienna, Reston, and McLean in Virginia; and from Miami and Boca Raton in Florida. As a meaningful touch, on each table was a flag of every country I had lived in—the Sudan, Egypt, Israel, Switzerland, England, and France. My children and their families continue to shower my wife and me with their love and spoil us on every day and every occasion. They and their dear children continually give us much joy and happiness, and I thank God for that.

Another celebration on a smaller scale was arranged on my eightieth birthday. Among the festivities, I particularly enjoyed an ode from my daughter, Evelyne, and her husband, David Klein, which, if the reader will indulge me, went as follows:

> Eli was a man from the Sudan
> who headed the Malka Clan;
> he left for the States for
> his children's sakes
> and in due course he found many fans.

> In White Plains he became a resident;
> with strangers he was never hesitant.
> He showed concern,
> he was willing to learn,
> and soon he was B'nai B'rith President.

> Now here is your 80th birthday;
> you're as active as in your heyday.

We wish you good health
(and also some wealth)
'til your hundred 'n twentieth birthday.

United States Business with the Sudan

Under pressure from my Sudan agents and clients, I resumed my efforts to supply the Sudan from the United States and the Americas, working under my new registered name Malka Export. With considerable effort in time and expense, I reached the major American exporters of the required commodities and tried everything. Yeast for the bakery industry, industrial chemicals for the plastic industry, fancy beef tallow for the soap industry, refrigerators, fire-fighting engines, constructional steel, wheat flour, wheat, sorghum, yellow corn, and fava beans and other agricultural products needed during times of crop shortages—for all of which the United States is a world source.

After some initial small successes, it was concluded that the United States was much too expensive for such far destinations as the Sudan when compared to European and Far East sources. A primary reason, particularly for agricultural products and steel, are the very high export subsidies that France and other European Common Market sources grant on their exports of these commodities, which allows their exporters to underquote considerably American unsubsidized prices. It is hoped that the General Agreement on Tariffs and Trade (GATT)[4] agreement, ratified by the Congress in 1994 will help the United States compete; but I do not think this will happen until the tariffs and subsidies are reduced to near zero, perhaps by the beginning of the twenty-first century.

Even under American aid, of which, until about 1985, the Sudan was receiving up to $200 million a year while under the rule of General Nemeiri, the cost of American products supplied under aid worked out too high compared to the cost of freely imported similar products from European Common Market and other sources. Another important reason for American products' being uncompetitive is the high cost of ocean freight to such far places as the Sudan when compared to the nearer ports of Europe, India, and some countries of the Far East because freight is an important part of the cost of most commodities.

4. GATT became the World Trade Organization 1 Jan. 1995.

Health, Work, and Conclusion

In the United States, I had a few health problems after the age of seventy-five; but thanks to the Almighty; the most advanced medicine in the world; the love and care of my wife, Bettina, and my children, Evelyne and Jeff, my problems have all been well treated and healed. In October 1984, At age seventy-six, I underwent a triple coronary artery bypass. In 1987 and 1989, I had cataract surgery and lens replacements for both eyes and also a gallbladder operation in 1989. In June 1990 and again in 1992, I had orthopaedic surgery to fix my left femur, fractured in a fall in Paris.

Through it all, I maintained my high spirits and continued all possible activities. I am now well healed, undergo periodic medical checkups, and pursue my usual activities with vigor and pleasure. I continue to learn, read, write, attend meetings, debates and celebrations, travel and take care of my affairs. My wife, Bertha (Bettina), and I enjoy our children, grandchildren, family, and friends.

For all this and for the life, sustenance, happiness, and independence, I thank the Lord, Creator of all life, and pray that He extends His favors to me in good health and spirit for many years to come. Amen.

30

❧

The Malkas

The Malkas are an old Sephardic Rabbinic family who left Spain for Morocco after the expulsion decree of 1492. They spent the next three centuries in Morocco, some of them leaving for Eretz Israel, usually to Tiberias, Safad, and Jerusalem, to fulfill the Messianic dream of populating the Holy Land.

In his extensive study of Jewish names, which he published in a voluminous exhaustive tome *Les Noms des Juifs du Maroc; Essai d'onomastique Judeo-Morocaine*, Abraham I. Laredo traces the origins of Jewish names and their transformations through history. Apparently during the period of Babylonian captivity, a number of Jewish names were changed into Babylonian and Chaldean names. Others took on the Aramean suffix of *Aleph* (Eng. A); and he specifically gives as an example the name *Malka*, which means king in Aramaic, equivalent to the Hebrew name *Melekh*.[1] He further adds that, through history, the same name can be traced through different forms such as the Persian *Ben Saahin*, the Hebraic *Ben Melekh*, the Arab *Sultan*, and the Spanish versions of *Soberano*, *Ibn Rey*, *Avenreyna*, *Aben Rey*, *Arasye*, and *Reino*.

The Malka name emerges through the pageant of Jewish history. Back when Sura and Pumbedita in Babylon were the centers of Jewish learning and from where the Babylonian Talmud originated, we find Rab Malka

---

1. The word *Melekh* consists of three vocalized route Hebrew letters: *mem*, *lamedh*, and *caph*. When the Hebrew *hé* (*h*) is added, it becomes *Malkah* (silent *h*), the Hebrew feminine of *Melekh* (Eng. queen). When the Hebrew *aleph* is added, it becomes the Aramaic *Malka* (Eng. king). In history, however, we find prominent Malka rabbis spelling their name sometimes with an Aramaic *aleph* (king) and other times with the Hebrew *hé* (queen).

Bar Mar Aha,[2] gaon (a title of respect for the head of a Babylonian Academy) of the Rabbinical Academy of Pumbedita in 771–775, and Mar Rab Malka[3] gaon of Sura around 885. There were also various noted cabalists, such as Nessim Malka and his son Judah Malka in Fez, authors of several important cabalistic books[4] in the fourteenth and fifteenth centuries; Salomon Ben Malka (or Avinmelcha) of Monzon, Spain, who appears in the writings of Francisco Ascensio, the town's notary in 1465–1475; Jacob Malka[5] of Fez, author of Ner Hamaarabi; numerous rabbis in Fez, Agadir, and Marrakech; and various others in Spain, primarily in Saragossa, Avila, Seville, Toledo, and Cordoba. Three Malkas are among the noted Sephardi rabbis of the twentieth century. My father, Rabbi Solomon Malka,[6] was chief rabbi of the Sudan from 1906 to 1949. His elder brother, Rabbi Yehiael Malka, was chief rabbi of the Southern District of Morocco. My cousin Rabbi Moshé Malka was ab Beth Din (vice-president) of the Rabbinical Court in Casablanca and is now chief Sephardic rabbi of Petah Tikvah in Israel.

My father used to tell me that his ancestors crossed from Spain to Tangier, the most northern port of Morocco on the Atlantic coast at the edge of the Strait of Gibraltar. Not very surprising in that Tangier and the Strait of Gibraltar[7] have long been the passageway between Europe and

2. Rab Malka Bar Mar Aha is mentioned in The Jewish Encyclopedia (London, 1907), 7:278.

3. Mar Rab Malka, gaon of Sura, is mentioned in The Jewish Encyclopedia (London 1924), 3:227.

4. Nessim Malka was a well-known cabalist rabbi of the fourteenth century and author of Sepher Zenif Melukhah and Imre Melukhah. His son Judah Malka, imbued with Plato's philosophy, wrote Uns Al-Gharib, introduction to Sepher Yezirab; Tafsir Yezirah, commentary on the Sepher Yezirah; Tafsir Pirque Rabbi Eli²ezer; Al-Miphtah; and Tafsir Es-salawat. They are mentioned in The Jewish Encyclopedia (New York: The Jewish Publication Society of America, 1907), 6:536, and in Yacoub Moshé Toledano, Sepher Ner Ha Mareb (Jerusalem: N.p., 5671), 41 and 47.

5. Jacob Malka of Fez is mentioned in Yacoub Moshé Toledano, Sepher Ner Ha Mareb, 138; and Joseph Ben-Naim, Sepher Malkhe Rabbanam ve Sepher Kebod Melakhim (Jerusalem: N.p., 5691).

6. Moshé Malka, Mikvé Hamaim (The water pool) (Jerusalem: Hamaarib, 1975), preface, nn. 5 and 7.

7. Gibraltar, the mount of Tarik (Ar. Jabal Tarik) is named after "Tarik" Ibn Ziad, who in 711 crossed from Africa to conquer Spain with an Arab Berber army, which is said to have included some Jews. Once across the Strait, he burned his ships and told his troops, "The sea is behind you and the enemy is in front, so where is the escape (Ar., Aina²l Maffar), you must go forward."

Africa. My brother Edmond, in his book *Sephardi Jews* states that, according to Jacob Malka writing in his book "Ner Hamaarabi" in the eighteenth century, Málaga in Spain, where he himself was born, was the stronghold of the Malka family.[8] In his book *The History of the Jews of Tangier,* my friend Rabbi Mitchel Serels, director of Jewish and Sephardic Studies at Yeshiva University, tells how Jews fleeing the Spanish Inquisition crossed to Tangiers and stayed at Wadi El-Yahud (Valley of the Jews) near Tangier.[9] From there, they spread throughout Morocco to places such as Melilia, Tetouan, Fez, Meknes, Casablanca, and the district of Tafilalt, where in the last century my father's immediate family has lived.

During the twentieth century and particularly after the Arab-Israeli wars, the Malkas, like many other Jews living in Arab countries, left for more hospitable states. Although Morocco has been one of the Arab countries where Jews were least ill-treated and where they were protected as "good citizens" by the ruling monarch, King Hassan II and before him by his father King Muhamed V, the majority of Moroccan Jews left for France and Israel. Because of the influence of French culture in Morocco, many Moroccan Jews, including some Malkas, were attracted to France, though others went to Israel.

Jews in Arab countries where the European cultural influence was English, like those of the Sudan, including my branch of the Malka family, tended to go to the United Kingdom, the United States, Switzerland, and Israel. Jews living in countries where the cultural influence was French, such as the Jews living in Egypt, tended to go to France and Israel.

In Paris, where I lived for several years, there are hundreds of French Malkas, all tracing their origins to the Moroccan Malkas. They are found in all professions and walks of life. None of them are directly related to the Sudan Malkas, except for the daughters and two sons of my first cousin Rabbi Moshé Malka. Victor, the elder, is the editor of *"L'Information Juive,"* the French Jewish Community newspaper and professor of Jewish and Hebrew Studies at the Sorbonne University. The younger son, Solomon, is the joint chief editor of *L'Arche,* the most ancient Jewish magazine in Paris. Solomon Malka was born the same year my father died (1949) and was named Shlomo after my father. I had the

8. Edmond S. Malka, 13.

9. M. Mitchell Serels, *The History of the Jews of Tangier* (Brooklyn: Sepher-Hermon, 1991), 1.

pleasure of attending his wedding in the historic synagogue of Rue des Rosiers in Paris.

Another distant cousin in Paris is another Victor Malka, now called Vittorio, and is the son of Joshua Malka, a distant cousin of my father and first cousin of my brother-in-law Makhlouf Malka. In the 1940s Joshua was living in Alexandria and noticed the writings of my father in *El-Shams*, the Jewish and Wafdist Zionist newspaper of Alexandria. He wrote to my father, and later his son Victor came to Khartoum to start his business career. Victor subsequently rose to become a senior executive and business consultant of Olivetti S.A. in Italy, the United States, and the European continent, and has kept in contact with me and my brothers and sisters to this day. There are now other Malkas in Canada, Brazil, Columbia, and various other parts of Europe and South America, and most trace their origins to the Malkas of Morocco.

In recent generations, many of the Sudan Malkas have married Ashkenazim. This was the case for two of my four brothers and myself and three of my six sisters. In my immediate family, both my children, who by lineage are half-Sephardim and half-Ashkenazi, have married Ashkenazi spouses so that their children are one-quarter Sephardic and three-quarters Ashkenazi and proud of their Judaism and their Sephardic and Ashkenazi heritage and history.

Appendixes

Bibliography

Index

APPENDIX A

✿

Record Book of Jewish Community of Omdurman, Sudan
Shebat 5668 (January 1908)

עשׂו   עמ״י   ב״נו

פנקס

הקהלה אשר לעדת ישׂראל

בעיר

אם דר—מאן

יע״א

בחדש שבט התרסח לפ״נ

Translation

My People Did
Notebook of
the Jewish Community of the Congregation of Israel
in the City of
Omdurman
in the Month of Shebat in the Year Hatirsah Lefag
5668 from the Creation of the World

❧

Record of Visit of Chief Rabbi
of Egypt & Alexandria Eliahu Hazan

27 Shebat 5668 (January 1908)

1

הפקר הקדושים הנעשים שלא ברשות ב״ד

Renunciation of Marriages That Are Performed Without the Consent of the Beth Din in Egypt

27 Shebat 5668 (30 January 1908)

הפקר הקדושין הנעשים שלא ברשות ב"ד

בע"ה
זך שבט תרס'ח
30 בינואר 1908

אנכי בדרך נחני ה' לראות את אחי הנפוצים במצרים העליונה היא סודאן, בבאי לעי"ת (עיר
תהלה) אם דרמאן יע"א (יכוננה עליון אמן) מצאתי פה קהל ועדה מישראל מעטי הכמות ורכי
הליכות, אנשים יראים וחרדים לדבר ה'. ועליהם נספחים כמה משפחות השוכנים רבוד בעי"ת
כרטום ועי"ת חלפאיה הסמוכים לה.

תחילת מעשי חשבתי לטובה להקהיל אותם ואדריכם באספתם להעיר את רוחם לסדר ולתקן
תקנות טובות ומועילות לישוב העדה. שלחתי והזמנתי אותם בכתבי הזמנה, וביום חמישי בשבת
ז"ך שבט התרס"ח בשעה רביעית אחר הצהרים, נקהלו היאודים (היהודים) בבית הכנסת אשר
בעי"ת אם דרמאן והיו עשרים איש לבד מסף ועמהם ש"ץ (שליח צבור) העדה, החכם במהר"ר
(בן מורנו הרב רבי) שלמה מלכא הי"ו (ה' ישמרהו ויחיהו). וקראתי באספתם את ההסכמה
הקדומה אשר חדשנו בארץ מצרים לגבולותיה בעצת נשיאי הקהלות הקדושות שלא יוכל
שום איש ישראל תושב או עובר ארח לקח"ש או לישא אשה אלא ברשות ובהסכמת הרב
המו"צ (המשכיל וצדיק) או גבאי הכפר בכפרים. ובמנין עשרה ומכללם שליח ב"ד (בית דין)
או הש"ץ (השליח צבור) בכפרים ובכתובה עשויה כהוגן. והעובר על זה להקדושיו קדושיו וכסף
הקדושין הרי הוא הפקר ב"ד גמור והאשה ההיא אינה מקודשת כלל ותנשא לאחר בלא גט כלל.
והעדים אשר ימצאום בקדושין הם פסלנו אותם פסול גמור, ככתוב ומפורש כ"ז (כל זה)
בהסכמה העשויה בארך התורה ותחתום בפנקסי ב"ד הצדק דעו"בי (דעיר ואם בישראל) נא אמון
ועו"בי מצרים יע"א משנת התר"ס אשר מצודתהו פרושה על כל ארץ מצרים לגבולותיה.

וכל הקהל כאחד הנמצאים בהאסיפה כביום הזה זה פה אם דרמאן, קימו וקבלו עליהם את ההסכמה
הזאת עליהם ועל זרעם אחריהם לדורות עולם עד בא לציון גואל אמן. וההסכמה הזאת אחרי
אשר יקראו אותה בקהל ביום השבת פ' (סדרה) ואלה המשפטים אשר שים לפניהם בהבהכ"נ
(בבית הכנסת) תהיה מונחת בכתל בהכ"נ (בית הכנסת) למופת לדור אחרון. ולמען האמת
והשלום ח"ש (חתם שם) פה אם דרמאן בש"א לשבט התרס"ח יה' יברך את עמו בשלום ביום
השבת ס' ואלה המשפטים. אחרי קריאת התורה דרשתי להם מענין היום על הדברים הנחוצים
לעדה. ואח"כ (ואחר כך) נקראה ההסכמה הנ"ז (הנזכרת) בקהל עם והיו עוד אנשים מאלה אשר
לא נמצאו ביום האספה וקים שנת

Signed by: הצעיר אליהו חזן ס"ט
Sealed with the official seal of Elie B. Hazan Grand Rabbin, Alexandrie
הצעיר אליהו חזן ס"ט רב ומליץ בה נא אמון יע"א
The Arabic reads: Eliahu Hazan Hakham Bashi Alexandria

Transcribed from the Sephardi (חצי קולמוס) script by Professor Roberta Barkan,
director, Jewish Studies Program, Purchase College, State Univ. of New York. Rabbi
Mitchell Serels, director, Sephardic Community Programs, Yeshiva Univ. provided
important advice. (See abbreviated translation in chap. 5, p. 34.)

APPENDIX A, DOCUMENT 2

Election of the First Jewish Community Council in Omdurman, Sudan

27 Shebat 5668 (30 January 1908)

בחירת נשיאי העדה

Election of the First Jewish Community Council in Omdurman

27 Shebat 5668 (30 January 1908)

בחירת נשיאי העדה

זך שבט תרס'ח
30 בינואר 1908

בהאספה הכללית אשר נעשית פה אם דרמאן בבה"כ'נ (בבית הכנסת) ביום חמישי בשבת זך שבט התרס"ח בשעה רביעית אחר חצות, אחרי ככלות עמן הסכמת הפקר הקידושין הכתובים מעלד"ז (מעבר לדף זה) יעצתי אותם לבחור מתוכם חמשה אנשי חיל הראוים למנות אותם ראשים על העם, ובדעות נעלמות נבחרו נבחרו האדון בן ציון קושטי הי"ו (השם ישמרהו ויחיהו) במספר תשעה עשר בוחרים מתוך עשרים בוחרים. וכן האדון נסים שלום הי"ו נבחר מתשעה עשר, והאדון אדוארד קאסטרו הי"ו נבחר מתשעה עשר, והאדון מנחם צאלח ה"ו נבחר מששה עשר, וכן האדון מאיר אפרים נבחר מששה עשר, וכן בהסכמת כל האספה נבחר האדון בן ציון קושטי הי"ו לנשיא הועד, האדון נסים שלום הי"ו סוכן, האדון אדוארד קאסטרו הי"ו מזכיר, האדון מנחם צאלח הי"ו והאדון מאיר אפרים יועצים וחברים בועד. על הועד לעשות פנקס מיוחד כניסות והוצאות מכל הכנסות הקהלה. ובכל שנה בחדש שבט יעשו אספה כללית לסדר לפניהם חשבון הקהלה, ולעשות בחירות מחדש על מינוי ראשי העדה. וכל דבר אשר יקשה מהם יקריבוהו אותו אל מ"ע (מאיר עינים) ב"ד (בית דין) הצדק דעו"בי נא אמון יע"א (יכוננה עליון אמן). הודענו כל זה במכתב רשמי למעלת האדון נשיא הארץ, האדון השר הגדול ריגינאלד ווינגאט י"רה (ירום הודו) למען יהיה הועד נודע לממשלת הארץ.

לצורינו נוחילה יבנה ערי יהודה ושבו בנים לגבולם ונדחי ישראל יקבץ מארבע כנפות הארץ אמן נהי"ז (נחתם היום הזה) היום זך שבט התרס"ח וה' יברך את עמו בשלום.
הצעיר אליהו חזן

Sealed with the official seal of Elie B. Hazan Grand Rabbin, Alexandrie

הצעיר אליהו חזן ס"ט רב ומליץ בה נא אמון יע"א

Transliteration of the Arabic inscription reads: "Mahdar ta'sis awal majlis lil ta'ifa al-yahudia bil Sudan bimadinat Omdurman fi yom 27 Shevat 5668 almuwafik 30 yanair 1908."
Minutes of the founding of the first Jewish Community Council in the Sudan in the city of Omdurman on the 27 day of Shevat corresponding to the 30th of January 1908.

Transcribed from the Sephardi (חצי קולמוס) script by Professor Roberta Barkan, director, Jewish Studies Program, Purchase College, State Univ. of New York. Rabbi Mitchell Serels, director, Sephardic Community Programs, Yeshiva Univ. provided important advice. (See abbreviated translation in chap. 5, p. 34.)

Appendix B

❧

Jewish Marriages in the Sudan 1907–1963

From Rabbi Solomon Malka's Register of Ketubot

Marriages Performed by Rabbi Solomon Malka from 1907 to 1949

Marriage Date	Place	Husband/Wife Names	Their father's names
18 June 1907	Omdurman	Baroukh Leilibh	Moussa Leilibh
		Hanna Sarah Wais	Samuel Hizgeil Wais
31 Jan 1908	Omdurman	Ben-Sion Coshti	Meyer Bechor Coshti
		Manna Shenouda	
27 June 1908	Omdurman	Shalom Hakim	Samuel Hakim
		Rosa Hindi	Suleiman Hindi
18 Dec 1909	Khartoum North	Yehuda Leon Franco	
		Gracia Wais	Samuel Hizgeil Wais
18 Jun 1909	Omdurman	Baroukh Moussa	
		Hanna Sara	Samuel Hizgeil Wais
22 Apr 1910	Omdurman	Yousef Ishag Mizrahi	Ishag Mizrahi
		Aziz Suleiman Benou	Suleiman Benou
27 Dec 1910	Omdurman	Ezra Marcos	Menahim Marcos
		Gamila Dwek	Nessim Dwek
12 Feb 1911	Khartoum	Yacoub Aelion	David Aelion
		Esther Satout Israel	Baroukh Israel
8 Jun 1911	Omdurman	Ibrahim Seroussi	Haim Seroussi
		Rosa Hakim	Shalom Hakim
20 Oct 1911	Omdurman	Leon Mannifker Cohen	Faibel Mannifker
		Liza (Lea) Kanzer	Boris Kanzer
5 Dec 1913	Omdurman	Emile Feinstein	Adolphe Feinstein
		Rachel Shapiro	Tzvi Shapiro
5 Dec 1914	Khartoum	Herman Berlenstein	Yosef Leb Berlenstein
		Rahma Baroukh	Baroukh Israel
26 Apr 1914	Khartoum	Charles Weinberg	Samuel Weinberg
		Mathilde Feinstein	Adolphe Feinstein
5 Sept 1915	Khartoum	Moussa Cohen	Ibrahim Cohen
		Oro Cohen Shakra	Moussa Cohen Shakra

215

Marriage Date	Place	Husband/Wife Names	Their father's names
28 Dec 1915	Khartoum	Moussa Harari	Eliaho Harari
		Esther Yetah	Aslan Yetah
12 Mar 1916	Omdurman	Gibrail Moussa Cohen	Moussa Cohen
		Latifa Nessim Dwek	Nessim Dwek Cohen
21 Jan 1917	Omdurman	David Yousef Gaon	Yousef Gaon
		Victoria Aslan Cohen	Aslan Cohen
3 Mar 1917	Omdurman	Eliaho Obadia Safadia	Obadia Safadia
		Rahma Farag Shoua David	Farag Shoua David
10 May 1917	Omdurman	Nessim Haroun Shama	Haroun Shama
		Zakia Obadia Safadia	Obadia Safadia
7 Jan 1918	Omdurman	Ibrahim Yousef Cohen	Yousef Cohen
		Flora Abdel Nabi Ani	Abdel Nabi Ani
20 Jan 1918	Omdurman	Leon Ortasse	
		Gracia Shalom Hakim	Shalom Samuel Hakim
1 Dec 1918	Omdurman	Menashe Yousef Levy	Yousef Levy
		Rachel Khidr Daoud	Khidr Daoud
8 Jun 1919	Omdurman	Yacoub Yousef Ades	Yousef Ades
		Sarina Shalom Hakim	Shalom Samuel Hakim
7 Oct 1919	Khartoum	Makhlouf Yaish Malka	Yaish Malka
		Esther Solomon Malka	Rabbi Shlomo Malka
31 Mar 1920	Khartoum	Yousef Nahman Berkowitz	Nahman Berkowitz
		Miriam Nahman Levitin	Dov Levitin
1 Aug 1920	Khartoum	Mathieu Ishag Sidis	Ishag Sidis
		Fortunée Zaki Sinai	Zaki Sinai
22 Jan 1922	Khartoum	Bernard Hizgeil Goldring	Ezekiel Goldring
		Fortunée Solomon Malka	Rabbi Solomon Malka
17 Dec 1922	Khartoum	Leonora Salem Greenberg	Salem Greenberg
		Alfred Israel Isidore Loupo	Isidor Israel Loupo
11 Feb 1923	Omdurman	Joseph Elie Tammam	Elie Tammam
		Flora Aslan Cohen	Aslan Cohen
25 Mar 1923	Khartoum	Nessim Ishag Gabra	Ishag Gabra
		Fortunée Farag Shoua	Farag Shoua

Marriage Date	Place	Husband/Wife Names	Their father's names
15 Nov 1923	Khartoum	Gibrail Ishag Pinto	Ishag Pinto
		Sarina Eliaho Cohen	Eilaho Cohen
1 Jun 1924	Khartoum	Aslan Haim Seroussi	Haim Seroussi
		Naima Abdalla Saltoun	Abdalla Saltoun
29 Jun 1924	Khartoum	Joseph Marco Dannon	Marco Dannon
		Gamila Elias Benou	Elias Benou
21 Aug 1924	Khartoum	Suleiman Kudsi	Haron Kudsi
		Simha Farag Shoua Daoud	Farag Shoua Daoud
5 Apr 1925	Khartoum	Julio Vago Moshé	Vago Moshé
		Fortuna Daoud Israel El-Eini	Daoud Israel El-Eini
15 Mar 1925	Khartoum	Armando Abraham Carmona	Abraham Carmona
		Gilda Berchmann	Abraham Berchmann
12 May 1925	Khartoum	Eliaho Yacoub Mashiah	Yacoub Mashiah
		Rahma Baroukh Israel	Baroukh Israel
24 Sep 1925	Khartoum	Moussa Yehuda Sasson	Yehuda Sasson
		Allegra Victor Levy	Victor Levy
16 Mar 1926	Khartoum	Daoud Farag Shoua Daoud	Farag Shoua Daoud
		Esther Ezra Baroukh	Ezra Baroukh
13 May 1926	Khartoum	Salih Haim Sasson	Sasson Ezra
		Nazima Yousef Abboudi	Yousef Abboudi
16 May 1926	Khartoum	Menashe Yacoub Yona	Yacoub Yona
		Rahma Haroun Levy	Haroun Levy
18 Dec 1927	Khartoum	Samuel Abraham Ishkinazi	Abraham Ishkinazi
		Sarina Ibrahim Ades	Ibrahim Ades
20 Mar 1930	Khartoum North	Isaac Yacoub Cohen	Yacoub Cohen
		Lizette Mourad Israel El-Eini	Murad Israel El-Eini
27 Mar 1930	Khartoum North	Abraham (Gurgi) Ezra Sasson	Ezra Sasson
		Allegra Solomon Malka	Rabbi Solomon Malka
22 Nov 1931	Khartoum	Maurice Adolphe Goldenberg	Adolphe Gedalia Goldenberg
		Rachel Solomon Malka	Rabbi Solomon Malka

Marriage Date	Place	Husband/Wife Names	Their father's names
9 Mar 1933	Khartoum	Daoud Ishag Daoud	Ishag Daoud
		Oro Elie Salamon Tammam	Elie Salamon Tammam
4 Nov 1934	Khartoum	Eliaho Solomon Malka	Rabbi Solomon Malka
		Dora Adolphe Goldenberg	Adolphe Gedalia Goldenberg
19 Aug 1934	Khartoum	Edgar Yacoub Ben-Rubi	Yacoub Ben-Rubi
		Rachel Yacoub Aeleon	Yacoub Aeleon
17 Mar 1935	Wad Medani	Elias Suleiman Benou	Sleiman Benou
		Aziza Saleh Baroukh	Saleh Baroukh
24 Mar 1935	Khartoum North	Yousef Ishag Gabra	Ishag Gabra
		Liza Yusef Abboudi	Yousef Abboudi
12 Aug 1935	Khartoum	Barukh Shoua Daoud	Shoua Daoud
		Hanna Jeanette Herman	Jeanette Herman
5 Apr 1936	Khartoum	Reuben Shaoul Cohen	Shaoul Cohen
		Alice Aslan Cohen	Aslan Cohen
12 Sep 1937	Khartoum	Maurice Elie Tammam	Elie Tammam
		Rosa Moussa Benaim	Moussa Benaim
13 Feb 1938	Wad Medani	Yousef Daoud Abdalla	Daoud Abdalla
		Rachel Saleh Baroukh	Saleh Baroukh
24 Jul 1938	Khartoum	Victor Ibrahim Heiman	Ibrahim Heiman
		Dina Samuel Menovitch	Samuel Menovitch
8 Sep 1938	Khartoum	Ezra (Cesar) Belilos	Ishag Belilos
		Rachel Mourad Israel El-Eini	Mourad Israel El-Eini
25 Feb 1940	Khartoum	Maurice Haroun Levy	Haroun Levy
		Flora Daoud Khaski	Daoud Khaski
14 Jul 1940	Khartoum	Max Gabriel	Elie Gabriel
		Sarina Solomon Malka	Rabbi Solomon Malka
22 Jul 1940	Khartoum	Jack Carmona	Daoud Carmona
		Sarah Palombo	
24 Jul 1941	Khartoum	Joseph Morino Soriano	Morino Soriano
		Nina Konein	Abramino Konein

Marriage Date	Place	Husband/Wife Names	Their father's names
19 Oct 1941	Khartoum	David Abramino Hemmo	Abramino Hemmo
		Perla Konein	Abramino Konein
27 Dec 1941	Khartoum	Yacoub Yousef Abboudi	Yousef Abboudi
		Jeanette Makhlouf Malka	Makhlouf Malka
8 Feb 1942	Khartoum	Joseph Berlenstein	Herman Berlenstein
		Esther Eliaho Safadia	Eliaho Safadia
8 Feb 1942	Khartoum	Sion Shoua	Shoua David
		Fortunée Saleh Baroukh	Saleh Baroukh
8 Mar 1942	Khartoum	Habib Hanan Cohen	Hanan Cohen
		Jeanette Gabra Cohen	Gabra Cohen
29 Mar 1942	Khartoum	Robert Braunstein	Abramino Braunstein
		Victorine Solomon Malka	Rabbi Solomon Malka
14 Mar 1943	Khartoum	Israel Daoud El-Eini	Daoud El-Eini
		Rachel Hizgeil Baroukh	Hizgeil Baroukh
16 Apr 1943	Khartoum	Saleh Baroukh	Baroukh Israel
		Rachel Ishag Gershon	Ishak Gershon
12 Mar 1944	Khartoum	David Nessim O'Hanna	Nessim O'Hanna
		Mary Yacoub Aeleon	Yacoub Aeleon
3 Sep 1944	Khartoum	Eliaho Shaoul	Shaoul Eliaho
		Leona Vago	Julio Vago
Nov 1944	Khartoum	David Solomon Malka	Rabbi Solomon Malka
		Jeanette Joseph Dannon	Joseph Dannon
27 May 1945	Khartoum	Ibrahim Abboudi	Yousef Abboudi
		Susan Ibrahim Sasson	Ibrahim Sasson
8 Au 1946	Khartoum	Ibrahim Daoud El-Eini	Daoud Israel El-Eini
		Flora Hizgeil Baroukh	Hizgeil Baroukh
2 Feb 1947	Khartoum	Mayer Makhlouf Malka	Makhlouf Malka
		Victorine Yacoub Ades	Yacoub Ades
3 Apr 1947	Khartoum	Asher Aeleon	Yacoub Aeleon
		Rosette Kramer	Maurice Kramer
15 Jun 1947	Khartoum	David Yacoub Aeleon	Yacoub Aeleon
		Mary Melida Masasini	Masasini
16 Oct 1947	Khartoum	Maurice Ibrahim Seroussi	Ibrahim Seroussi
		Rose Aslan Seroussi	Aslan Seroussi

Marriage Date	Place	Husband/Wife Names	Their father's names
22 Feb 1948	Khartoum	Zaki Abraham Nessim Dwek Lili Gabra Pinto	Abraham Nessim Dwek Gabra Pinto

Marriages Performed by Rabbi Haim Siboani

13 Aug 1950	Khartoum	Eliaho Yousef Abboudi Juliette Ibrahim Cohen	Yousef Abboudi Ibrahim Cohen
1 Apr 1951	Khartoum	Edmond Solomon Malka Yvonne Sasson Levy	Rabbi Solomon Malka Sasson Levy Smouha
21 Aug 1952	Khartoum	Moussa Sasson Levy Allegra Makhlouf Malka	Sasson Levy Smouha Makhlouf Malka

Marriages Performed by Rabbi Massoud El-Baz

4 Jan 1953	Khartoum	Ishak (Zaki) Saltoun Esther Yousef Gabra	Abdalla Saltoun Yousef Gabra
11 Oct 1953	Khartoum	David Suleiman Ani Rose Samuel Dayan	Suleiman Ani Samuel Dayan
10 Jan 1954	Khartoum	Lazar Samuel Dayan Gracia Zaki Saada	Samuel Dayan Zaki Saada
28 Mar 1954	Khartoum	Ezra Hizgeil Baroukh Marcella Saleh Baroukh	Hizgeil Baroukh Saleh Baroukh
15 Aug 1954	Khartoum	Yacoub Ibrahim Seroussi Claudette Maurice Goldenberg	Ibrahim Seroussi Maurice Goldenberg
22 Aug 1954	Khartoum	Jack Suleiman Ani Sarina Ibrahim Cohen	Suleiman Ani Ibrahim Ani
23 Dec 1954	Khartoum	Isaac Gabriel Pinto Norma Ibrahim Sasson	Gabra Pinto Ibrahim Sasson
25 Dec 1955	Khartoum	Edward Shehata Mizrahi Nella Jack Bigo	Shehata Mizrahi Jack Bigo
29 Jan 1956	Khartoum	Jacque Ibrahim Cohen Lucienne Cesar Wahba	Ibrahim Cohen Cesar Wahba

Marriage Date	Place	Husband/Wife Names	Their father's names
14 Apr 1957	Khartoum	Zaki Daoud Ishag	Daoud Ishag
		Beatrice Yousef Aslan Cohen	Yousef Aslan Cohen
29 Apr 1957	Khartoum	Isaac Mayer Joseph Cavaliero	Joseph Cavaliero
		Janine Blanche David Behar	David Behar
18 Aug 1957	Khartoum	Elie Aslan Seroussi	Aslan Seroussi
		Lizette Joseph Soriano	Joseph Soriano
24 Sep 1957	Khartoum	Edward Aslan Seroussi	Aslan Seroussi
		Amy Rudolphe Heber	Rudolphe Heber
10 Nov 1957	Khartoum	Shaoul Yousef Matalon	Yousef Matalon
		Mary Marc Bossidan	Marc Bossidan
12 Jun 1958	Khartoum	Josef Aslan Seroussi	Aslan Seroussi
		Chichilla Ittamar Sagrani	Ittamar Sagrani
30 Nov 1958	Khartoum	Gabi Joseph Tamman	Joseph Tammam
		Lina Angelle Ibrahim Mourad	Ibrahim Mourad
15 Nov 1959	Khartoum	Albert Samuel Ishkinazi	Samuel Ashkenazi
		Hanna Regina Yousef Daoud	Yousef Daoud
1 Jan 1960`	Khartoum	Salvator Daoud Shoua	Daoud Shoua
		Rita Stulmacher	M. A. Stulmacher
10 July 1960	Khartoum	Moussa Shaoul	Shaoul Eliaho
		Rachel Daoud Shoua	Daoud Shoua
4 May 1961	Khartoum	Solomon Goldenberg	Maurice Goldenberg
		Elizabeth Drig Bat Abraham	E. Drigg
4 Mar 1962	Khartoum	Roger Cohen	Isaac Cohen
		Adiba Cohen	Shalom Cohen
4 Apr 1963	Khartoum	Yacoub Seroussi	Ibrahim Seroussi
		Flora Lola Cohen	Yousef Cohen
21 Mar 1963	Khartoum	Yitzhak Zaki Yousef Gabra	Yousef Gabra
		Viola Bat Abraham Cohen	Abraham Cohen

Marriage Date	Place	Husband/Wife Names	Their father's names
24 Mar 1963	Khartoum	Moshé Ben-Samuel Dwek	Samuel Dwek
		Naomi Bat Daoud Ishak	Daoud Ishak
3 Nov 1963	Khartoum	Joseph Ben-Samuel Ishkenazi	Samuel Ishkinazi
		Dolly Bat Daoud Ben-Sion Coshti	Daoud Ben-Sion Coshti

Malka-Goldenberg Family Tree

The Malka Family

Mimon Yehouda Malka
b. 1830 Tafilalt Province, Morocco
d. 1895 Tafilalt Province, Morocco

Yehiael Malka (Rabbi)
b. 1864 Tafilalt Province, Morocco
d. 1932 Tafilalt Province, Morocco

Solomon Malka (Rabbi)
b. 1878 Asephalo, Tafilalt, Morocco
d. 4 Apr 1949 Khartoum, Sudan
m. 1896
Hanna David Assouline
b. 1882 Tinghir, Tafilalt, Morocco;
d. 26 Aug 1951 Khartoum, Sudan

Alia Malka
b. 1880 Morocco
d. 1949 Tiberias, Palestine

Esther Malka
b. 1900 Tiberias, Palestine
d. 1974 NYC, USA
m. 7 Oct 1919 Khartoum
Makhlouf Malka

Fortunée Malka
b. 1904 Tiberias, Palestine
d. 1960 Israel
m. 22 Jan 1922 Khartoum
Bernard Goldring

Eliaho S. Malka
b. 7 Nov 1909 Omdurman, Sudan
m. 20 Dec 1973, Paris, France
Bertha Waldman
b. 10 Feb 1920, Egypt
m. 4 Nov 1934 Khartoum
Dora Goldenberg
b. 1 Dec 1914 Egypt
d. 5 Jan 1966 Switzerland

Jenny Hanna Malka
b. Oct 1935 Khartoum, Sudan
d. 29 Mar 1942 Khartoum, Sudan

Jeffrey Solomon Malka
b. 10 Sep 1940 Khartoum, Sudan
m. 5 Nov 1967 Philadelphia, Pa, USA
Susan Gelfand
b. 31 Aug 1944, Philadelphia, USA

Dorothy Jacqueline Malka
b. 30 Jun 1971 NYC, USA
Jennifer Elizabeth Malka
b. 4 Dec 1972 Wilkesbary, PA, USA
Deborah Ann Malka
b. 10 Nov 1974 Falls Church, VA, USA
Judith Emily Malka
b. 27 Oct 1980 Falls Church, VA, USA

Evelyne Malka
b. 14 Jul 1945 Khartoum, Sudan
m. 30 Jun 1974 NYC, USA,
David C. Klein
b. 10 Feb 1941, Newark, NJ, USA

Alexander E. Klein
b. 6 Sep 1977 NYC, USA
Lauren Deborah Klein
b. 30 Nov 1981 Portchester, NY

Allegra Malka
b. 12 Sep 1911 Omdurman, Sudan
m. 27 Mar 1930 Khartoum North
Abraham Sasson

Rachel Malka
b. 7 May 1913 Khartoum, Sudan
m. 22 Nov 1931 Khartoum, Sudan
Maurice Goldenberg

Samuel S. Malka
b. Oct 1917 Omdurman, Sudan
d. 21 Jul 1986 NJ, USA
m. 1939 Cairo, Egypt
Giselle Kramer

Sara Malka
b. 13 Sep 1915 Omdurman, Sudan
m. 14 Jan 1940 Khartoum, Sudan
Max Gabriel

Edmond S. Malka
b. 4 Mar 1916 Omdurman, Sudan
m. 1936 Cairo, Egypt
Ida Goldenberg

Victorine Malka
b. 10 Apr 1920 Khartoum
d. 24 Apr 1996 USA
m. 29 Mar 1942 Khartoum
Robert Braunstein

David S. Malka
b. 30 Oct 1923 Khartoum, Sudan
m. 5 Nov 1944 Khartoum, Sudan
Jeannette H. Dannon
d. 26 Dec 1996, NJ

The Goldenberg Family

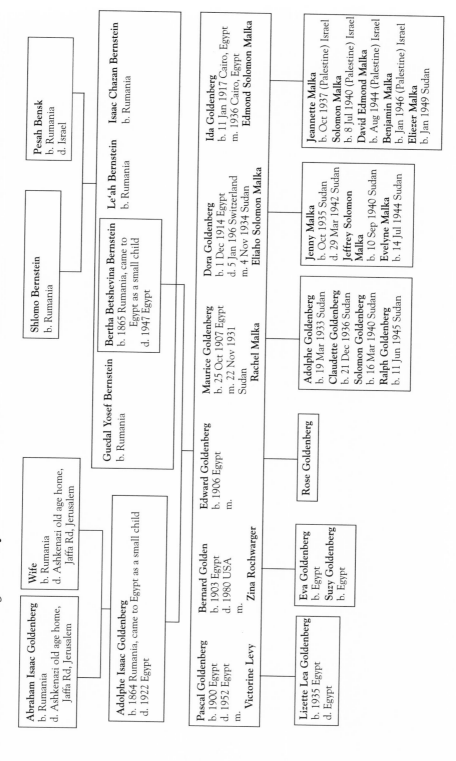

Abraham Isaac Goldenberg
b. Rumania
d. Ashkenazi old age home,
Jaffa Rd, Jerusalem

Wife
b. Rumania
d. Ashkenazi old age home,
Jaffa Rd, Jerusalem

Shlomo Bernstein
b. Rumania

Pesah Bensk
b. Rumania
d. Israel

Adolphe Isaac Goldenberg
b. 1864 Rumania, came to Egypt as a small child
d. 1922 Egypt

Guedal Yosef Bernstein
b. Rumania

Bertha Betshevina Bernstein
b. 1865 Rumania, came to
Egypt as a small child
d. 1947 Egypt

Le'ah Bernstein
b. Rumania

Isaac Chazan Bernstein
b. Rumania

Pascal Goldenberg
b. 1900 Egypt
d. 1952 Egypt
m.
Victorine Levy

Bernard Golden
b. 1903 Egypt
d. 1980 USA
m.
Zina Rochwarger

Edward Goldenberg
b. 1906 Egypt
m.

Maurice Goldenberg
b. 25 Oct 1907 Egypt
m. 22 Nov 1931
Sudan
Rachel Malka

Dora Goldenberg
b. 1 Dec 1914 Egypt
d. 5 Jan 196 Switzerland
m. 4 Nov 1934 Sudan
Eliaho Solomon Malka

Ida Goldenberg
b. 11 Jan 1917 Cairo, Egypt
m. 1936 Cairo, Egypt
Edmond Solomon Malka

Lizette Lea Goldenberg
b. 1935 Egypt
d. Egypt

Eva Goldenberg
b. Egypt
Suzy Goldenberg
b. Egypt

Rose Goldenberg

Adolphe Goldenberg
b. 19 Mar 1933 Sudan
Claudette Goldenberg
b. 21 Dec 1936 Sudan
Solomon Goldenberg
b. 16 Mar 1940 Sudan
Ralph Goldenberg
b. 11 Jun 1945 Sudan

Jenny Malka
b. Oct 1935 Sudan
d. 29 Mar 1942 Sudan
**Jeffrey Solomon
Malka**
b. 10 Sep 1940 Sudan
Evelyne Malka
b. 14 Jul 1944 Sudan

Jeannette Malka
b. Oct 1937 (Palestine) Israel
Solomon Malka
b. 8 Jul 1940 (Palestine) Israel
David Edmond Malka
b. Aug 1944 (Palestine) Israel
Benjamin Malka
b. Jan 1946 (Palestine) Israel
Eliezer Malka
b. Jan 1949 Sudan

APPENDIX D

Gellatly Hankey Group of Companies

Gellatly Hankey Group of Companies

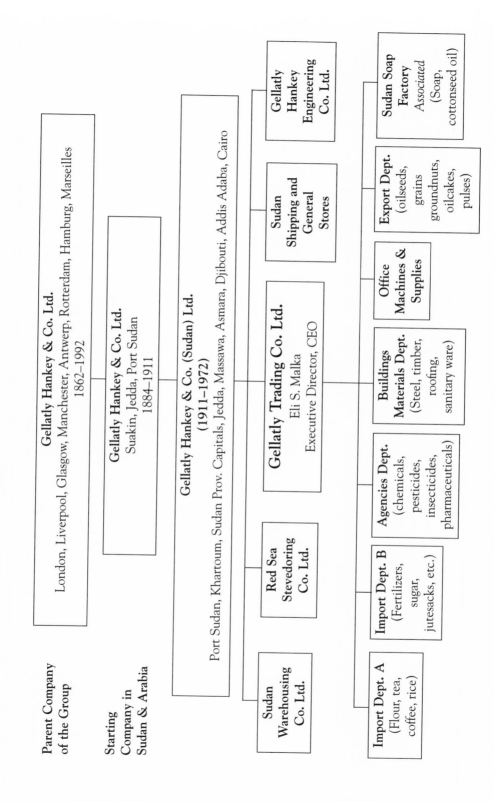

Parent Company of the Group

Gellatly Hankey & Co. Ltd.
London, Liverpool, Glasgow, Manchester, Antwerp, Rotterdam, Hamburg, Marseilles
1862–1992

Starting Company in Sudan & Arabia

Gellatly Hankey & Co. Ltd.
Suakin, Jedda, Port Sudan
1884–1911

Gellatly Hankey & Co. (Sudan) Ltd.
(1911–1972)
Port Sudan, Khartoum, Sudan Prov. Capitals, Jedda, Massawa, Asmara, Djibouti, Addis Adaba, Cairo

Sudan Warehousing Co. Ltd.

Red Sea Stevedoring Co. Ltd.

Gellatly Trading Co. Ltd.
Eli S. Malka
Executive Director, CEO

Sudan Shipping and General Stores

Gellatly Hankey Engineering Co. Ltd.

Import Dept. A
(Flour, tea, coffee, rice)

Import Dept. B
(Fertilizers, sugar, jutesacks, etc.)

Agencies Dept.
(chemicals, pesticides, insecticides, pharmaceuticals)

Buildings Materials Dept.
(Steel, timber, roofing, sanitary ware)

Office Machines & Supplies

Export Dept.
(oilseeds, grains groundnuts, oilcakes, pulses)

Sudan Soap Factory
Associated
(Soap, cottonseed oil)

Bibliography

Angel, Marc D. *Voices in Exile, A Study in Sephardic Intellectual History*. Hoboken, N.J.: Ktav, 1991.

Bacon, Karen. "The Case of Ethiopian Jews." *Madda Journal*, Yeshiva Univ. New York, 1992.

Benbassa, Esther. *Un Grand Rabbin Sepharade en Politique*. Paris: Presses du CNRS, 1990.

Blake, George. *Gellatly 1862–1962*. Glasgow: Blackie & Son, Ltd., 1962.

Metz, Helen Chapin. *Sudan: A Country Study*. 4th ed. Federal Research Division, Library of Congress Department of the Army, DA PAM 550-27, 1992.

Churchill, Winston. *My Early Life. A Roving Commission*. New York: Scriber's, 1987.

Coren, Alexander. *Personalities from Jewish Communities in Europe*. Ramat Gan, Israel: Royal Printing, 1989.

Dobrinsky, Herbert. *A Treasury of Sephardic Laws and Customs*. Hoboken, N.J.: Ktav, 1986.

Elazar, Daniel J. *The Other Jews. The Sephardim Today*. New York: Basic, 1988.

El-Rai El-Am (Public opinion). Editorial, "Al-Ginsia al-Sudania" (Sudanese nationality), n.d.

Farwell, Byron. *Prisoners of the Mahdi*. New York: Harper and Row, 1967.

Gerber, Jane S. *The Jews of Spain. A History of the Sephardic Experience*. New York: Free, 1992.

Ginzberg, Louis. *The Legends of the Jews*. Philadelphia: The Jewish Publication Society of America, 1968.

Great Jewish Personalities in Ancient and Medieval Times: Moses, David, Jeremiah, Philo, Akiba, Saadia, Halevi, Maimonides, Rashi, Abrabanel, Baal Shem Tov, Vilnagaon. Edited by Simon Noveck. Vol. 1.

Holt, P. M., and M. W. Daly. *A History of the Sudan. From the Coming of Islam to the Present Day*. 4th ed. New York: Longman, 1988.

Josephus Flavius. *The Life and Works of Josephus Flavius.* Bk. I, *Antiquities of the Jews,* chap. 10. Translated by William Whiston. New York: Holt, 1973.

Jewish Encyclopedia, The. 12 vols. New York: The Jewish Publication Society of America, 1907.

Krämer, Gudrun. *The Jews in Modern Egypt.* Seattle: Univ. of Washington Press, 1989.

Laredo, Abraham I. *Les Noms des Juifs du Maroc. Essai d'onomastique Judeo-Marocaine* (The names of the Jews of Morocco). Madrid: Consejo Superior de Investigationes Cientificas, Instituto B. Marias Montano, 1978.

Les éditions du Scribe. *Juifs D'Egypte Images et Textes* (Jews of Egypt, pictures and texts) 2d ed., 1984.

Levy, Nomi. "American Diplomatic Relations with Sudan, 1977–1985." Master's thesis, Cambridge Univ., 1993.

———. "The Mangled Mask of Empire: Ceremony and Political Motive in the Anglo Egyptian Sudan." Senior thesis, Columbia Univ. 1993.

Malka, Edmond S. *Sephardi Jews—A Pageant of Spanish-Portuguese and Oriental Judaism Between the Cross and the Crescent,* Edmond S. Malka, 6715 Deeb Street, #15, Port Richey, Fl 34668, 1979.

Malka, Eli S. "Jews in the Sudan." *Bʾnai Bʾrith Magazine,* Oct., 1936.

Malka, Elie. *Essai de Folklore des Israélites du Maroc.* (Essay on the folklore of the Jews of Morocco). Geneva: Librairie Menorah, n.d.

Malka, Jacob. *Ner Hamaarabi.* (Candle or light of the west) Jerusalem, 1932.

Malka, Moshé. *Mikvé Hamaim* (The water pool). Jerusalem: Hamaarib Press, 1975.

Malka, Solomon. *Frontiers of Jewish Faith.* 3 vols. Translated by Edmond S. Malka. Reproduced by Edmond S. Malka, 6715 Deeb Street, #15, Port Richey, Fl 34668, 1977.

Malka, Solomon. *Rabbinical Records of Jewish Marriages in the Sudan (1907–1963).*

Malka, Solomon, and Eliahu Hazan. *Pinkas hakehilla de adat Israel be Omdurman* (Notebook of the Jewish community of Omdurman), 1908.

Malka, Victor. *La Memoire Brisee des Juifs du Maroc* (The heart rending memory of the Jews of Morocco). Paris: Editions Entente, 1978.

Messing, Simon D. *The Story of the Falashas: The "Black Jews" of Ethiopia.* Hamden, Conn.: Balshon Printing, 1982.

Morehead, Alan. *The Blue Nile.* New York: Dell, 1968.

———. *The White Nile.* New York: Dell, 1969.

Netanyahu, Benjamin. *A Place among the Nations: Israel and the World.* New York: Bantam, New 1993.

Rapaport, Louis. "The Ancient Origins of Ethiopian Jewry," *Jerusalem Post,* International ed. 1 June 1991.

Revue de Droit de Vivre (The right to live), May 1993.

Roth, Cecil. *A History of the Jews: From the Earliest Times Through the Six Day War.* Rev. ed. New York: Schocken, 1970.

————. *The Marrano Jews.* New York: Harper & Row, 1966.

Serels, M. Mitchell. *The History of the Jews of Tangier.* Brooklyn: Sepher-Hermon, 1991.

Shamir, Yitzhak. *Summing Up: An Autobiography.* Boston: Little, Brown, 1994.

Slatin Pasha, Rudolph. *Fire and Sword in the Sudan: Fighting and Serving the Dervishes.* London: Greenhill, 1990.

Santob De Carion. *Jewish Wisdom in Christian Spain: The Moral Proverbs of Santob De Carion.* Translated by T. A. Parry. Princeton: Princeton Univ. Press, 1987.

Schoenberg, Harris Okun. *A Mandate for Terror: The United Nations and the PLO.* New York: Shapolsky, 1989.

Stillman, Norman A. *The Jews of Arab Lands.* Philadelphia: The Jewish Publication Society of America, 1979.

Toledano, Yacoub Moshé. *Ner Hamaarab. Toldot Yisrael BeMaroc* (Light of the west). Jerusalem, 1911.

————. *Sepher Ner Ha Mareb.* Jerusalem: N.p., 5671.

Ye'or, Bat. *The Dhimmi: Jews and Christians under Islam.* London: Fairleigh Dickinson Univ. Press, 1985.

Index

(References to illustrations are in italic)

233

Jewish Community Board (Sudan), 60–61

Jewish Community Executive Committee (Sudan), xi, 61

Jewish Encyclopedia, The, 203nn. 2–4

Jewish Golden Age, 137

Jewish Monthly (B'nai B'rith Magazine), xii, 88, 91, 93, 99

Jewish Recreation Club (Khartoum), 66–69, 186; bar mitzvah celebration at, 181; construction of, 60; dancing at, 68, 69, 185; Goldenberg sisters and, 179; probable destruction of, 50

Jewish Theological Seminary (New York), 110

Jewish Union for Education (Egypt), 91

Jews in Modern Egypt, The (Krämer), 90–91, 103–4, 115

"Jews in the Sudan" (Eli S. Malka), xii, 99

J. M. Cattaoui e Figli (firm), 104

Jordan, 116, 133

Josephus, Flavius, 80

Juan Carlos, king of Spain, 137

Juba, 165, 174–75

Juifs d'Egypte: Images et Textes, 102, 154–55

Juliana, queen of the Netherlands, 141

Kabalists. *See* Cabalists

Kaddish, 154n. 3

Kahan, Harry, 82, 83

El-Kahira. *See* Cairo

Kahn, Jean, 95

Kalpakian, Sarkis, 62

Kaminsky, Esther, *185*

Kaminsky, Israel, 52, *185*

Kampala, 174, 176

Kanarek, Herbert, 98–99

Kane, Jimmy, 54

Kane, Trudy, 54

Kanouns, 137n. 4

Kantzer, Boris, 25

Kanuri tribes, 6

Kasher meat, 31, 82–83, 190

Kashta, king of Cush, 5n. 6

Kasparian, Edmond, 170

Kasr Avenue (Khartoum), 9, 37, 67, 71

Kassala, 79, 130

Kawa, George, 62

Kenana District, 168

Kenesseth Rab Moshé (Cairo), 154–55

Kenisah El-Kebira (Cairo), 155

Keniset Al-Ismailia (Cairo), 107–8, 153, 154, 155

Kenya, 112, 160, 174, 176

Keren Hayesod, 139

Keren Kayemet, 139

Keystone Co., 52

Khaled, Sayed Khalafalla, 123–24

Khalil, Prime Minister Sayed Abdalla, 117, 126

Khartoum, 64; ancient Egyptian culture and, 5; bombing of, 48; cinema houses of, 67, 186; coffee imports of, 175; demonstrations in, 123, 130; departure from, 119; diplomats killed in, 130; Egyptian Jews in, 24–25, 51–52; Ethiopian Airways service to, 80; export companies in, 173; family life in, 183–89; features of, 7–11; Gellatly Hankey operations in, *162, 163*, 165, 166, 170–71; German Jews in, 53–54; home ownership in, 129–30, 160, 183–84; horsebean restaurants in, 172; irrigation headquarters in, 112; Khatmiya headquarters in, 65; Kitchener recapture of, 10, 56; Mahdi capture of, 14–15; Malka businesses in, 32, 33, 205; mamours of, 111; matza incident in, 116; merchants of, 57, 62; municipal engineer of, 144; name of, 4; railway service to, 100; schools of, 149, 180; sports in, 66–67, 156; travel from, 102, 115–16, 172n. 4, 174, 196; visitors to, 68, 70–75, 77–78, 122, 179; in World War II era, 114; Yemenite Jews in, 85

Khartoum B'nai B'rith Lodge. *See* Ben-Sion Coshti Lodge No. 1207

Malka, Rabbi Solomon, xi, 27–36, 149,
203; assistants of, 39; B'nai B'rith
and, 87; Brodie and, 75;
circumcisions by, 31, 43–44, 77; on
Community solidarity, 61, 96; death
of, 36, 45, 152; *Eilam Shar'ei* and,
113; Emmanuel and, 77–78; example
set by, 57; government officials and,
55; I. H. Herzog and, 72, 74; home
expenses of, 158; IDF descendants of,
146; immigration by, 20, 26, 27, 29;
Mandeel and, 22; marriages by,
219–24; memorial plaque for, 44–45,
46; H. Nahum and, 104; at party, 53;
pilgrimage suggested by, 195–96;
portrait of, 28; 54; reinterment of, 47;
rented synagogue and, 37; seders of,
151–52; Sokolov and, 71; Tafilalt
relatives of, 204; Tefilin and, 156; in
World War II era, 48; writings of,
39–40, 62, 205
Malka, Solomon (b. 1949), 204–5
Malka, Solomon Edmond, 145
Malka, Susan Gelfand, 145, 191
Malka, Victor, 118n. 3, 204
Malka, Victorine, 145, 198
Malka, Vittorio, 205
Malka, Yehiael, 27, 29, 203
Malka Bar Mar Aha, Rab, 202–3
Malka Export (firm), 200
Malka family, 202–5; genealogy of, 227;
New Jersey members of, 143; Spanish
expulsion of, 138; successful members
of, 144; "Tanta Lodge" member of,
89
Malka Mobaso Corporation, 191, 192
Malka Trading Co., 192, 193–94
Maller, Israel, 196
Malouf Sons (firm), 129
Mamelukes, 64n. 2
Manchester, England, 41, 56, 168
Mandeel, Suleiman, 16, 22
Mandel, Robert A., xiii
"Mangled Mask of Empire, The" (N.
Levy), 145
Mangoes, 175

Mani, Simon, 89
Al-Mansura, 90
Marawi, 6, 24, 64–65
Marcos, Ezra, 25
Marcovitch, Maurice, 51, 66
Marnignone, Joseph, 21–22
Marnignone, Josephine Levy, 21
Marrakech, 203
Marranos (Anusim), 16
Marriages, 35, 205, 213, 219–26
El-Masalma (Omdurman), 30
Mashiah, Elie, 25
Masliah, Rabbi, 36
Masons (Freemasons), 90
Massawa, 83, 165, 174
Massoud, Ibrahim, 118n. 3
Matza, 116
"Mayer." See Maher
May Revolution (1969), 128, 129, 161
May Trading Co., 129, 161, 173. See also
Gellatly Trading Co. Ltd.
Mazuki, Eugene, 62
McFarlane, D., 177, 178
McLean, Va., 194
Meadi, 53n. 1
Mecca, 19n. 1
Mediterranean countries, 65
Mediterranean Sea, 4, 112, 197
Mediterranean Towers (Fort Lee),
191
Meir, Rabbi Ouziel Ben-Zion, 196
Melekh (the word), 202
Memorial Hospital for Cancer and
Allied Diseases (New York), 142
Menasce, Behor David Levy de, 107
Menasce, Baron Behor Jacques de, 107
Menasce, Yacoub de, 107
Menasce family, 106, 107
Menasse, Joseph, 62
Menasse, Yacoub Levy, 104
Mendel, Suleiman, 16, 22
Menelik I, emperor of Ethiopia, 79–80
Menorah symbolism, 86
Mère de Dieu School (Cairo), 179
El-Merghani, Sayed Ahmed Uthman,
132

Tilche family, 107
Tile manufacture, 33
Tokar, 168
Toledano, Aaron, 145
Toledano, Jeannette Sasson, 145
Toledano, Rabbi Yacoub Moshé, 145,
    203nn. 4, 5
Torah: on Abrahamic Covenant, 31n. 3;
    bar mitzvah reading of, 156; at
    Comboni College, 88; on menorah,
    86n. 2; on Moses, 108, 110; on
    nedabas, 41; obedience to, 151; on
    Sha'ar Hashamaim, 153n. 1; on
    shemittah, 41; Yemenite Jews and, 81
Torah Im Derekh Eretz, 78
Torah scrolls (sepharim), 31, 38, 49–50,
    156
Torquemada, Tomás de, 92, 138
Toulon, 85
Trade. *See* Commerce
Treaty of Lausanne (1923), 103
Tripoli, 35–36
Trucco & Co., 116
Truman, Harry S., 84, 141
Tueta, David, 197
Tueta, Giselle Goldring, 146, 197
Tueta, Reuven, 146
Tueta, Shai, 146
Al-Turabi, Hassan, 130, 132, 133
Turetsky, Rabbi Arnold, 199
Turkey, 12, 27n. 1, 76, 103, 121
Turkish language, 104
Tuval, Esther Malka, 146
Tuval, Yehuda, 146
Twenty-first Lancers, 17

Uds, 137n. 4
Uganda, 4, 112, 160, 174, 176
Ultra Orthodox Jews, 153
El-Umma (newspaper), 117
Umma Party: DUP and, 132; Electoral
    Commission and, 125; A. R. El-
    Mahdi Pasha and, 45, 117; in 1964
    election, 127; PDP and, 126;
    supporters of, 122–23

Unilever Brothers (firm), 171
Unionists (NUP), 125, 126, 127
Union Juive pour l'Enseignement
    (Egypt), 91
United Kingdom. *See* Britain
United Nations: French representative
    to, 136n. 1; Israeli representative to,
    176n. 1; partition vote by, 44;
    secretary general of, 107; Shalom son
    and, 21; Sudanese membership in,
    126
United Nations Association of the
    United States, 191
United Nations Educational, Scientific,
    and Cultural Organization
    (UNESCO), 100
United States: Abboudi business in, 64;
    Abboud regime and, 127; birthday
    guests from, 199; B'nai B'rith in, 86,
    88, 94, 96–99; civil war in, 4;
    education in, 180; entry permit issue
    and, 84; exports of, 200; Hakim
    immigration to, 21; Israeli relations
    with, 195; Jewish immigration to,
    204; Vittorio Malka business in, 205;
    Malka immigration to, 120, 145,
    190–91, 194; El-Nemeiri and, 79,
    130; roasted snacks in, 172; Seroussi
    trade in, 64; Shuggi immigration to,
    169; Sudanese in, 62, 143, 144;
    Temple of Ramses II and, 100;
    terrorist sought by, 133; travel from,
    197; Treaty of Lausanne and, 103;
    Zakhari businesses in, 173. *See also*
    American Jews
United States Army, 191
United States Congress, 195, 200
United States Department of Education,
    145
Unity High School (Khartoum), 180
Universal Declaration of Human Rights,
    136n. 1
University Hospital of Geneva, 120
University of Geneva: Danielli at, 180;
    Evelyne Malka at, 120, 173, 181,
    190–91

University of Geneva School of
Medicine, 181
Upper Egypt. *See* Egypt
USINOR Steel (firm), 193

Vegetable oils. *See* Oilseeds
Vermicelli, 32
Veyrier, 190
Vichy government, 95
Victoria, Lake, 4, 112, 176
Victoria Avenue (Khartoum), 9, 37, 67,
71
Vienna, Va., 194
Vietcong, 85
Vietnam War, 191
Villars sur Ollon, 180, 188
Virginia, 194
"Voice of the Turtle" (musical group),
137n. 4

Wadi El-Yahud, 204
Wadi Halfa, 23, 100, 165, 187
Wad Medani, 64; cotton plantations in,
41; development projects in, 61;
Egyptian Jews in, 25; electrical
service in, 52; Gellatly enterprises in,
165; touring in, 173
Wad Sayedna, 11
Wafd (political party), 115, 205
Wais, Samuel Hizgeil, 25
Waiters, 9
Watania Cinema (Khartoum), 186
Waxler, William, 97
Weather, 11, 83, 188, 189
Weinberg, Charles, 25
Weiss, Herbert, 53, 54
Weiss, I., 51, 66
Weiss, Lisa, 53, 54
Weiss, Richard, 53–54
Weizmann, Chaim, 44
West Africa, 5n. 6
West Bosham, 164
Westchester Jewish Community,
199

Westchester Jewish Conference Israel
Action Committee, 195
Westchester-Putnam Council of B'nai
B'rith, 92
Western Europe, 78
White ants, 168
White Nile, 4; Albert Falls and, 176;
bridge on, 9; cotton cultivation and,
168; in Cushite era, 5; Jebel Awlia
Dam on, 8n. 9, 72, 112
White Nile Province, 122
White Plains B'nai B'rith Unit 5249,
91–92, 96–97, 98–99, 152,
194–95
Whittingham College, 181
Wholesale trade. *See* Commerce
Wild animals, 174–75, 176–77
Wilson, Sir Charles, 14
Wingate, Sir Reginald, 17, 163,
177
Wolf, J., 52–53
Wolf, Mrs. J., *53*
Women's lodges, 89–90, 97
World Jewish Congress, 139, 141
World Organization of Jews from Arab
Countries, 141
World Sephardic Federation: N. Gaon
and, 57, 107n. 3, 134, *135*, 137,
153n. 2; projects of, 138, 139
World Sephardic Federation Board of
Governors, 137
World Trade Organization, 200n. 4
World War I, 136n. 1
World War II: airmen lost in, 48–49;
anti-Semitism in, 114–15; B'nai
B'rith and, 88, 93; import business
and, 166; notables' visits in,
70–74; outbreak of, 107; service
in, 62
World Zionist Organization, 70, 179
Wycombe Abbey, 181

Yacoub, Tadessa, 78–79
Yemenite Jews, 81, 85
Yemenite music, 82